W9-BMF-228

THE
WOLF PRINCESS

THE
WOLF
PRINCESS

CATHRYN CONSTABLE

SCHOLASTIC INC. / NEW YORK

Text copyright © 2013 by Cathryn Constable

All rights reserved. Published by Chicken House, an imprint of Scholastic Inc.. *Publishers since 1920.* CHICKEN HOUSE, SCHOLASTIC, and associated logos are trademarks and/or registered trademarks of Scholastic Inc.
www.scholastic.com

First published in the United Kingdom in 2012
by Chicken House, 2 Palmer Street, Frome, Somerset BA11 1DS.
www.doublecluck.com

No part of this publication may be reproduced, stored in a retrieval system, or transmitted in any form or by any means, electronic, mechanical, photocopying, recording, or otherwise, without prior written permission of the publisher. For information regarding permission, write to Scholastic Inc., Attention: Permissions Department, 557 Broadway, New York, NY 10012.

Quotations from *Old Peter's Russian Tales* by Arthur Ransome reprinted courtesy of the Arthur Ransome Literary Estate.

Library of Congress Cataloging-in-Publication Data

Constable, Cathryn.
The wolf princess / Cathryn Constable. — 1st American ed.
p. cm.
Summary: Sophie Smith is an orphan stuck in a boarding school in London, but at night she dreams of Russia and wolves — then, on a class trip to Saint Petersburg, she finds herself and her two friends deliberately separated from the group and whisked off into the silver forest of her dreams, where a mystery awaits.
ISBN 978-0-545-52839-9
1. Wolves — Juvenile fiction. 2. Princesses — Juvenile fiction. 3. Orphans — Juvenile fiction. 4. Boarding schools — Juvenile fiction. 5. Russia (Federation) — Juvenile fiction. [1. Wolves — Fiction. 2. Princesses — Fiction. 3. Orphans — Fiction. 4. Boarding schools — Fiction. 5. Schools — Fiction. 6. Russia (Federation) — Fiction. 7. Mystery and detective stories.]
I. Title.   PZ7.C76498Wol 2013   823.92 — dc23
2012040544

10 9 8 7 6 5 4 3 2   14 15 16 17

Printed in the U.S.A.   23
First American edition, October 2013

The text type was set in Centaur.

Book design by Whitney Lyle

C. M. R. S

CHAPTER ONE

The Forest

"Hold my hand, Sophie. We have to leave!"

It was her father's voice. She couldn't see him, but she knew, somehow, that his hair was disheveled and that he was wearing his tatty overcoat, the one with the hem that hung down like a ragged wing. He slipped his hand into hers, clasping it tight, and together they ran through the frozen silver forest. She knew where they were going. Always the same place — a place conjured from his stories, dreams, and memories. At the edge of the trees, they stopped. Their breath scrolled out before them and the snow fell like a heavy lace curtain. Flakes as large as moths fluttered in front of her eyes.

"Wait, Sophie," he said. *"She's coming. Can you see her?"*

And his words called up a young woman in a long cloak, her face hidden beneath a hood. Sophie glimpsed a tendril of dark blonde hair. It was covered with snowflakes that changed to diamonds as she watched.

"Who is she?"

She couldn't hear her father's answer, but he gripped her hand a little tighter and he sang to her . . . that lovely song whose words she had forgotten. Sophie wanted to ask her father about the woman, but now the song had become a story. He wouldn't stop telling her the story.

It was winter. It was snowing. There was a girl lost in the woods. And — Sophie felt her chest tighten with fear — *a wolf* . . .

She felt her father's hand slip out of hers.

"Don't leave me!"

But he was no longer there. And the sadness and the fear got mixed up with the snowflakes and covered everything.

"Sophie!"

No! This voice was from another place. She didn't want to answer.

She pressed her face into the pillow, trying to climb back into the forest. To hold herself in the strange dreamtime, where she could taste the cold, clear air like a mixture of peppermints and diamonds . . . feel the forest all around her . . . hear the snow creak beneath her feet . . .

"Are you awake?"

Sophie sighed and moved her hand across the bedspread as if to brush snow from it.

"I am now, Delphine."

She tried not to sound grumpy. But the day at the New Bloomsbury College for Young Ladies had started and it would not be stopped. It was too late for dreams.

She turned onto her back and stared at the ceiling. Why did real life have to be so dull? Why did boarding school seem so . . . *beige*? She looked around at the three narrow wardrobes, three flimsy bedside cabinets, and three scratched desks and chairs, and wished for . . . something else. Something beautiful, however small. Enormous branches of cherry blossom in an agate urn . . . panels of lace at the window . . . candlelight . . . In this cramped, shabby London room, there would never be any beauty or excitement. No secret notes or espionage. No adventures.

Just school.

Delphine sat up in bed and stretched. Yellow hair flowed around her face and shoulders. She looked like a marble princess on a church tomb who had just woken up after a thousand years of restful sleep.

"What's the weather doing?" Weather only mattered to Delphine, of course, so she could decide what to do with her hair. And Sophie's bed was next to the window. Delphine asked the same question every morning.

Sophie sat up. For a moment she gazed at the photograph of her father on the windowsill. The picture had caught the dreamy, quizzical expression she thought she remembered, as if he had just seen or heard something that interested him. She pulled back the curtain.

The window looked out onto a narrow street of tall houses, and she had to crane her neck to get any view of the sky. Even when it was wild with sunshine, the street was dank and depressing. Today, beads of rain drizzled down the dirty panes, so there was hardly any need to check the sky, which happened to be the normal London color — dishwater gray.

"It's amazing how much water there is in the sky above London," Sophie said.

"It's been like this for four days," Delphine replied. "Do you think the rain ever gets bored? Do you think it ever wants to do something else with itself other than fall on drab old London?"

"It rains in Paris, doesn't it?" Sophie said.

"Of course! But even the rain in Paris is beautiful."

"I wish it would snow," Sophie whispered. She wondered if the dream of the winter forest would come again. Could she make it come back?

"Snow? Are you mad?" Delphine shuddered. "It ruins your shoes."

"But that wouldn't matter," Sophie said. "We would wake up and everything would look so different . . . Maybe it would even *be* different. Like a fairy tale. Wouldn't it be amazing if, just for once, it was cold enough for snow?"

"Such weather is only perfect on the *piste*," Delphine said firmly. "With skis attached to your feet." She stretched again and yawned prettily, like a cat. "Shall we wake Marianne?" She swung her long legs over the edge of her bed and wiggled her toes. The nails were painted metallic green. "If we don't, she'll miss breakfast again."

"What is this fascination with breakfast?" A girl with thin dark hair emerged from under a brown quilt cover, her face bleary and puffed with sleep.

"Hey! It speaks!"

The girl blinked like a mole and felt around on her bedside cabinet for a pair of slightly bent wire glasses, then pushed them onto her face. "Why are you walking around on tiptoe, Delphine?" she said.

"To improve circulation," Delphine responded, then stopped and threw her head between her knees to brush her hair. "And this is to prevent wrinkles."

"That's ridiculous," sniffed Marianne. "There's absolutely no scientific evidence for that."

"And you haven't got any wrinkles," Sophie pointed out. "You're much too young."

"It is the French way," Delphine shrugged, as if that were answer enough. She flicked her head back up, then twisted her hair into a bun on the side of her head and pierced it with a hairpin. Being half French seemed an awful lot of work, Sophie thought. And took an awful lot of time.

"Oh, but there *is* something to wake up for today!" Marianne kicked back her quilt with an unexpected burst of energy. "It's Thursday. We get the results of our geography test!"

Sophie groaned. It was always such an effort not to feel squashed between Marianne's high academic standards and Delphine's equally high grooming standards. Mostly Sophie couldn't be bothered to resist the pressure; she'd got used to the feeling of being squashed by now, anyway.

She checked her watch. "We'd better get dressed."

"Give me twenty minutes," Delphine said, pulling on a pale pink silk robe and heading for the bathroom.

"Twenty minutes?" Marianne made a face.

"I couldn't take that long even if I did everything twice," Sophie said.

"Which is why I look like me . . . and you look like . . ." But whatever Sophie looked like, Delphine couldn't find the word for it. She stopped suddenly and stared, as if something had just occurred to her.

"What?" Sophie said.

"You're actually quite pretty," Delphine said. "Good eyebrows. Perfect skin. But no one notices because you always forget to brush your hair. And don't even get me started on that school sweater you wear — it's full of holes."

"Well, it's the only one I've got. And stop staring at me like that!"

Delphine shrugged. "You should think about these things."

"But why?" Sophie said. "No one ever takes any notice of me."

"There's no point saying anything to her, Delphine," Marianne said, putting on her robe. "She's happy the way she is."

Delphine wagged her finger. "Trust me, one day you will want to make a good impression."

"Well, I'm never going to meet anyone important," Sophie said. "So it won't make any difference if I have holes in my sweater or not."

"You wait!" Delphine said. "Someone important could turn up today!"

"That's about as likely as snowflakes in summer," Sophie laughed.

CHAPTER TWO

The Visitor

They were seriously late for breakfast. The smell of damp toast rose to greet them as they made their way down the back stairs, their shoes squeaking on the linoleum floor. Just as they reached the bottom, they heard a heavier tread ahead of them and saw the corduroy-suited figure of their deputy headmaster. He turned as they tried to slip past him.

"Good morning, girls," he said brightly, checking the time on his watch. "You'd better hurry." His gaze rested on Delphine. "I would think about finding a less time-consuming hairstyle in the future, Delphine, if I were you."

Sophie put her head down, stared hard at the floor, and tried to make herself invisible. She knew she could get past most teachers without them really noticing she was there. It was one of her most useful skills.

But not this morning.

Mr. Tweedie cleared his throat. "Sophie?" he said, just at the very moment when she thought she had escaped. "A word?"

"But I'll be late for breakfast, sir," Sophie said. "You said so yourself."

"It won't take long. I'm sure the others can get you something."

Delphine and Marianne took the hint and made a dash for the refectory, Delphine mouthing "sorry" as she went.

Sophie tried to avoid Mr. Tweedie's concerned gaze. He didn't so much frown as crumple up his face when there was a problem. "It's the sweater, Sophie," he sighed.

Sophie tried to rearrange the offending knitwear so that the holes weren't so apparent.

"And your shoes," he continued. "Ballet shoes — the sort tied to your feet with ribbons — aren't on the uniform list, are they?"

She shook her head.

"I wonder, Sophie, if you've written to your guardian yet about your clothes? We did agree you were going to do that, didn't we?"

At the word guardian, an image of Rosemary — a middle-aged woman with blonde-gray hair cut in a boyish crop, sitting poker-straight on a stool in her small, neat kitchen — flashed in front of Sophie's eyes. She and Rosemary had nothing in common with each other, were not related in any way. But rain, a borrowed car, her widowed father's tiredness, and an unexpected turn on a dark country road had all combined one night in a fatal cocktail to make Rosemary and Sophie lifelong companions. As the only friend of the family the authorities could reach after the accident, Rosemary had taken Sophie in as a temporary measure, until a relative of the newly orphaned child could be found. But Sophie's father had not lived what Rosemary called a "settled life." Sophie's mother had died when Sophie was a baby, and her father had taken her to live in many different places. He'd talk about magical journeys, about the next place they would go. Friends were scarce and, it became apparent, relatives were nonexistent.

"Rosemary is very busy," Sophie said, putting a finger into one of the smaller holes in the sleeve of her sweater and hooking it over her fingernail in an attempt to hide it. She looked up at Mr. Tweedie's crumpled, kind face and smiled with more confidence than she felt. "She really does have a lot on her plate at the moment, and I don't like to bother her . . ." Sophie didn't want to add, *when she is away.* Better that the school didn't know just how much time Rosemary spent out of the country. It would only cause problems.

"But it's not just the sweater or the shoes, Sophie, it's

all your clothes." Mr. Tweedie sounded strained. "Everything you wear is just so . . ." He stopped. "You must understand that it's not that I mind, but it's better for you if you blend in. Look in the Lost and Found." Mr. Tweedie gave her one of his *I-mean-it* faces. "Before Mrs. Sharman sees you."

In the refectory, Sophie took a thick white plate out of the plastic box stacked next to the counter, chose the least bruised banana and a glass of watered-down orange juice, and put it all on a tray. Then she joined Delphine and Marianne at the long trestle table. They were the last, and already the kitchen staff were moving around and clearing things away.

"What did Tweedie want?" Marianne had propped her physics textbook up against her bag on the table. Sophie remembered there was a test today. She'd completely forgotten.

"Sweater alert."

"He does go on," Delphine said. "You should just agree with everything he says. That usually stops him."

"He's got to do his job," Marianne said, her eyes still scanning the page. "Did you know that the angle of incidence is equal to the angle of reflection?"

Delphine rolled her eyes.

"And did *you* know it's the first of March?" Sophie said quickly, trying to distract Marianne. "That means the list should go up this morning."

"What list?" Delphine took a small piece of butter and placed it on the edge of her plate. From this she put an even tinier piece on her knife and spread it on a minuscule fraction of toast. She then bit into the buttered toast, before repeating the procedure. Sophie calculated that at her current speed, it could take Delphine up to ten minutes to finish one slice. (Marianne, no doubt, would be able to calculate it to the second.)

"Where we're going in the last week of term," Sophie said, peeling the banana. "The class trip."

Delphine shrugged. "You know we won't get to go anywhere interesting or exciting. They save those for year twelve."

"We'll probably get Cooking Country-Style in Thomas Hardy's England," Sophie sighed.

"Or Franco-Belgian Battlefields," added Marianne, raising her gaze from the textbook. "If we're really, really lucky."

"Well, that's all right if you've only ever been to the coast of Cornwall," Delphine said.

"But I love Cornwall!" Marianne protested.

"It's just not very *chic*, is it?" Delphine went on. "Not like the Île de Ré, where you can wear tailored shorts and nice little canvas shoes."

"I want to get on the Saint Petersburg trip," said Sophie.

There. She'd said it. And she'd promised herself that she wouldn't. She knew from experience with Rosemary that asking for anything was the surest way of not getting it. She bit her lip. There'd be no chance now. If only she'd kept her mouth shut for just a while longer.

"Dream on!" Marianne laughed, stuffing the textbook into her bag. "You know there's no hope of that." Deep down, Sophie knew she was right. Only those taking Russian for A-level exams had any chance of going.

"Anyway, why would anyone in their right mind want to go to Saint Petersburg before the summer?" Delphine shivered. "It will be far too cold in March."

"But snow in Russia! That's the whole point!" Sophie hugged her arms to her chest. "Anyway, I'm used to the cold. Rosemary's flat is freezing. She thinks central heating is immoral."

"It *is* very bad for the planet," Marianne said primly. "But how do you keep warm without any proper clothes?"

"Rosemary gave me an old mink jacket to wear in bed."

"So, central heating is immoral, but killing innocent animals for their fur is fine?" Marianne said.

"Well, they're very old furs. The animals would be dead by now anyway. And it feels like wearing something from a different world . . ."

"*That's* not the point!"

"But don't you ever lie in bed at night and think about being someone else?" Sophie continued.

Delphine raised one perfect eyebrow. "Someone other than me?"

"When I wear that coat," Sophie rattled on, "I'm not plain old Sophie Smith . . . I feel like I'm some beautiful countess, running away from an empty life of parties and balls to find my destiny . . . with the Cossacks . . . and I am traveling across Russia wrapped in furs on a night train . . . and under my pillow" — she knew she sounded crazy, but she couldn't stop — "are a box of sugar mice and foil-wrapped chocolate cats with red sequins for eyes . . . and . . . a . . . p-pistol." She reached the end of the sentence because she hadn't known how to stop before saying "pistol." By the expression on Marianne's face, she might as well have said "penguin."

"A pistol?" Delphine's face creased in incomprehension. "What do you . . . ?"

Sophie decided to brave her friends' incredulity. She would just say it. "I need the pistol to shoot the bears and the wolves."

"Do you really think a bullet from a pistol would stop a bear?" Marianne snorted. "They are seriously vicious creatures when they're angry. Think Sharman in one of her moods . . . and then some!"

Delphine went back to applying butter to her toast as if she were giving it a manicure. "I need a pool and blazing sunshine." She looked thoughtful. "Of course, a yacht is always a bonus."

"Too much outdoors!" Marianne laughed, heaving her overstuffed rucksack onto her shoulder and draining her glass of water. "Just give me a library and a fire."

"But shall we go and check the bulletin board anyway? Do we have time?" Sophie said. Maybe it wouldn't be Saint Petersburg, but she wanted to know where she would be spending Easter. Rosemary would probably make some excuse about not being at home, as usual. When Sophie was young, Rosemary had made the best of it by hiring a series of au pairs and doing the best to ignore the disturbance to her ordered, career-focused life. Boarding school, the minute Sophie was old enough, came as a blessed relief to both of them, but holidays were not on Rosemary's radar.

"Yes, but we can't be late for physics. I'll test you on the anthropic principle on the way, if you like," Marianne offered.

Delphine and Sophie made a face at each other as they made their way out of the refectory, taking the prohibited shortcut through the library. Neither of them had a clue what Marianne was talking about. That didn't bode well for the physics test.

Marianne sighed at their blank expressions. "The anthropic principle was posited by Robert Dicke, a cosmological scientist, in 1961 to deal with the presence of incredible coincidence in the universe."

"It's not a coincidence that you're boring me silly," Delphine muttered. "I don't remember anything about this from class."

"She's going to get an A-plus again," Sophie sighed. "Marianne must be the only girl in the school to get more than a hundred percent on a physics test."

"But it's so interesting!" Marianne burst out. "How else can you explain why we are here?"

"Because we're taking a shortcut through the library?" Sophie offered.

"No. Here. With a capital H. Everything has been working toward this moment, don't you see? The precise level of weak nuclear force that allows stars to shine, that allows matter to coalesce and form planets, oxygen, water . . . Only a slight variation and our whole world would fall apart."

Sophie and Delphine kept walking.

"Don't you see?" Marianne was in full flow. "We are here, wherever we are, because we can *only* be here. There is no other place for us."

Sophie tried to imagine that the whole of the universe had been working toward this one moment — she, Sophie

Smith, walking toward the bulletin board — but, as with most of Marianne's Big Ideas, she gave up.

Delphine breathed, "Fascinating," and nodded her head as if she were taking it all in, but Sophie could see she was already scanning the far end of the corridor where a group of girls was standing around the bulletin board, laughing and talking excitedly.

Sophie hung back and crossed her fingers. *I know it can't be Saint Petersburg,* she said to herself. *But just this once, could the office have made a mistake and accidentally put my name down on the wrong list? I won't eat any more of Marianne's chocolate-covered cherries or use Delphine's toothpaste or that lavender shampoo her mother sends from Paris, and I'll look for a sweater in Lost and Found right now and I'll be good for the rest of my life . . .*

They got closer to the gaggle of girls. Delphine pushed to the front.

"Oh, typical!" Millie Dresser, a drab girl in the grade above, looked fed up. "I've got the battlefields." She stomped off in a huff.

Sophie couldn't bear to look. She was just going to stare in the opposite direction and wait until Delphine told her. While she didn't know, there was still a chance . . . The voices rose, screams of "Lucky you!" or "That will teach you to be rude in geography!" rolled around her. The tension was unbearable.

"Well?" She nudged Delphine's back. "Where are we going?"

Delphine got as far as saying, "Cooking Country-Style —" when the bell rang for the start of classes.

Sophie's heart sank. A familiar feeling of disappointment. She was so stupid to have thought anything beautiful or even different would happen in her life.

"Bad luck," Marianne said, looking sympathetic.

Sophie turned away — and was confronted by Mr. Tweedie, no longer looking remotely understanding.

"I meant it, Sophie," he said, his voice strict. "Change your sweater!"

"Mr. Tweedie!" Sophie and the deputy head jumped as the figure of Mrs. Sharman, the headmistress, strode toward them, the embodiment of female determination, excellence, and academic achievement. Her highlighted hair was blow-dried into enormous flicky curls that the morning's rain had done nothing to deflate. Accompanying her was a tall, thin woman wearing a silk headscarf and improbably large sunglasses.

Mrs. Sharman launched a brief professional smile, like a rocket, at Mr. Tweedie. "Could you spare me one of your girls? Delphine, perhaps?"

"Girls? Girls?" the deputy head replied in confusion, as if, in a school full of them, he had never heard of such a thing as a "girl."

Mrs. Sharman, extending her smile, nodded graciously at this hapless example of the more feeble gender. "To give our prospective parent here a tour of the school, of course!" she cried, waving her hand loosely in the direction of the visitor. "Mrs. . . . Mrs. . . . ." The woman said nothing, and merely examined her nails, which Sophie noticed with fascination were painted navy blue. Mrs. Sharman pursed her lips in irritation.

Sophie said, "Delphine's gone to physics."

The headmistress's head swiveled to take in the child who had spoken without being spoken to.

Sophie swallowed. "I could go and get her for you."

Mrs. Sharman gasped. Her eyes widened. "Sophie!" She managed to make the name sound like a curse. "Your sweater!"

Mr. Tweedie cleared his throat. "We were just discussing the sweater . . ."

Mrs. Sharman pulled Sophie's arm toward her as if it were a scientific specimen. "There are *actual holes!*"

"I'll change," Sophie mumbled.

"You most certainly will!" the headmistress snapped. It was clear that she was not just referring to the sweater. She dropped Sophie's arm and clamped the professional smile back in place. "Bring me Delphine! I will see you later, Sophie Smith."

"Sophie Smith?" The visitor turned sharply, peering

over her sunglasses at Sophie. Her eyes, Sophie saw, were enormous and very pale blue, surrounded by feathery lashes. The voice was rich and low.

Sophie felt her cheeks burning as the woman looked her up and down, taking in everything, including the holes in her sweater. Oh, why hadn't she looked in Lost and Found before breakfast? But just as she turned to go, the visitor's hand shot out and clutched her elbow. Sophie looked up. The pale blue eyes were fixed on her. Unless she wrenched her arm out of the woman's grasp, she was stuck.

"I am happy with *this* young lady . . ."

"Oh, you don't want *her*." The headmistress frowned. "She is not the pupil for you." When the woman didn't let go of Sophie's elbow, as expected, Mrs. Sharman explained. "We have a very few places at New Bloomsbury College for Young Ladies for students who are on *reduced fees*." She mouthed the last two words as if this might somehow spare Sophie's feelings. "Due to *family circumstances* . . ." She raised her eyebrows, implying this would explain Sophie's orphan status, her unbrushed hair, and the holes in her sweater. "We take our charitable status very seriously! However, I must stress that the majority of girls at New Bloomsbury College come from impeccable families."

The woman seemed to consider what Mrs. Sharman had said. Then she smiled slowly. She included Mr.

Tweedie in this gift, and Sophie noticed with astonishment that he blushed. The visitor bent toward him like a heavy tulip and, lightly touching his arm, said in her exotically accented English, "We see *your* classroom?"

Mr. Tweedie stammered something, and the headmistress hissed, "It might be better if you started with the science labs. But Sophie is not available. She has a class."

"Sophie Smith is girl for me!" the woman laughed. "We will make good team!" Still gripping Sophie's elbow, she maneuvered her toward the door to the playground. "He has stopped raining! Now I see ground where you *play!*"

Sophie glanced over her shoulder. Mr. Tweedie's face was looking crumpled again, and Mrs. Sharman's smile had vanished, her mouth a perfect O.

Then Sophie felt herself pushed through the door, the visitor's hand firmly in the middle of her back.

CHAPTER THREE

The Photograph

They stepped into the cramped courtyard that passed for a playground. The woman seemed to forget Sophie immediately. She took off her sunglasses, opened her bag, and got out a pack of cigarettes. The box had a large red heart on it, and the word *Kiss*.

"Oh, but you can't smoke!" Sophie gasped.

The woman's enormous blue eyes opened even wider.

Sophie said, "Not on school premises. It's against the rules." Had the woman heard her? Understood her? She had already put a cigarette in her mouth.

"We are outside!" she pronounced. "In fresh air! I *need* cigarette!" But after a second, she took it out of her mouth, unlit.

Sophie looked around the dismal yard. What could she say about it? Valerian was growing out of the brickwork, and the paint on the window ledges was flaking.

The pavement seemed to sweat. The presence of such an exotic, glamorous creature against this drab background made the school seem even more inhospitable than usual.

"So," Sophie started, "this is our playground. The science labs . . ."

The woman wasn't listening. She was rummaging in her handbag again. "I take photograph!" she said, lifting a small camera to her face.

"I think that's against the rules as well . . ." Sophie blushed.

"To show my daughter. In Saint Petersburg."

"You are from Russia?" Sophie blurted out. Of course! She should have known! The woman's voice, her scarf, her charm, set her apart. Her father had always said it was the most romantic country on earth. And anyone could see that the woman in front of her could not have wandered in from some sorry old corner of England. She could only have stepped out of a land of palaces and poetry.

Flash!

"Turn your head to side!"

Sophie, startled, did as she was told.

Flash!

"How old is your daughter?" Sophie asked.

The woman waved her hand dismissively. "Ten . . . eleven, maybe. Natalya very clever. All her teachers tell me they are blessed to have such clever child in their class.

She can do any sums!" The woman snapped her fingers. "Like that! In head!"

Sophie wondered what such a mathematical prodigy would make of Mr. Webb, the school's only math teacher, who had taken to talking about the insanity of numbers and how they persecuted him.

The woman rearranged her silk scarf so that the over-sized designer logo was more apparent. "I tell them it is because I prepare all her food. Finest food. From import. All organeek!" She glanced up at the sky. "Now it will rain. I do not like rain."

"Well, maybe the science labs —" Sophie began, though the rain had stopped and didn't look like it was starting again.

"I do not like science labs. I *must* speak with nice English man. *Ooocheeetel.* This is word for *teacher* in my language." The way she pursed her lips as she said the word made it sound like a more fascinating job than Sophie could ever have imagined, possibly than Mr. Tweedie could ever have imagined. "But first . . . leep-steek! Take me somewhere I can make beauty face." She puckered up her mouth, and gave Sophie a sly look. "You have room where sleep?"

Ten minutes later, Sophie was still waiting outside her own room. The woman seemed to be taking rather a long time just to apply some lipstick. Eventually, she emerged in a storm cloud of scent and with a determined air.

"Photograph at window," she said. "Is your father?"

"Yes . . ." Sophie said cautiously. But why, she thought, had the woman been looking around the room rather than at her own face in the mirror?

"He lives abroad?"

Something in her voice made Sophie reluctant to answer. She hated questions about her father, but the woman's direct, uncaring tone made it even worse.

"No. He's . . ." She hesitated.

"Dead?"

Sophie nodded.

But why did that make the woman smile? Without another word, she turned and sashayed off down the corridor. She did not ask Sophie to follow her.

She had looked, Sophie thought uneasily, almost triumphant.

Sophie paid no attention in French. The dream of her father and the winter forest, the holes in her sweater that had caught Mr. Tweedie's eye, the strange Russian woman . . . the day was beginning to feel unreal. The *assistante* warbled on, but Sophie stared out of the window, trying to turn the wet London plane trees into a forest coated in snow. If only she could have gone to Saint Petersburg! She stared hard at a couple of Japanese tourists, dressed in leg warmers and trench coats, with manga-style spiked hair, and half closed her eyes to see if she could get them to become duelists, meeting in the half-light of dawn. Perhaps the taller one could be a poet, if she imagined him with a hat to cover the pink streaks in his hair. And the other one could be a lieutenant, and they had quarreled over a game of cards . . . no . . . the taller one had stolen the other's stallion and ridden it until it was lame . . .

"Sophie Smith!"

She jumped. "Yes? Sorry, I mean, *Oui?*"

Someone behind her laughed. She looked at the board. It had become quite full of new vocabulary since she had started staring out of the window. Mademoiselle Deguignet asked her a question. From the tone of her voice, it sounded like it wasn't the first time she'd asked it. Marianne turned around and mouthed something: the answer, most likely, but despite Marianne's best efforts Sophie could not work out what she was saying.

At that moment, Mrs. Hingley, the school secretary, entered the room. She was at her most officious, her dumpy frame outlined by a too-tight sweater and skirt, her mean little mouth made to seem even smaller and meaner by her shocking pink lipstick. She had a short conversation with Mademoiselle Deguignet, stared at Sophie with scarcely disguised suspicion, then stomped out again.

"It seems you are required in the headmistress's office, Sophie." The *assistante* looked surprised.

Sophie heard her chair scrape far too loudly as she stood up. Mademoiselle Deguignet winced and the laughter broke out again. This must have to do with the sweater. How she wished she had looked for one in Lost and Found before breakfast! She'd had no time since then — and now she had to face Mrs. Sharman again. Sophie left the classroom and walked as slowly as possible toward the office. She felt sick.

"Sophie!" She turned to see Delphine running toward her.

"What are you doing?"

"I told Mademoiselle Deguignet I needed to go to the loo . . ." Delphine pulled off her sweater and handed it to Sophie. "Quick. Swap! Mrs. Sharman will have a fit if she sees you in that old thing again."

Gratefully, Sophie pulled off her sweater and handed it to Delphine, who knotted it around her shoulders: It made her look chic and hid the worst of the holes.

"*Bonne chance,*" her friend whispered.

Sophie knocked on the secretary's door. Her pulse was racing and she knew her cheeks were red. She licked her lips nervously and put her head around the door when she was told to enter. Mrs. Hingley's Jack Russell terrier, in his basket under the desk, started to growl.

Mrs. Hingley directed Sophie into Mrs. Sharman's office with a grumpy nod.

The headmistress was checking figures on a spreadsheet. Her glasses rested halfway down her nose. Without looking up, she said, "I've just called your guardian, but she's not at any of the numbers we have in your file. Do you happen to know where she might be?"

Sophie stood in the middle of the office. She was quite a long way from the desk, but felt it would be inappropriate to advance any farther. Where *was* Rosemary, exactly? She had a feeling March was the month she went to Majorca to play bridge.

Mrs. Sharman sighed and looked up. "What exactly did you do today, Sophie?" she asked.

"Er . . ." Sophie began.

Mrs. Sharman frowned. "When you took the visitor into the playground? Did you say something to her?"

"I told her she couldn't smoke," Sophie said.

Mrs. Sharman shook her head. "Anything else?"

Sophie pulled at the sleeve of Delphine's sweater. Much softer than hers. Probably cashmere. "I don't think so."

"Unbelievable," Mrs. Sharman said under her breath. She stood up. "Well, whatever you did, our extremely *wealthy* visitor from Saint Petersburg is convinced that *you*" — and here she shot Sophie a look of utter disbelief — "would be able to persuade her friends to send their daughters here. Apparently, her friends are very wealthy, too." Mrs. Sharman took off her glasses. "She asked a lot of questions about you; she seemed to be interested — pleased, even! — to know just how poor you are!" Mrs. Sharman shook her head as if nonplussed. "I began to wonder if she hadn't understood what I was saying! However, against my better judgment, I am going to send you on the trip to Saint Petersburg, Sophie Smith."

Sophie stood very still, not daring to breathe. Had she heard correctly? She balled her fists and dug her fingers into her palms.

"Of course," Mrs. Sharman went on, "I think the woman is quite wrong — which is why I will also send Marianne and Delphine. *They* are the sort of girls who show the benefit of a New Bloomsbury College education!"

On the way back to French, Sophie allowed herself several footsteps to savor the thought that, for the first and only time in her life, something wonderful and magical had happened. Then she sighed.

There was just one problem. A big one.

Rosemary.

CHAPTER FOUR

The Piece of Glass

Sophie was right to be pessimistic. The paperwork for the trip came back in a large brown envelope with one of Rosemary's scrawled notes paper-clipped to the top: *No can do. Much too expensive.* In another pen, she had added, *Away for most of school holiday. Best get yourself invited to a friend's.*

Sophie stuffed the envelope into her bedside drawer, then lay on her bed and stared at the leaden sky. She could understand Rosemary not wanting to spend the money: She knew there wasn't much of it around for Sophie, and the little there was had been earmarked for school fees. Rosemary was keen on Sophie's "education" largely because it meant they had to spend very little time together.

It was hard not to think about how different things could have been if . . . No. She wouldn't allow herself to think about her father. Nothing would bring him back.

Sophie straightened the photo on the windowsill. She

tried hard every day to remember everything she could about him, but he was starting to fade. She couldn't stop it. And trying to remember him was like trying to remember a dream. Sometimes she had a sudden memory of climbing onto his knee to put her finger in the cleft of his chin, or snatches of a song he sang in the car, or the way he used to laugh as he wiped her face after he'd let her use ketchup for lipstick . . . but she couldn't force these memories to come without them feeling damaged in some way. And she couldn't remember his voice. All she really knew about the night he had died — through listening to Rosemary on the phone years later — was that it was dark and it was raining and her father had borrowed someone's car to drive home after his poetry reading.

"Have you handed in your form?" Delphine had come back to the room to pick up a forgotten workbook. She plucked it off her shelf and pushed it into her oversized Chanel handbag.

"No." This would make it even worse. Her two closest friends were going on the trip . . . and they didn't even want to go. Delphine kept going on about how cold it would be, and Marianne said she was actually *interested* in Thomas Hardy's cooking.

Delphine raised one eyebrow.

"It's Rosemary," Sophie muttered. "I need her permission and she won't give it."

Delphine put out her hand. "Give the form to me."

Sophie handed the envelope to Delphine, who whisked a pen out of her pocket.

"But you can't!" Sophie gasped. "That's illegal."

"Look, the office isn't going to check. They just want a signature. The only time they go back and check is if something goes wrong. And nothing ever goes wrong on a school trip, does it?" She dashed off a signature with a flourish. "Anyway, I'm doing Rosemary a favor. Mrs. Sharman will send home anyone who isn't traveling, and she won't want to be stuck looking after you while everyone else is on the trip. So it's better for everyone if you come with us."

"But what about the cost?" Sophie said, her stomach heavy.

Delphine shrugged. "It'll go on her school bill. And by that time it will be too late. She'll just have to pay up."

"I don't feel very happy about this," Sophie whispered.

"You don't have to feel happy," Delphine said. "You just have to hand it in at the office and start thinking about what you're going to pack." She shook her head. "Or should that be *not* pack?" She laughed. "My mother still talks about the little English orphan who came to stay in Paris for a whole week with a plastic bag as her luggage."

"I didn't need anything else . . ." Sophie started to say, although the image of Delphine's mother opening the door of the small but incredibly chic apartment, and shaking her head as if Sophie were from another planet, made her scalp tingle with embarrassment.

"Don't worry." Delphine sounded confident. "My mother is sending me some clothes from Paris. There's bound to be a few things that will fit you."

Sophie held the signed form in her hands. Could she do it? She looked at the signature and realized that this was more than just a piece of paper: She was holding snow and a forest and a dream in her hand. Of course, it wasn't *her* dream, it could never be her dream, but the thought of going to Saint Petersburg, to Russia, made her scalp tingle in a different way. She had glimpsed something magical, as if a butterfly had landed on a boring textbook. For a moment she remembered the glamorous visitor who had made it possible, then the sense of unease she had felt in her presence. She put them both out of her mind.

She would go!

"Can't you move your stuff, Delphine?" Marianne kicked two metal suitcases out of her way as she crossed the room. "I knew you didn't have a headache! You just wanted extra time to pack!"

It was the day before the end of term and, by Sophie's reckoning, only fifteen hours and seventeen minutes until they left for Saint Petersburg.

"Normally, I would have laid everything out at least two days in advance!" Delphine picked up a canvas tote from the floor. The suitcases remained where they were. "But of course in London you are expected to pack in half an hour!"

"We're not going until tomorrow!" Marianne said, throwing her math books onto her bed. "Why all the fuss?"

Delphine ignored Marianne and started wrapping a pile of cashmere sweaters in tissue paper. "Can I put some of my clothes in your bag, Sophie? I've no more room in mine." She looked across at Sophie's small pile of clothes and frowned. "Although I hope you're taking more than that."

Sophie laughed. "Do I need anything else?"

Delphine sighed. "What about a dress? For the evening? It said on the itinerary that we were going to the ballet. You can't go to the ballet in Saint Petersburg in a pair of jeans."

Sophie dug out a little sequined summer dress from her narrow wardrobe and held it up. It had looked pretty in the summer, she thought, with flip-flops. But now, in the gray London light, she knew it looked cheap and flimsy. A couple of the sequins were hanging down from the hem on long threads. And it wouldn't be warm enough for Russia.

Delphine shuddered. "Don't worry," she said. "You can borrow something of mine, like I said." She looked suspiciously at Marianne. "Have you even started packing yet?"

"It'll get done." Marianne lay full-length on her bed, reading a guidebook on Saint Petersburg. "But you know, all I really need to take is a happy smile!" She beamed over the pages at Delphine. "My mother says it's the most important thing to wear!"

"Oh yes, I can just see it on the catwalks," Delphine mused. "Clothes by Yves Saint Laurent . . . lunatic grin by Marianne!"

She ignored the book thrown at her head and calmly put several shoe boxes into Sophie's rucksack, placing Sophie's clothes carefully on top. "What's this?" she asked, picking up an old-fashioned wooden pencil box. She stuck her fingernail in the tiny indent and slid the lid to one side.

"Just . . . stuff . . ." Sophie said. "I'll put it in my rucksack."

Delphine picked out a heavy gold cuff link.

"My dad's," Sophie muttered.

A small piece of lace was next to come out. "It must have been from one of my mother's summer dresses," Sophie said.

Delphine put them carefully back in the box. "And this?" she asked, unfolding a piece of paper that looked as if it had been torn from a magazine. Inside was a large colorless stone on a piece of old string. It looked like a piece of dirty glass.

"I don't know, really," Sophie said. "It's just something of my dad's. He used to hold it up to the light and it would suddenly have all these other colors in it."

"Prism," said Marianne.

"What?" Delphine held the glass up and little sprinkles of light seemed to jump out.

"Refraction!" Marianne said. "When light is split up into its component parts. Like in a rainbow. Don't you *ever* pay attention in physics?" She added, "It looks a bit like my lucky druid stone."

"*Mon Dieu*," Delphine muttered. "How can you be so superstitious *and* so clever?" She held the piece of glass up to her ear. "It'd make a nice earring, though."

"Except there's only one." Sophie sat down on her bed. "I don't have a pair of anything. Rosemary got rid of most of my parents' things in one of her big spring cleanups."

"I'm surprised she hasn't got rid of *you* in one of her cleanups!" Marianne said, trying and failing to lighten the mood. "Sorry," she added.

"I wonder what it would be like to be one of a pair . . ." Sophie whispered. "Or a *family* . . ."

There was an awkward silence and then Delphine said softly, "It's all right being the only one, Sophie. It means you're unique."

Sophie smiled, although she didn't feel happy. Talking about her parents always made her feel their loss more keenly. She took the box from Delphine, wrapped the piece of glass back up in the torn magazine page, and put it neatly back in the box. Then she put the box in her rucksack. Her father had promised to take her on a magical journey. Of course, he probably meant traveling by flying carpet, or charging along in a time machine. She couldn't manage either of those, but she would take what little she had left of him with her. That way *she* could take *him* on a magical journey.

She was really going!

She allowed herself to think about it — really think about it — for the first time. Of Russia. Of vast lily pads of ice slipping down the inky river Neva. Of uprisings and royal bloodshed. Of the story of the poet who fought a duel on a bitter frosty dawn for the sake of his skittish young wife. And everywhere — under the hooves of the horses pulling sleighs through the streets, on the onion domes of churches, or covering the parks of ornate baroque palaces — snow.

CHAPTER FIVE

The Station

Twenty English girls stood underneath the clock in the Moskovsky Vokzal train station, waiting for their host families to arrive. The early start from school, the excitement of the flight from England, and the taxi across the city had left them all exhausted.

Miss Ellis, their language teacher, clapped her hands. "We are now in Russia!" She spoke loudly, as if she were addressing a huge crowd rather than a group of twenty schoolgirls. "Remember — and this especially means you, Nadine" — she glared at a sixteen-year-old whose hair had been backcombed into a Marie Antoinette birds' nest and who was picking the silver varnish off her nails — "that you are ambassadors for your country! You are ambassadors for womanhood! You are ambassadors for New Bloomsbury College!"

Sophie didn't care about being an ambassador. She

was in Saint Petersburg! She was actually here. Not only that, there was a blizzard outside. Real, proper snow. Wild, magical weather instead of London drizzle. And the station itself was as beautiful as a *palazzo*. She felt as if she were already somewhere enchanting, somewhere full of possibilities.

Sophie looked out over the crowded concourse. Men wore fur hats. Their faces, under the lights, were the color of the meat in a pork pie. The women looked bored and disdainful in long fur coats, but glamorous and foreign with their bright, waxy lipstick and thick black eyeliner. In between the crowds, young soldiers in greatcoats wandered around, their faces impossibly clean, their eyes sleepy. They carried large black machine guns on leather straps over their shoulders.

As the crowds parted, Sophie noticed a woman at the station café, beautifully if showily dressed in a long tapestry coat with a high fur collar. Unlike many others in the station, she wore no hat. Her short hair, which curled around her wide cheekbones like orchid petals, was very black and almost as shiny as her high patent-leather boots. Every few seconds, the woman checked the time on her watch and glanced over to the station clock above Sophie's head. Sophie found her concentration fascinating. What was the woman so concerned about that needed such careful attention to the passing of time? Perhaps she was a countess, smuggling secrets, about to take the train through the snows and the forests to some dangerous assignation with a foreign agent? Or was she about to start work on a cosmonaut base, training brave young Russians to travel to the stars? Or was she even, Sophie wondered as she watched the woman lift a tiny cup to her lips, a famous ballerina who simply wanted to find some anonymity away from adoring audiences and a grueling dance schedule?

Delphine, dressed in a gray-and-silver tweed coat, a soft silk scarf at her neck, and a gray man's homburg hat pulled down low over her loose blonde curls, pointed her toe and photographed her shoe.

Marianne, wearing her navy school coat, jeans, and sneakers, nudged her in the ribs. "Why are you taking photographs of your feet?"

"For my visual diary!" Delphine explained. "Don't you think my shoes are pretty? And the herringbone pattern of my tights? I'm going to make a film when we get back to London."

"Your feet?" Marianne repeated. She shook her head and waved her guidebook at Delphine. "With 'all the splendors of the Tsars' to be seen, you're going to make a film of your feet?"

Sophie slipped her copy of the itinerary out of her rucksack. Their hostess was called Dr. Galina Starova.

That sounded like a good name. A glamorous name. *What would a woman with a name like that be like?* Sophie thought. She decided she would greet her in Russian — if she didn't become tongue-tied at the last minute.

How would she say hello? *"Strast-vooo-id-tye,"* she muttered.

This Dr. Starova, decided Sophie, was probably responsible for scientific research at a top secret institute. She would be beautiful and clever, but also do wicked things like smoking, playing cards, and wearing fur. She would be an excellent shot. She would definitely be wearing thick black eyeliner and too much lipstick.

"Paj-hal-ster." It would be good to be able to say "please."

By the end of the week, Dr. Starova and Sophie would be firm friends and write to each other for the rest of their lives.

"Spar-see-bar." And always useful to say "thank you."

Sophie liked the way her tongue rolled around in her mouth as she said these words. They seemed so much more meaningful than just "please" or "thank you." It amused her the way the vowels just knocked into each other. There was nothing polite or clipped about Russian, nothing very kind or courteous about the sound of the words. Nothing limited. They sounded rich and fat, like someone laughing. Dr. Starova would teach her how to speak Russian, she just knew it. And for once, Sophie would be good at something.

A middle-aged couple with a sulky-looking girl approached the group. The woman was holding a piece of paper. Miss Ellis spoke to them in what appeared to be very stilted Russian, then checked her clipboard and called out, "Lydia? Lydia Sedgwick? Come on! Oh, will someone pinch her and get her headphones off? Can she not go for three seconds without blasting her brain with rap music?"

Lydia, looking slightly dazed, pushed her headphones off as her Russian hosts shook hands with her. Before the man had picked up her suitcase, however, she was pulling them back on.

"Honestly . . ." muttered Miss Ellis.

Other families arrived, and girls were quickly ticked off the list and accompanied out of the station. By six forty-five, only Miss Ellis, Sophie, Delphine, and Marianne were left.

Miss Ellis's own host, the head of modern languages at School 59, was standing slightly to one side, looking bored. He wandered over to Miss Ellis and they had a conversation that involved lots of looking at watches and shrugging of shoulders.

"Miss Ellis?"

Sophie gasped.

It was the woman from the café, the one with the short black hair and the tapestry coat. She had appeared as if from nowhere.

"I am sorry to be late. I am Dr. Galina Starova." She smiled at Miss Ellis's host and the man grinned foolishly, his bored manner completely extinguished. "Dr. Karenin! I have heard so much about you!"

The man stood taller and his shoulders seemed to broaden under his thick overcoat.

"You will excuse me." The woman leaned toward Miss Ellis as if she were about to tell her a great secret. "My car, he would not start. The weather!" She showed a set of extremely even, incredibly white teeth. Her eyelids gleamed with pearly blue eye shadow, which made her pale eyes look even larger.

The way she bent like a tulip toward Miss Ellis, the slow smile, that rich voice, the enormous pale blue eyes . . . Now Sophie wanted to gasp again, but felt too astonished. She'd been watching this woman at the café without realizing that she'd seen her before.

She turned to Marianne. "It's her!" she whispered.

"Who?" Marianne looked around.

"The woman who came to our school."

"What woman?"

But before Sophie could reply, Miss Ellis snapped, "Well, at least you're here." She did not bother to hide her irritation. "It is very late for the girls, Dr. Starova. They are very tired after their long journey."

"But of course." Dr. Starova looked serious. She placed a gloved hand on Miss Ellis's arm, and glanced across at Dr. Karenin, lowering her eyelids once more. "I understand. You worry! But now I am here and girls all safe!" She turned to the girls and opened her eyes wide. "So, we say good-bye to Miss Ellis and charming Dr. Karenin, and we hurry into night. Snow not worry us!" She almost pushed Miss Ellis away. "Good-bye! See you Monday!"

Miss Ellis gave Dr. Starova a quizzical look, then turned to the girls. "Please be on your best behavior," she said, staring at Sophie meaningfully, then started walking briskly toward the Metro. Dr. Karenin shook himself as if from a daydream, and followed slowly behind, but he kept glancing over his shoulder, as if he were no longer eager to leave the station and the mesmerizing Dr. Starova.

"Wave good-bye, girls!" Dr. Starova beamed.

Sophie, Marianne, and Delphine waved limply to their teacher's unseeing back. Dr. Starova watched the escalator intently, waiting until Miss Ellis and her host had completely disappeared.

Then Sophie couldn't stop herself. "It's you!" she cried.

The woman narrowed her pale eyes and looked at Sophie, then quickly looked away again. "Who else could I be but me?" she said.

"I mean, it's you. From the school. You came to my school. In London." Sophie wasn't sure if she was making herself clear. "I showed you the playground," Sophie insisted. "You took my photograph. To show Natalya."

"Who?" The woman frowned.

Sophie felt confused. Had she got it wrong? "Natalya, your daughter . . ."

The woman waved her hand airily. "Ah, yes. Perhaps. I travel often. I visit many schools!" She smiled approvingly at Delphine. "That is good coat. Good for Russian weather." She reached out and stroked the fabric. "Is designer?"

Delphine smiled. "Of course!"

"So now," announced Dr. Starova, checking her tiny wristwatch, "we run for train!"

They scarcely had time to pick up their bags before Dr. Starova was marching smartly toward the platforms. Sophie, seeing that Delphine was struggling, took one of her suitcases and Marianne the other. They set off after the elegant figure of their host, feeling awkward and out of place, trying to get past commuters and travelers who were not in the habit of moving to accommodate three hobbling schoolgirls.

"Where's she going?" Delphine said. "Why aren't we taking the Metro?"

"Just don't take your eyes off her," Marianne replied, her breathing shallow. "If we lose her, I don't get the feeling she'll come back for us."

"Quick!" Dr. Starova called over her shoulder as they reached a platform. "The train is leaving. We must not miss him. Next train tomorrow!"

The girls immediately upped their pace, almost breaking into a run as the woman strode alongside an old-fashioned-looking train, which seemed to go on for miles. Eventually, Dr. Starova thrust her tickets at a uniformed guard standing at the farthest door, fluttering them like a fan under his nose and laughing coquettishly. He waved them on without looking once at the tickets.

"We are just in time!" she said, smiling at them all.

The girls struggled up the steps with their bags, Dr. Starova doing nothing to help.

"Turn right! Second compartment!" she called. "Hurry!" She stepped lightly up behind them, banging the door shut.

The train jolted, then began to move.

CHAPTER SIX

The Train

"Hurry!" Dr. Starova urged, pushing past them. "We must find our carriage!"

Sophie felt a delicious combination of fear and excitement. This was not the glamorous sleeper she had imagined, but it would do. She was on a train in Saint Petersburg. Who cared if she wouldn't have time to put chocolate cats under her pillow as she did in her fantasy Russian journey? After all, they wouldn't be traveling very far; soon they would be in Dr. Starova's home, enjoying Russian food and meeting the rest of the Starova family, including Natalya, the math prodigy.

"Watch it!" Marianne turned to Delphine as they tried to maneuver their suitcases along the narrow corridor. "I need *both* my legs!"

"Too slow!" Dr. Starova pushed past them and disappeared into a compartment ahead.

The girls struggled on. They had to stop to let another passenger pass, but finally they caught up and put their bags down. They were in a cramped cabin with four narrow red seats and a small drop-down table.

Dr. Starova drew the curtain behind them. "We good!" she said.

Delphine got out her phone. "Would you mind if I took a photograph of your coat? My mother is a fashion editor in Paris and she likes me to send her pictures of things that have caught my eye. Is it vintage?"

Dr. Starova took off her coat and folded it carefully. "No photographs. I stop them many years ago." Then she took Delphine's phone out of her hand and turned it off.

"You can't do that!" Delphine said.

Dr. Starova shrugged and handed it back. "But if I let you take photograph, I must let everyone take photograph!" She smoothed her claret wool skirt over her hips before sitting down.

The train was picking up speed. Dr. Starova reached into her handbag and brought out a jeweled compact, an old-fashioned-looking thing that nevertheless seemed exotic and precious in the bare train carriage. She snapped it open, ran her tongue over her teeth, arched her eyebrows, pushed a curl back from her forehead, and pursed her lips. "Every hour men want photograph . . . It must stop!" She snapped the compact shut. "So!" she said. "This your first time in Russia?"

The girls nodded.

"Voy gavaritye parruski?"

The girls stared at her.

"What did you say?" Sophie asked. She thought the last word might be something to do with the word for *Russian,* but didn't want to risk looking silly.

"That funny." And then the woman laughed. A short, sharp laugh, like a slap. "You not understand Russian?"

Marianne looked stung. "I have memorized the alphabet," she said.

"And we are very keen to learn," Sophie added quickly.

"You two are," muttered Delphine.

"Of course!" Dr. Starova was still smiling, but her eyes had assumed a more watchful expression. She stared out of the window at the blizzard and the black night. The train was now rattling along at high speed. She turned back to the girls.

"So, I think because you not need school until Monday, we spend weekend with my friends!" She had a curious habit of making everything sound as though it were an announcement of enormous importance, and that the girls should be incredibly pleased with her. "They have *dacha.* Do you know what that is?" Her eyebrows flew up. "It's . . . little house . . . in country . . . for holidays and weekends. North of city." Dr. Starova was speaking rapidly but smoothly, as if she were rehearsing lines for a play.

Sophie couldn't think what to say. She was sure that Miss Ellis had told them they would be going to a suburb of Saint Petersburg called Stary Beloostrov, which wasn't in the country at all. "We aren't going to your apartment?" she asked.

"We go to country." Dr. Starova looked faintly annoyed. "I told you."

"But I have to go shopping tomorrow," Delphine said.

"Shopping?" Dr. Starova said this word as if it were the most lunatic thing she had heard.

"I have to get special notebooks for my mother. From the shop on Nevsky Prospekt. And a chocolate carriage from the shop near the Stroganov Palace." Her cheeks became pink. "That's really important."

"But how you send chocolate carriage to your mother?" Dr. Starova said. "It not possible!"

"But that's the most important thing. She needs the carriage by Tuesday. She's doing a shoot. A Cinderella jewelry shoot. For a magazine!"

Dr. Starova shrugged. "I know this shop. There is no more carriage. Only . . ." She thought for a moment. ". . . chocolate yacht! Rich people in Russia not want carriage. They want yacht!" She smiled at Delphine.

Delphine looked as if she was about to say something else, but Dr. Starova turned her head away and looked out of the carriage window. The conversation was clearly over.

The train slowed down. It jolted and stopped. They were at the first station. Sophie saw people crowding on the platform and heard large, loud Russian voices. Dr. Starova looked out of the window. There was a crease between her eyes, as if the girls were irritating her now. She didn't say anything.

The train picked up speed again as it left the station. Dr. Starova reached into her handbag and brought out their tickets. She checked the names and handed one to each of the girls in turn. They were large, the paper faintly marbled, incomprehensible Russian letters swarming all over them. She glanced at her watch. "I think we arrive by nine," she said. "It not far."

"But that's two hours away!" Marianne said. "How can you say that's not far?"

"We are in Russia." Dr. Starova looked even more irritated. "It is large country." She smoothed her skirt again.

"This isn't on our itinerary!" Marianne pulled a piece of paper out of her coat pocket, unfolded it, and read out the details. "It says we will be staying with our host families in Saint Petersburg!" She thrust the paper at Dr. Starova. "See? You can read it for yourself!"

Dr. Starova took the paper from Marianne, held it far away from her, as if she needed glasses, then shrugged, as if what was written on the paper was of no interest to her.

"I will fetch you some tea," she said, standing up and sliding into her coat. She put Marianne's itinerary in her pocket. "I think perhaps you thirsty."

"Thank you very much." Sophie smiled, trying to be polite. "I'm sorry . . . we're not being ungrateful . . . it's very kind of you . . ."

The woman picked up her handbag.

"We're just a bit tired," Sophie added, although she wasn't sure that Dr. Starova had heard as she slipped quickly out of the compartment.

"Do we want to go to the country?" Delphine asked. "I'm not sure I want to. I don't care what Dr. Starova says about chocolate yachts! I don't want to leave Saint Petersburg. I have a lot of shopping to do."

"She's just trying to do something nice for us," Sophie said. "Show us a bit more of Russia."

"But what am I going to do about the chocolate shop?" Delphine said, her voice wound tight. "And the notebooks? What will I tell my mother? She's relying on me."

Sophie reached across and squeezed her hand. "We'll sort it out."

Delphine took a deep breath and squeezed Sophie's hand back.

"Just think. Everyone else is taking the cooking course," Marianne sighed. "Probably drinking hot chocolate with marshmallows and playing Scrabble . . ."

The train slowed down for another station, this one much less busy. Sophie watched the dark-coated figures get off the train, their breath escaping in great clouds. She tried to read the letters of the name of the station, but couldn't make head nor tail of them.

"It's odd how Russian looks so foreign," she said, more to herself than to her friends. "It's so frustrating not even knowing where to start."

She watched a woman walk quickly up the platform, her hands thrust into her pockets, her arms close to her side. Black hair like petals and a tapestry coat.

"Dr. Starova!" she called, banging on the window.

The woman's eyes flicked toward their carriage, but she kept on walking.

"That couldn't have been Dr. Starova," Marianne said, shifting in her seat. "She said she was going to get us some tea."

"Why would she need to get off the train to get tea?" Delphine looked puzzled. "It can't have been her."

The train started to pull out of the station.

"Did anyone see her get back on?" asked Sophie. The others shook their heads.

They sat silent for a couple of moments, each of them waiting for Dr. Starova to pull back the curtain and step into their compartment.

After a few more minutes, Sophie said, "She's not coming."

Marianne said, "There are one hundred and forty million people in Russia. The chances are it was just someone who looked like her."

Sophie shook her head. "It's no use, Marianne. It *was* Dr. Starova I saw on the platform. She's left us on the train."

There was a longer silence. Sophie felt her heart pick up speed in time with the train. They were now slipping farther and farther away from the station, through the blizzard, into the vast, empty countryside. But where were they heading?

It was unbearable. Sophie stood up.

"What are you doing?" Marianne said.

Sophie didn't know. She stared out of the window but saw only her own face staring back.

Delphine said, "You got it wrong, Sophie. Dr. Starova *must* be on the train because . . . if she got off . . ." She turned a blank face to Marianne. "Do you know where we're going?"

Marianne looked down at her ticket. She stared very hard at the writing. "I learned the alphabet," she whispered. "I ought to be able to read what it says."

Sophie sat down again. She and Delphine waited quietly.

After a minute or so, Marianne looked up. It was clear she was upset. "I'm really smart," she whispered. "I know I am. But I don't understand what's written on the ticket." She took her glasses off and rubbed her eyes.

Sophie said, "I think that says Saint Petersburg." She pointed to the top left-hand corner.

"Even I knew it said that," Delphine said. "It's two words."

Marianne chewed her lip. "I'm sorry," she said. She folded her ticket up and put it in her pocket. And then, her face crumpling, she whispered, "What are we going to do?"

Sophie tried to think, but she felt like her brain was as full of swirling snowflakes as the night outside. She simply could not make sense of what had happened. Their three reflections in the window seemed very small as the train hurtled through the night.

"Let's call the conductor." Delphine got up and pulled the curtain open. She stepped out of the compartment, but then froze. "We won't know how to explain to him," she gasped. "We can't speak Russian."

Sophie, realizing that her Russian amounted to just three words, said, "We'll just have to make him understand somehow."

"Understand what?" Delphine looked on the verge of tears. "That we've been left on a train? That we don't know where we're going?"

She came back into the carriage, drew the curtain closed again, and sat down. She took off her hat and raked her hands through her hair.

Marianne had her thoughtful face on. "Let's think about this logically," she said. "Did someone forget to tell us something? Miss Ellis seemed a bit stressed."

"I'm going to call her." Delphine got out her phone. She tapped at the screen and put the phone to her ear. Sophie held her breath. Delphine shrugged. "It just rings and rings. I can't even leave a message."

"*Beel-yet!*" The conductor, a small wiry man wearing a peaked cap on the back of his head, pulled back the curtain. He stood with his hand out. The girls didn't move. He smiled and said more loudly, "*Beel-yet!*"

"What does he want?" Marianne asked.

The man said, "Teekits!"

Sophie handed hers over. He looked at it, looked at her, and made a strange clicking noise in the back of his throat. He shook his head and said something under his breath. Then he shrugged, checked both Marianne's and

Delphine's tickets, and left. They heard him walking up the corridor, yelling, *"Beel-yet!"*

"At least we've learned one word," Marianne said, folding her ticket up and putting it away.

"He looked surprised," Sophie said, staring at her ticket as if she would suddenly become able to read Russian, or find the answer to their situation printed on it. "I wonder why?"

Within minutes, they found out.

The conductor reappeared and picked up their bags, moving them into the corridor.

Marianne said, "What's he doing? Why is he taking our bags?"

Delphine pulled at the man's sleeve. "Leave my things alone!"

The conductor ignored her. Sophie got the impression that, although a small man, he was used to getting people off trains without any bother. And without losing any time.

Sophie and Marianne found themselves moving toward the door. But Delphine stayed in her seat. She folded her arms, crossed her legs, and stared straight ahead. The conductor took her by the shoulder. She shook him off. He took her shoulder more forcefully. Sophie saw her wince.

"Come on, Delphine," she whispered. "This won't help."

Delphine's mouth became harder as the conductor maneuvered her out of the compartment. But despite the determined angle of her jaw, her resistance was just for show. The whole episode seemed to have achieved a dynamic and an inevitability of its own, as if they were moving through a dream.

The train slowed down. The conductor opened the door. Snow flew into the train.

"There must be a mistake!" Sophie said desperately.

The conductor shrugged. "Maybe mistake on teekit," he said. "No station! Only old platform. But you leave where teekit say."

Then he threw Sophie's rucksack out into the night before picking up the first of Delphine's suitcases with two hands.

It was as if Delphine suddenly came to life. She screamed at him in French to put the suitcase down, how dare he, she would kill him with her bare hands if he so much as touched anything of hers. And then, as the suitcases went out into the night, she cried, *"Mes vête-ments!"* And pushing past the others, she leaped from the train.

The brakes squealed and the conductor yelled, *"Uiditye!"*

Marianne turned her head as if it were filled with concrete. "What did he say?"

To Sophie, her voice sounded far away. She had a sense that she was looking at everything through very thick glass. Even if she spoke, she wasn't sure that Marianne would hear her.

The man bellowed, *"Von. Out!"*

Marianne's suitcase was thrown into the snow. And now the conductor clamped a small white hand around Marianne's arm as if he would throw her, too, from the train.

Confused, frightened, but unable to know what else they could do, both girls jumped down, into the dark and the fury of the storm, and onto a narrow platform that was completely covered in deep, deep snow.

CHAPTER SEVEN

The Hut

Sophie and Marianne clung to each other as the lights of the train floated off into the night. The wind snapped at their fingers and faces and screamed in their ears. Snow jabbed and stung their eyes.

They were nowhere. This was no longer even a station. How could they have been put off the train here?

Delphine was gone. It was as if she had jumped into nothingness, another world, perhaps.

All Sophie could think was that they couldn't stay on the platform, if it even *was* a platform. This snow, this wind, was not romantic, as she had thought it might be from the safety of the train station. It was vicious and savage. They had to find Delphine so they could get out of the cold, find shelter, just so they could think about what to do next.

Sophie squinted her eyes, concentrated really hard, and tried to peer through the dark and the driving snow.

"Delphine!" she yelled. But her voice was whipped away to nothing by the wind. She took a step forward, dragging Marianne with her. "We have to get out of the storm!"

Another step, and then, not knowing how, she found herself tipping forward into snow, a live creature at her feet. She screamed and tried to crawl away, but the creature grabbed her foot. It was sobbing and calling her name.

"You idiot, Delphine!" Sophie cried. "What are you doing?"

"My suitcases! I need to find my suitcases!" Delphine scrabbled frantically in the snow.

"You'll have to leave them!" Sophie yelled back. "We'll find them later!"

Delphine shook her head, refusing to give up.

"I can't see!" Marianne wailed. Her glasses and hair were completely coated in white.

"Don't take your glasses off!" Sophie grabbed Marianne's arm to stop her. "If you drop them, you'll never find them!"

"But what are we going to do?" sobbed Marianne.

Sophie turned her back to the wind, and peered into the night. There! A black square behind the furious snowflakes. A waiting room? A hut?

"I think there's shelter over there!" she shouted. "Hold hands. We mustn't fall onto the tracks!"

She wasn't sure they had heard, but then felt Marianne grasp her frozen hand. She grabbed Delphine, pulling her up, and this time met with no resistance.

The three girls shuffled through the blizzard to the hut. The wind screamed. Sophie could feel her teeth knocking about in her mouth. Finally, they reached a door of split and weathered wood. Sophie attempted to turn the handle, but cried out when she touched the metal: It was so cold it had burned her fingers. She pulled her sleeve down over her hand, tried again. After a shove and a kick, the door gave.

Bringing swirling capes of snow with them, the girls fell out of the storm and into the hut, closing the door with their shoulders. The sound of the wind — a sound as wild and distressing as a wounded animal — was instantly muted. They leaned against the door, getting their breath back. Sophie felt snow melting on the back of her neck and dripping slowly underneath her collar. She turned to look at her surroundings.

It wasn't what she had expected to find. It was as if her father had opened the pages of a book and pointed to the illustration. A line drawing of a log cabin, just waiting for the woodcutter to return.

There was a small black stove, which, judging by the warmth of the room, had been burning for some time. In front of it were a stack of logs, three wooden chairs, and a small table. The thick white cloth had been ironed with so much starch it was as stiff as cardboard, with sharp creases where it had been folded. On this a loaf of dark bread, a bread knife with a bone handle, and white butter had been laid out on a battered metal tray. There was also a plain white jug, and three small horn cups. Through a small window they could see furious swirls of snow. The contrast between the scene in front of them and the savagery of the storm outside was such a surprise that none of the girls seemed able to move.

"What are we going to do?" Marianne shook her head as if a fly were annoying her. "I think and think, but I can't think what to do!"

Sophie squeezed her arm reassuringly. "We're going to wait for the next train back to Saint Petersburg."

"But what if it doesn't stop?" Marianne cried.

Delphine took out her phone. She pulled off wet gloves with her teeth and turned it on to check for a signal. "Nothing!" She threw the phone on the floor.

Sophie took a deep breath, and then bent down and picked it up. "Come on, Delphine," she said. "We have to stay calm."

"Calm? Are you mad? No, don't answer that. We already know you're insane. Telling us that Russia would be exciting. And we believed you!"

Sophie handed Delphine her phone.

"Oh, what's the use!" Delphine turned away. "The whole trip is stupid!"

"Not stupid, Delphine," Sophie said quietly. "Just different from what we expected."

She calmly took her friends' hands and led them toward the table. She felt that she must speak slowly to them, as if they were wild animals that would startle easily. She mustn't make too much of anything. Keep it normal. "Come on, Delphine." She tried to smile. "We can rest here for a short while and sort everything out. Let's eat."

Sophie took off her soaked coat, and the others followed suit.

"Well, I *am* hungry!" said Marianne. The snowflakes had melted into little diamonds of water on her glasses. She took them off and wiped them on her sleeve, then put them back on, picked up the bread knife, and started sawing into the loaf.

Delphine said, "But it isn't for us. What if the owner comes back?"

Marianne spread the bread with thick waves of butter. "Well, we're in the middle of nowhere in Russia in a blizzard. I'm sure whoever it *is* for won't mind."

Sophie cut and buttered a thick slice. "I'm hungry, too," she said, and realized she really was.

"Perhaps this is like one of those mountain refuges," Delphine reasoned. "Things are left for people who get stuck on the mountain at night."

Marianne nodded, her mouth full of bread.

"But we're not on a mountain," Sophie said, biting into her bread. It was delicious: soft but with a smoky taste, as if it had been cooked in a wood-fired oven. "We're in Russia — somewhere." And she shivered, but not with cold. She thought she should feel anxious about their situation, but somehow she wasn't. Surely this was an adventure? Wasn't this what she had hoped for in her beige boarding-school room?

"I've got a little money in my pocket — in euros." Delphine was helping herself to bread and butter now. "We could leave some here as payment. People usually don't mind you taking things as long as you pay."

They sat in front of the fire and ate their strange little meal in the strange little hut. Their first sip of the rich juice in the horn cups made them smile.

"It's . . . it's . . . cherry!" Marianne laughed.

And when they saw Marianne's crimson mustache, it made them all feel better.

"This hut . . ." Sophie began, thinking. She looked around. "It reminds me of somewhere. A photograph . . . no, a picture." She frowned, trying to secure the half-remembered image. "It's as if a woodcutter is going to appear out of a forest."

Marianne glanced nervously at the door. "I hope he's a friendly one."

"Yes, now I remember," Sophie said slowly. "There was a picture in a book I had when I was little. My father read it to me. The hut was just like this." It made her feel safe to talk about her father and the book and the stories. "He would sit on the edge of my bed and read to me until I fell asleep." She felt a lump form in her throat. "When I started living with Rosemary, that was the hardest thing to get used to . . . I really missed his voice at bedtime."

Why was she saying this? What was she thinking? She put a piece of bread in her mouth, as if that would help get rid of the lump in her throat. She needed to stop thinking about how things had changed since he had died.

"I don't see my father much," Delphine shrugged. "And even when I do see him, he doesn't really seem to see me." She smiled as if she wanted to make herself believe she didn't care. Sophie put her arm around her friend. Delphine dropped her head onto Sophie's shoulder. "Sorry about the phone," she mumbled. "And saying you're mad . . ."

"Argh!" Marianne dropped her cup and ran to the door.

"What's the matter?" Sophie and Delphine cried.

"There's something under the table!" she yelled, her hand on the door handle.

But before she could wrench open the door, a large

black cat appeared from beneath the thick white tablecloth.

"Marianne!" Delphine laughed. "It's a cat! A big, beautiful cat!"

The creature rubbed itself against Sophie's legs, allowing her to stroke it behind its ears, and then lay down in front of the fire.

"He's not dangerous, Marianne," she said.

Marianne came back to her seat, looking slightly foolish.

"It's not so bad here, is it?" Sophie said. "Anyone who can have a cat as splendid as you must be all right." As if the cat had understood, he stretched one large, square paw across Sophie's foot.

"I wonder what he's called?" said Marianne.

"Something serious, like Alexey, or Sergei," Sophie decided.

"Don't Russians always have two first names?" Delphine said. "I'm sure that's what Miss Ellis said."

"You're right," Marianne smiled. "The men's second names always end in 'ich.' That's the name they take from their father."

"So if this cat's father was called Dmitri," Delphine said, "he'd be called Alexey Dmitrivich."

"Oh, let's call him Sergei Sergeyevich," Sophie said. "Doesn't that sound magical? It's the sort of name that would make anyone sound important, even this big, fat black kitty cat . . ."

They were quiet for a few moments, wriggling their toes in the warmth.

"Do *you* have any other names . . . other than Sophie?" Marianne said. She took a sip from her horn cup.

"Of course not. Just plain old Sophie Smith." Sophie wrinkled her nose. "But then, I don't have any extra anything, do I?"

"No extra money . . ." added Delphine.

"No extra sweaters . . ." Marianne caught the mood.

"Definitely no extra sweaters," Sophie agreed. "Just holey ones. No extra family, either." She gave her friends a half smile.

"Families are overrated, in my opinion," Delphine said. "They're not all they're cracked up to be."

Marianne offered Sophie the last crust of the loaf. "Oh, I don't know. Spending time with my parents is lovely."

"If you like playing Scrabble," Delphine said.

"Well, I do!" said Marianne with enthusiasm.

"Although when my mother saw your dad at New Bloomsbury's open house," Delphine went on, "she liked his cravat and that weird jacket he was wearing."

"She also told him the impoverished English look was going to be all over the catwalks next season," Marianne added. She opened the door of the stove and put more wood on the fire.

Sophie picked up the cat and put it on her lap. The animal settled down happily, his body becoming relaxed and heavy. "Why don't we take turns staying awake so that we don't miss the next train back to Saint Petersburg?"

"That's a really good idea," Delphine said, settling herself further into the little chair and closing her eyes.

"And it will mean that the fire won't go out," Marianne added, stifling a yawn. "Because whoever is awake can make sure there's plenty of wood on the stove. And listen out for the train."

"Will you hear it above the wind, Sophie?" Delphine said cheekily.

Sophie didn't mind being on first watch. She didn't mind if she kept watch all night. She was far too excited to sleep. Being here in this Russian hut, stirring up these memories of her father and those stories, felt somehow right — as if it was where she was meant to be, however ridiculous that sounded.

"Sergei has excellent hearing," she replied, stroking the cat's haunches, and the creature started a deep purring.

What was the story her father had told her? she wondered, as her friends' eyes closed and their breathing became steadier. She could only remember the picture in the book, the hut in the woods that was so similar to this one it felt as if she had stepped into that picture and was now sitting inside the story. If only she could hear her father's words . . .

And as she stroked the cat, she felt that the wind was no longer hostile, but was calling up images and pictures in her mind, of bear cubs and magical horses and beautiful maidens dressed in *sarafans* and a child carved from snow. And . . . a hummed tune, which, after seven years, she still remembered quite clearly, although the words had slipped away from her memory. Then, beneath the wind, a voice, a familiar voice, that seemed to be right inside her head. What was it saying . . . ?

"Oh, gray wolf," says the little snow girl . . .

Yes, that was how it went. The snow girl. She was called . . . *Snegurochka*? And what did she say to the gray wolf?

"I have lost my way and it is getting so dark, and all my little friends are gone."

Yes, she remembered now — there was always a tiny, delicious pause before the next line. The voice would become lower, pretend to be threatening.

"I will take you home," says the old gray wolf.

And she would always feel so scared. She wanted to tell the snow girl not to go with the wolf!

"Oh, gray wolf," says the little snow girl, "I am afraid of you.

I think you would eat me. I would rather go home with some-one else . . ."

She hadn't heard his voice, the voice of her father, as clearly as that for a long time — not since the first few weeks she had spent with Rosemary, in fact. Lying in the dark in her room, she would have whole conversations with him . . . but Rosemary had shouted at her and said she was "weird" and it had to stop. From that day he had stayed silent. It was as if her father didn't want to upset her guardian.

"I will take you home," says the old gray wolf. It was the story her father had told her: Those were his words. She had been the snow girl and he had been the wolf. She knew she was meant to be frightened of the wolf, but because it was her father's voice, she always felt sad when the wolf ran away.

The cat's purrs were so loud they filled the room. Sophie looked up to see moonlight at the small window and a broad slice of silver on the floor. She had fallen asleep!

Sergei sprang down onto the floor and sat looking at her, as if he expected her to do something. *Fool!* She had been the one on duty. What if they had already missed a train? She must not let her friends down.

Feeling determined, she got up, pulled on her coat, and went to the door.

CHAPTER EIGHT

The Stranger

Sophie stepped out onto the platform. The moonlight made everything glitter and a light flurry of snow danced about in the dying wind. All around were the narrow, dark triangles of pine trees, each branch laden with snow, waiting like passengers for something to happen. Every so often, the weight of the snow would be too much for one of the branches and the snow would suddenly slide off and land with a satisfying thud, sending up a white cloud of snowy dust. Then the branch would spring up, light again at last.

The air was cold, and it made her catch her breath. There was a brisk scent of pine needles as well as the softer smell of snow. Sophie's face was already tingling. She knew she should be anxious — she had fallen asleep when it was her turn to listen for the train, after all — but seeing this forest coated in thick drifts of snow and moonlight, breathing air so clear it seemed to sparkle inside her lungs, made her feel full of excitement. This was not like the silver forest her father had taken her to in her dreams. But then, that would be impossible.

Marianne and Delphine stumbled out of the hut, both in their coats, bleary-eyed.

"Oh, you are clever, Sophie!" Marianne said.

"Am I?" Sophie dragged her gaze away from the trees to look at her friend.

"We knew you wouldn't let us down," Delphine cried, clapping her hands.

"Really?" Sophie was puzzled. What were they talking about? Then, seeing her friends staring into the forest behind her, she turned to look.

In the distance, coming toward them on tracks she couldn't have seen due to the deep drifts of snow, was a magnificent white steam train, with two enormous lights, like twin moons, at its front. She felt momentarily disoriented.

"But it's coming from the wrong direction . . ."

The others were too excited to listen. They were jumping up and down on the platform, yelling.

There was a long blast on the whistle, an accompanying joyous screech of metal, and the train slowed down and finally stopped right where they were standing. A cloud of steam enveloped them.

And then, as they laughed with relief, the door of the engine opened and out stepped a man as tall as a bear, with black hair and beard. He was dressed in a white tunic with a black belt around the middle and gold buttons across one shoulder and all down one side. His black trousers were tucked into long black boots.

He walked toward the girls through the folding, spiraling steam, then bowed. As he stood upright again, he smiled broadly, showing square, white teeth. His eyes crinkled at the edges as if he were about to tell them a tremendous joke.

"At last!" he said over the hissing of the engine. "Marianne, Delphine, and my dear, dear Sophie! You are safely here at last!" His voice sounded exactly as Sophie thought a Russian voice should sound. Fat and roly-poly, the words knocking into each other like bowling pins.

The man bowed once more. "I am sorry I was not here to meet your train. Russian blizzards . . ." He shrugged. "But you were comfortable?" he went on anxiously. "You found the hut? I prepared everything in advance."

The girls nodded, then looked at each other. It was as if they were each waiting for one of the others to say something. Sophie, who had felt so comfortable in the hut, now felt less sure about what to do. It felt rude to have a discussion in front of the man about whether they should go with him or not, but then . . . they didn't know him!

The man opened another carriage door and stood to one side, holding it with one hand, the other stretched out toward them. "But make haste! We must get out of the cold. Frost bites more deeply than the wolf!"

Through the steam, Sophie saw the head of an animal painted in silver on the side of the train. Mouth open, teeth bared, as if about to snap its fierce jaws shut on the soft body of its prey. A wolf.

"My luggage . . ." said Delphine.

"I will dig it out!" said the man.

His openness and assurance appeared to give Delphine confidence. She stepped toward him. "Come on!" she called over her shoulder as she took the man's hand and climbed up the step.

"He knows who we are, but who is he?" Marianne whispered.

"I don't know," Sophie replied.

"I'm not sure we should go."

"Well, we can't stay here."

"But we shouldn't go with him if we don't know who he is."

"Please do not delay," the man said, looking more serious and glancing at the sky. "The blizzard will soon return."

Marianne looked back at the hut. "What about the cat?" she asked.

"He belongs here," Sophie answered. "And we don't."

Somehow that seemed to make up both their minds and Marianne and Sophie allowed themselves to be steered up the steps of the train and into an old-fashioned carriage. As she stepped inside, Sophie gasped in delight. Yes, this was the train she had imagined while wearing Rosemary's mink jacket, sleeping in that chilly spare room! The sort of train that began adventures.

There was a pretty chandelier hanging from the ceiling, silver-gray banquettes with deep-set buttons, wooden cupboards above, and heavy, lace-edged blinds at the window. Sophie noticed that, although it was all very beautiful, many of the fabrics looked fragile and worn, like pieces in a museum.

Marianne stood uncertainly by the window and watched the man pluck the luggage out of the snow. He threw the suitcases up into the driver's cabin as easily as if they were empty, slammed their carriage door shut, and walked to the front of the train.

"We still don't know where we're going," Marianne said.

"Back to Saint Petersburg!" Delphine said. "You heard him!"

Marianne shook her head. "He didn't say anything about Saint Petersburg."

"And the train came from the other direction," added Sophie.

Steam billowed past the windows, there was the screech of iron wheels on track, and the train shunted forward. The chandelier tinkled and sprinkled light over them.

"He's been sent to fetch us," Delphine said firmly. "He knows our names. Where else would he be taking us?"

The train gathered pace and slipped into the snow-covered forest.

"I've lost my ticket," Marianne said, slumping down onto a banquette. "I hope he doesn't ask to see it."

Before the girls could say anything more, the man reappeared. He seemed even taller and larger now that he was in the daintily appointed carriage. He rubbed his hands together and said, "It is very cold in the forest. I must make sure that you are kept warm." He turned and took three pale fur traveling rugs from a wooden cupboard.

He gestured to Sophie to sit down. "You must be tired after your long journey," he said, tucking the fur under her knees and then turning his attention to the other girls. Marianne bit her nails and glanced out of the window as if she might still try to get off. The man seemed unaware of her anxiety. "I must first attend to the furnace in the driver's cabin," he said. "A matter of moments, only."

"You're the driver, too?" Marianne looked dazed.

"The train almost takes care of itself." The man smiled. "Which means I will have time to serve you a midnight picnic and your first glass of proper Russian tea. I will prepare the *samovar!*"

He rubbed his hands together and beamed at the girls as if he had just given them a present.

"Miss Ellis definitely got confused," Delphine whispered once the man had left the carriage. They could hear him singing cheerfully, and the sound of cutlery and plates being placed on a tray.

"Or Dr. Starova didn't explain things properly," Marianne added.

An image of the woman in the tapestry coat sipping coffee and checking the station clock dropped into Sophie's mind. Dr. Starova struck her as the sort of woman who knew exactly what she was doing. She thought of her visit to the school — her certainty at wanting Sophie to do the tour, her deftness in taking Sophie's photograph in the playground. And then looking around her room, asking about her father . . . In Sophie's memory, there seemed to be a point to all that the woman had done that day, to her waiting in the station café until the last possible moment at the station, although Sophie still could not understand what that point was.

"Perhaps . . ." Sophie started to say, just as the man reappeared with a small dish of pancakes.

"Blinis!" he said proudly. Each pancake had a dollop of thick white cream and pearls of pale gray on top. "With caviar!"

There was a question to which they desperately needed the answer, but none of them had had the courage to ask it. Sophie wished that Marianne wouldn't go quiet in these situations; her reticence, as she sat observing everything like a little owl, had its drawbacks. And Delphine was sometimes a bit *too* forthright.

"Would you mind telling us . . ." Sophie felt heat sliding over her cheeks.

The man smiled encouragement as he handed them each a plate with a blini.

Delphine, using her most sophisticated voice, finished Sophie's sentence. ". . . who you are?"

The man took a second to answer, as if he might be translating what they had said into Russian. And then he burst out laughing. "The journey to fetch you has made me forgetful!" He took a deep breath, bowed deeply to each of the girls in turn, and then said, in solemn tones, "I am Ivan Ivanovich, majordomo at the Volkonsky Winter Palace!"

Delphine simply nodded, as if she had known this all along. Sophie thought she might have laughed if she didn't feel so confused.

Marianne turned to Sophie with a questioning look and mouthed, "What?"

Delphine was still nodding. "This palace place . . ." she said. "Is it in Saint Petersburg?"

The man shook his head. "Why, no!"

"Oh!" Delphine frowned and stopped nodding.

Marianne made a funny little noise, like air escaping from a balloon. "But we thought" — her voice had a catch to it, as if she were about to cry — "that you had come to take us back to Saint Petersburg."

"That's why we got on the train," Sophie added.

"But why would I take you back to Saint Petersburg when you are to be guests at the palace?" The man called Ivan Ivanovich looked baffled.

Marianne looked even more worried. Sophie wanted to go and sit next to her, put her arm around her thin shoulders. It usually made her feel braver if she could comfort someone else.

Marianne swallowed. "We wondered if there had been a mistake," she explained. "We were left on the train."

"And then," added Sophie, "kicked off the train."

Ivan Ivanovich still looked puzzled. "I think you have had a long journey and you are tired," he said. "We still have a long way to go until we arrive in the Volkonsky forest. The princess —"

"Princess?" Delphine choked on her blini.

"Her Serene Highness, the Princess Anna Feodorovna Volkonskaya!" Ivan said. "She requested your presence and I was sent to fetch you!"

Sophie looked at Delphine and Marianne. They looked as shocked as she felt. None of them seemed to know what to say. Instead they watched Ivan lighting a small bundle of twigs with a flourish and pushing them into a cavity below a dented, but highly polished, silver urn with a spout in the middle. Within seconds, the fire was hot enough to make the water inside the urn hiss. He set out a tray with glasses and a dish of ruby-colored jam, then turned a tap on the spout. Hot tea splashed into the first glass.

"Put a spoonful of jam in your tea." He smiled encouragingly at Sophie. "It is how Russians drink it!"

Sophie stirred a spoonful of jam into the dark, steaming liquid, then put the glass to her lips and inhaled a smoky, bitter scent, like tree bark dipped in sugar. But after the first strange mouthful, she found herself wanting more, delighted at the warmth that chased away all of the cold locked in her body.

Ivan Ivanovich smiled. "This is what a good Russian tea will do for you!" he said. "It brings heat to the body.

That is very important when there are twenty degrees of frost on the thermometer." He poured a glass for himself, spooned in some jam, and stirred the tea, looking suddenly serious. "And of course, tea is the only thing to relieve *toska*."

Marianne looked puzzled as she bit into her blini. "What is *toska*?" she asked.

"The word does not have a good translation in your language, but it is a sadness, a melancholy that afflicts the Russian soul. So, as a remedy, we drink tea!" He raised his glass in a salute.

"But you still haven't explained," Sophie burst out. "You are being very kind and it's very good of you to come all this way to fetch us, but we weren't told anything about a palace . . . or a princess . . ."

"It isn't on our itinerary," said Marianne, rather sternly.

"And I would *definitely* have remembered if there had been anything about a princess," Delphine added.

"You will meet the princess tomorrow. You will never have met a more cultured or beautiful woman."

Delphine tucked her hair behind her ear and smoothed her coat. "I'm used to meeting important people," she said.

"Delphine!" Marianne rolled her eyes and tried to kick her, but the fur rug had been wrapped too tightly around her knees.

"You do not need to worry about meeting the princess," Ivan said, his voice grave. "She is a woman of enormous grace and intelligence." He sighed. "I owe the Princess Volkonskaya everything. Fifteen years in the army and then one mistake. A coward tells lies about me and I am thrown out of the army. I cannot return to my village: The shame would kill my mother. So I live on the street. One summer night, the princess walks past. She sees a man crushed by lies, his honor torn to shreds." He smiled. "But she sees more. She sees *trust*. She gives me a new life at the Volkonsky Winter Palace."

Marianne fished her guidebook out of her battered leather bag. "Where is that?" She turned to the index and started looking through the entries.

"Beyond the White Lake," Ivan said. "But you will not find the Volkonsky Winter Palace in any guidebook. It is a diamond in the snow, a palace of dreams, so remote it has been forgotten and the noble Volkonskys erased from the history books."

He stepped across the carriage and pressed on the paneling. A door slid back to reveal a cabinet, fitted out as a compact traveling bathroom. He opened a deep drawer in a cupboard and brought out more furs and pillows, toothbrushes and nightgowns, putting a pile next to each of the girls.

"It would be well if you try to sleep," he said. "Our journey is long and I do not wish you to be weary. The princess is anxious to meet you. I know you will want to make a good impression."

He bowed and left them.

"What did I tell you scruffy English girls?" Delphine looked triumphant. "I said you would want to make a good impression one day!"

"At least I haven't brought the sweater with the holes," Sophie replied, but her mind was spinning with the images Ivan's words had conjured up. A princess? A winter palace? And all too remote for anyone to know about?

She had wished for adventure — and now it was happening.

The train ran along over the rails, the wheels clicking like castanets. There was something so reassuring about this sound, about the velvety warmth of the train carriage, that made the girls feel quite happy to brush their teeth and put on the thick nightgowns Ivan had laid out for them. They lay down on the banquettes, tucking furs around them.

"Fancy being taken to stay in a palace." Marianne put her glasses on top of her suitcase. "And meeting a princess."

"I told you," Delphine said, yawning. "All this fussing

over tickets and itineraries and stations. Nothing ever goes wrong on a school trip."

Sophie buried her fingers in the fur pelt. The skin crackled like paper; it must be very old. There were no sugar mice under her pillow, or chocolate cats, no pistol to guard against the bears and the wolves. Yet she was in Russia, on a train, and it was real, not just a London daydream.

She could hardly have imagined this elegant carriage. The reality was even more wonderful than her dreams, and made her realize the bleakness of her bedroom in Rosemary's flat. Nothing had been done to make it inviting or cozy, perhaps because Rosemary was hoping that Sophie's stay would not be for much longer, that she would get her spare room back. *Was all my dreaming, all my imagining, just an attempt to wish that bleak, small life away?* she wondered. It was hopeless. Better to admit who she was, to accept that she was not remarkable.

She watched Delphine sit up and braid her hair, every movement precise. She looked somehow "right" in the train carriage. Sophie felt she must look ridiculous by comparison, an impostor. And she wasn't smart like Marianne, either. She didn't deserve to be here. She wasn't special or interesting, however much she wanted to be.

She sat up and moved the blind to one side to peer out. The moon, like a great diamond button, hung low in

the sky. Every so often, the forest — which at times was
so close that the branches scraped the windows with their
snow-laden fingers — opened out into an expanse of
moonlight. Sophie glimpsed wooden buildings with low,
carved roofs set about with tumbledown fences, everything glimmering with its coating of frost, before the
curtain of trees swept back in and extinguished the scene.

She didn't know how long she remained like that, gaz-
ing out at Russia, before she sensed a movement at the
doorway. She turned.

"Be careful of the moon, little Sophie," Ivan Ivanovich
whispered. "It will bewitch you. Before you know it,
you can no longer live in the day, but only in the world
of dreams."

CHAPTER NINE

The Vozok

Sophie was woken by the smell of warm bread and hot chocolate. The train whistle hooted loudly and she felt the carriage begin to slow.

Delphine had tipped her head upside down and was brushing her hair vigorously. She flicked her head back up and her hair cascaded over her shoulders. "When we meet the princess, don't stare and don't speak — unless she speaks to you."

"Good morning to you, too," said Sophie.

Marianne murmured, "Too early!" into her pillow, and went back to sleep.

Ivan appeared with a tray and boisterously announced, "We have entered the forest!" He put down the tray and pulled up the blinds. "Hurry with your breakfast, young ladies! Next stop, the Volkonsky Winter Palace!"

Sophie had just enough time to eat, dress, and to wake Marianne before the train stopped with a blast of steam. As the cloud cleared, Sophie saw they were surrounded by the scarred, slender trunks of silver birch trees. The Volkonsky forest. That sounded beautiful. But as she looked deeper into the graceful trees, she frowned, feeling something . . . What was it?

She was still trying to place it when Ivan, now dressed in a full-length sheepskin coat that was belted at the middle, brought in a pile of furs and coats.

"So now we must dress for a Russian winter! First you put your feet into the *valenki*." He held out thick, heavy boots. "Made of felt," he explained. "They keep your feet warm."

Delphine, looking as if she didn't believe him, nonetheless put her feet into the boots.

"And then the *shuba*." Ivan held up a felt coat, lined with fur. "For Marianne!" He helped her into the long coat.

Marianne said, "I can't move my arms."

Ivan Ivanovich placed a sheepskin hat on her head. "We take a shawl," he said. "We wrap it over and around the *shuba*, over your hat, covering as much of your face as we can, and then we cross it, like this, at the back."

He tied the shawl tightly, then darted across the carriage and started opening drawers in a small dresser. With a flourish, he brought out three boxes. Inside each one was a pair of dark gray gloves. "Sealskin!" he beamed. "Now you will avoid frostbite. The Volkonskys made their fortune from salt and diamonds. But their *first* fortune was from fur trapping. These are lined with cashmere, and have never been worn!"

"I feel very peculiar," Marianne whispered to Sophie.

"You look wonderful," said Sophie, but she couldn't help giggling.

Ivan Ivanovich held out a *shuba* for Delphine.

"Thank you, that's very kind," she said, pulling on her exquisite gray tweed coat. "But I have my own clothes. I couldn't meet the princess dressed like —"

"To freeze is not good. You wear the *shuba*, Delphine" — his voice dropped — "or you die."

Delphine shrugged, as if she couldn't care less, but she allowed herself to be dressed, just like Marianne.

Ivan glanced out of the window. "We must hurry!" he said, putting a scarf on Sophie's head. "We must not keep the *vozok* waiting!"

"The *vozok*?" Marianne said, pulling the shawl down so that she could speak. "Isn't that a sort of sleigh?"

"How clever you are, Marianne!" Ivan smiled.

"You mean we're not at the palace yet?" Delphine asked.

"A short drive along the ice road," Ivan said.

"A road made out of ice?" Marianne asked. "That doesn't sound at all safe."

"A frozen canal," he explained. "But quicker and safer than driving through the woods." He frowned slightly, as if something had just occurred to him.

"I think I'd rather go through the woods, if you don't mind!" said Delphine.

"What's in the woods?" said Sophie.

Ivan would not look at them. He spoke quietly. "The ice road is the safest way . . . at this time of year. There are . . . wild animals." He smiled then, and said something in Russian. "My mother would always say to me, when I left her cottage to go and play with the children in the village: A sheep that strays is the wolf's gain!" He stood back to observe the girls. "What a picture!" he smiled. "We'll make Russians of you yet."

They were so trussed up that he had to help them from the carriage and onto the platform. The air was bright and hard and made the girls gasp. Sophie's eyes watered, the teardrops stinging. She felt suddenly grateful to Ivan for taking such care in wrapping them all up like parcels.

"Our luggage!" Delphine's words came out on a cloud of mist. "Don't forget the luggage! I can't meet the princess looking like this!"

"I will fetch it later!" Ivan cried, steering the girls away from the train. Their feet crunched on the granular ice. He looked anxiously at the sky as snowflakes danced around them. "We must hurry. The storm will find us."

Although Ivan had told them it was past midday, it seemed to Sophie that there was only trembling twilight, all that the sun could manage in the depths of a northern winter. Sophie looked through the tiny snowflakes at the sprinkling of stars that glittered in the opaque, dark sky.

"Did you hear that?" Marianne's voice was muffled through the shawl.

"I can hardly hear a thing wrapped up like this!" Delphine said.

Sophie stopped to listen. "Bells!" she said. "I can hear bells."

Then she looked up. Just ahead of them, his head poking around the trees as if curious to see the visitors, stood a black horse with a wild mane. Behind him a low sleigh on delicate, curved runners seemed to float atop the snow. There was a high leather-upholstered bench for the driver to sit on, and behind it a deep, wide seat piled with fur rugs. A hood had been pulled up to keep any flurries of snow off the passengers. It looked as if it had been driven straight out of another century, Sophie thought. She wanted to laugh, suddenly, at the Russian-ness of it all. They might have expected a car, or a jeep, given the depth of snow, but this horse and the sleigh were perfect.

The animal snorted and shook his head, and the bells on the reins jangled. Standing on the other side of the horse, holding his bridle, was a boy. There was a light dusting of frost on his shoulders, as if he had been standing there for some time.

"You see? We must not keep Viflyanka waiting!" Ivan Ivanovich boomed.

The boy craned his neck around the horse's head and stared at each of the girls in turn. *Viflyanka*, Sophie thought. *Russians have such remarkable names.*

Ivan laughed. "Viflyanka is a very impatient horse!"

Ah — the *horse* was called Viflyanka. But who was the boy? Sophie wondered how old he was. The same age as her? No, older. Dark, straight eyebrows underneath the sheepskin hat. A flat snub nose. Dark blue eyes fringed with very black lashes. He didn't smile.

As the girls approached, the boy nodded to Ivan and then to Marianne and Delphine as they each climbed into the *vozok*. His expression was closed. Sophie stood next to the *vozok*, waiting. She didn't want to stare at him, but she could see, out of the corner of her eye, that he had a tiny scar in the middle of his cheek, shaped like a crescent moon.

Sophie pulled the scarf from her face. "Thank you for waiting. It must have been very cold. Your horse is beautiful." She reached out and patted the animal's thick, muscular neck. The horse snorted as if he approved of her kindness.

·The boy glanced at her, then his expression changed to something Sophie couldn't read. *"Voy Volkonsky?"*

Sophie shook her head. "I don't understand —"

"Dmitri!"

At Ivan's command, the boy stepped back immediately. He stared at the ground. Sophie could see the scar on his cheek jumping, and his pale cheeks were flushed.

Ivan spoke to him harshly in Russian. The boy appeared to fold into himself. Perhaps Ivan felt he had been too hard on him, because after a second, he put his hand on the boy's shoulder and patted it. Then he turned and winked at Sophie. His black beard was covered in tiny pearls of ice.

"Don't let Viflyanka hear you say he's beautiful. He's so vain." The horse snorted and shook his head. "But no one can pull a *vozok* like he can!"

Ivan hurried her into the sleigh. As he tucked them all under bearskin rugs, he said quietly but firmly, "It is not polite to talk to the servants."

"I just wanted him to know that I thought it was kind to wait for us," Sophie started to say.

Ivan shook his head. "It is not kind. It is what Dmitri has to do. He has no choice." He sighed. "It is kinder not to notice him. That means he has done a good job. If you speak to him, it is difficult."

"But how can I not speak to people when they are helping us?" Sophie said. "It's so rude."

Ivan shook his head. "Things are different here," he said. "The princess does not want you to make friends with grooms and cooks. It is better for you if you understand."

The boy was already sitting at the front of the *vozok*. Ivan climbed up next to him and, standing up, shook the reins. *"Poshawl!"* he called out, and the sleigh began to move.

"You've never been to a house in the country? With staff?" Delphine whispered. "Of *course* you mustn't speak to them."

"Actually, I don't think that's quite true . . ." Marianne began. But the harness bells rang out over the *shushhhhhh* of the sleigh, drowning out the rest of her sentence.

Sophie felt a wave of panic. She wasn't like Delphine, used to staying in grand houses. Whenever she stayed with friends, she got confused over which knife and fork to use, what to do with her dirty laundry. But how ridiculous to be worried about things like that, she thought then, when she hadn't been worried about being abandoned in the middle of Russia in a snowstorm.

"Gei! Geiiiiiiii!" The words were flung at Viflyanka's wild black mane. "See?" Ivan called back to the girls. "He is stronger than greed chasing money!"

As if he understood the words, Viflyanka snorted and pulled harder, his neck thrust forward, his hooves shaking off the snow as if it were no more than mist. Branches, like black veins, scratched at the sky as the *vozok* skirted the edge of the forest. The slender pale trees reminded Sophie of something . . . *Wait. She's coming . . .* It was her father's voice! And this forest, with its pale trees and snowdrifts, seemed so like the one in her dream . . . Except there was no cloaked figure, no sense of sadness. Instead, she felt curious, awake, and alive in a way she had never felt before.

Marianne reached across and squeezed her arm. "What is it?" Her eyes, blinking behind their glasses, were full of concern.

"The trees. I feel as if I've seen them before . . ." Sophie said. She was about to add, *in a dream,* but Marianne nodded and mumbled, "Déjà vu," adding something about how it could occur when your emotions were more intense.

Sophie didn't answer, but found herself wishing that Ivan would let them go into the forest. They weren't sheep, after all. Straying from the path could hardly hurt them, could it? What had Ivan said about wild animals? Would she see in the forest the gray wolf from her father's story? Or something else? The cloaked figure from her dream, with snowflakes in her hair?

A large break appeared in the trees, and Ivan steered Viflyanka straight toward it. They shot through and Sophie found they were traveling through what appeared to be a long white corridor of clipped hedge, silvered by frost. Arches had been cut in the hedge at regular intervals, and tall statues stood sentinel; wrapped in thick burlap and heavy rope, they looked like men waiting to be shot.

The *vozok* slipped past a frozen ornamental lake, then creaked alarmingly as it slid almost vertically down a bank.

"The Volkonsky ice road!" Ivan yelled into the wind.

They were on the frozen canal. The *vozok* flew along it as if on wings. Sophie could hear the thud of Viflyanka's hooves on the ice. She wondered how he did not slip — he must have special shoes, she thought. When she finally had the courage to look up, she saw, at the end of the ice, the palace.

I want to remember this, she told herself. *I want to remember this exact moment when I'm really old. The moment I first saw the Volkonsky Winter Palace.*

It looked like a Greek temple: bone-white with pillars all along the front, like bars of a cage. The effect was delicate, almost like a skeleton, and the palace seemed to hover at the end of the ice, as if it were about to dissolve into something less solid.

What an extraordinary place! Sophie thought. It seemed ridiculous and yet marvelous at the same time, that anyone could have been brave enough and foolish enough to build such a palace here, in a world made out of winter.

But at the same time, she loved the fact that someone had been so crazy as to try. Her father had once told her that he had persuaded her mother to marry him by filling an entire car with roses. He'd arrived at the house she shared with Rosemary and piled the flowers on the doorstep. It was crazy, stupid, foolish. And yet . . . She smiled to herself. She knew her father would have loved this place just for the romance of its setting.

"Can you see it?" Ivan cried. "What do you think?"

Marianne and Delphine were still hiding under the blankets.

"It's magical!" Sophie shouted. And then she laughed. The palace really did look as though it had just appeared out of the snow and the forest, conjured up by a spell.

At last they reached the end of the ice. Viflyanka's neck muscles bulged as he dragged the *vozok* up the shallow bank. He slowed to a walk now that the deeper snow dragged on the runners once more.

"*Haiiiiiiii!*" Ivan pulled Viflyanka's head around. After a short struggle, the horse surrendered and trotted compliantly across the snow to the palace's vast double doors. Now that they were closer, Sophie could see that the imposing façade, though beautiful, was badly damaged. Paint peeled away from the cracked stucco. Blank windows were shuttered, the glass long gone.

Sophie felt disoriented. Close up, the palace was not

what it appeared to be. This was more like the moments before a dream ended, when things dissolved into reality. It made her feel sad that such a grand building had fallen into such a state of neglect, that even this grandiose dream was no more than a falling-down building.

Ivan jumped down, his knees bending deeply. He strode up to the horse and patted his neck, stroked his bobbing nose, speaking to him as if they were equals. Then he held out his hand to help the girls down.

Delphine and Marianne seemed dazed from the cold and the speed of the ride. They looked very small and very young standing next to Ivan. But Sophie could have carried on riding in the *vozok* for the rest of the day. She looked back down the ice road, toward the forest. How big was the Volkonsky estate? Perhaps she could persuade Ivan to take them on a drive.

"I was right about Viflyanka," she said as Ivan held out his hand to her. "He is a beautiful horse."

Ivan put his finger to his lips. "Remember, no compliments! He's vain enough as it is!"

The boy jumped down from his seat and took the horse's head. He stared at Sophie quite openly. Sophie pulled down her shawl and tried smiling in what she hoped was a friendly way. The boy looked as if he might risk talking to her again, but, seeing Ivan watching them, must have thought better of it. He took the bridle, pulled at the horse's head, and the pair walked forward to the edge of the portico and out into the snow.

"He always gallops faster on the way home," Ivan said. "He knows he is going back to his stable."

But what about the boy? Sophie thought. *Where was he going?* Watching the boy and the horse walk away like that, Sophie felt awkward and sad. She hoped that the stable was warm, but felt that it would not be the case. She suddenly had the impulse to run after them. She could have helped to unhook the brave Viflyanka from the *vozok*, put down fresh straw, and make the horse feel comfortable. She'd really rather do that than meet a princess. She sighed and turned away. If only she could leave the princess to Delphine.

Waves of snow had drifted against the double doors. Ivan brought out an enormous iron key from the folds of his sheepskin coat and placed it in the lock. It took both his hands to turn it. He kicked one of the doors hard, the snow falling off his boots, and it swung back on its hinges.

Ivan stood to one side, his hand stretched out, just as he had at the train. "Welcome to the Volkonsky Winter Palace," he said. "Welcome home!"

The three girls stepped over the crust of snow and into the palace. Behind them the door closed with a deep, dull thud, as if everything that had happened before that moment was now shut out.

CHAPTER TEN

The Winter Palace

Ivan had called it "a diamond in the snow," which had made Sophie think of vast frost-white rooms, glittering and cold. But what they stepped into was a palace of shadows, of twilight, everything cobweb-colored. The hard, freezing air of the park outside had been replaced by the smell of dust and time-shredded fabrics, as if no doors or windows had been opened for decades.

They stood in an atrium flanked by tall gilt mirrors, the glass spotted with pools of black, and chairs covered in dust sheets. Candles, almost burned down to the wicks, flickered from drunkenly arranged sconces on the walls. A grand staircase twisted up and up, into the shadows, winding around a chandelier as large as a boat. Sophie could just see it underneath a cloud of ripped and frayed muslin.

It didn't look like a "palace of dreams," either. Perhaps this was the real reason it would not appear in any guidebook. Who would make the journey to come here? It was so dilapidated.

Sophie saw Delphine's face settle into a sulky frown. This clearly wasn't the sort of grand country house she was used to visiting. But Sophie didn't care that the building looked half forgotten. To her, that made it more precious, like finding something that no one else much cared for.

"I thought Dr. Starova said we were going to a *dacha*," Marianne muttered.

"And I thought Ivan said the Volkonskys had a fortune," whispered Delphine.

Ivan seemed to sense their unease. He stamped the snow off his boots rather too enthusiastically. "Make some noise!" he shouted, his voice echoing around them. "No Russian likes to leave snow on their shoes!"

Obediently, the girls kicked the snow from the toes of their *valenki*.

"Apart from a few servants," Ivan spoke gravely, looking at Delphine, "the palace has been empty and locked up for nearly a century."

A draft sidled up to them then, as if the palace were sighing, and the candles quivered, throwing extraordinary shadows that looked like prancing animals. Some larger movement caught Sophie's eye at the top of the staircase, but when she peered up she saw nothing.

"Why did the Volkonskys leave?" she asked.

"The revolution," said Ivan simply, as if that were explanation enough. "One dreadful night in 1917 destroyed the family forever."

"That was when Russia got rid of the Tsar," Marianne said, seeing Delphine's incomprehension. "It caused the downfall of the Russian Empire and led to civil war and the birth of the Soviet Union."

"How do you know?" Delphine looked suspicious. "We haven't studied that in history."

"I read the guidebook," Marianne said. "It's important to know about the country you're visiting."

"Those are the facts," Ivan said. "But they hardly describe the reality." He sighed. "When I first arrived here, shortly after the princess had taken up residence, I was heartbroken that such a gem, such a jewel, had been so badly treated." He shook his head. "Any true Russian would feel a deep and heavy sadness when they walked along corridors that had once echoed with music, parties, and happy family life." Then he smiled. "But the Princess Anna Feodorovna Volkonskaya has sworn to change the fortunes of the palace or die!"

He smiled awkwardly as the girls looked at each other. "The princess decided you would be most comfortable in the old nursery. It is a part of the palace where the heating still works."

They followed Ivan up the staircase. "Please," he said quietly as they climbed past a section of the balustrade that had fallen away, "watch your step. The soldiers ruined so much the night they hunted down Vladimir, the last Volkonsky prince."

"What do you mean?" Sophie whispered.

"Twenty revolutionaries on horseback broke into the palace, intent on murdering the young prince. He knew they would come, of course: Such acts of violence had happened across even this remote province. But Prince Vladimir did not meet his would-be murderers with prayers. He strolled down the stairs in the uniform of the Imperial Hussars, a decanter of vodka in his hand. When told he was an enemy of the people, he spat on the boots of the commanding officer. And then he said that he would be happy to speak to them, but only with his family around him. He ran up this very staircase, and they chased him on horseback. Can you imagine what it must have felt like to have twenty horsemen gallop up these steps after you?"

Sophie turned and looked down the broad stone stairs. She would never have been able to run up them fast enough to escape twenty horsemen. "But why did he do that?" She suddenly wanted to know why the young man had behaved in such a foolhardy manner. "Why didn't he hide? Or try to escape?"

"A good question, young Sophie," Ivan replied. "And one that shows a finer understanding of the prince than that of those who pursued him. For why would he — the bravest man in the Tsar's army — run away?"

They had reached the top of the stairs. Ivan turned to them. His eyes shone in the candlelight. Ahead of them was a wide corridor, which the stubs of candles in the few sconces barely illuminated. "The prince ran down this corridor to the gallery, where there is a painting of almost every Volkonsky that ever lived." Ivan sighed. "There he waited for the horsemen."

Sophie stared down the corridor. In the distance she could see a pair of double doors, lyres painted on the panels, and the same fierce creature she had seen painted on the door of the train. The pairing of those small harps and the snarling wolves seemed odd, as if someone expected the wolves to sing. She could almost hear the snorting of the horses, their hooves on the stone, the yells of the men.

"He must have been so afraid," she whispered. "What happened then?" She simply had to know.

"Without ceremony or respect for his rank, observed only by the family portraits," Ivan said, "they shot him."

Sophie gasped. She felt almost sick.

"That's dreadful," said Delphine solemnly.

"They said that, as the soldiers raised their rifles,"

Ivan continued, "the prince offered them all a cigarette and laughed."

"He doesn't sound very clever," Marianne said.

"Not clever?" Ivan looked insulted. "He was the most passionate, intelligent man! A poet. A musician. A mathematician. And that was why he could laugh when confronted with those rifles. Because in those last few moments," Ivan said, "the prince knew he had not died in vain: He had given his young wife and child time to escape into the forest."

"So he did it to help them?" Sophie said. "But it's still awful. Because the princess must have left the palace knowing that he would die, that she would never see him again."

And as she said these words, she thought again of a figure walking through a frozen forest. But was it a dream, or a memory of her father's story? The more she tried to fix it in her mind, the less solid it seemed, dissolving just as her vision of the palace had done.

"Not awful!" Ivan replied. "Noble!"

He stopped in front of a pair of carved doors, the panels warped and peppered with small holes. There were painted cartouches of young girls in togas carrying flutes. The handle was a brass animal's paw. Ivan reached into his pocket and brought out another key, much smaller than the one to the front door. It was dark and rusty and wouldn't, at first, fit into the lock. Muttering under his breath, Ivan freed the mechanism and the doors swung apart.

"It is not the largest bedroom in the palace, but I trust you will be comfortable."

The room might once have been grand, but like the rest of the palace it seemed to have been locked up and forgotten about for years. On each of the three narrow metal beds, made up with fur rugs and clean, fat-looking pillows, were a pile of clothes and a piece of white paper with a name on it. Sophie could see that the writer had used the English alphabet, but the hand was unmistakably foreign, with loops and curlicues. Her bed was next to the window, just as it was at school. Between the beds were small bedside tables. A few chairs stood awkwardly in the empty space, and leaning against a wall was a long plain mirror, cracked down one side.

Seeing Delphine frown at the clothes, Ivan explained. "I will bring your luggage this afternoon, Miss Delphine. However, the contents of your cases will not be needed immediately. The princess loves her guests to dress up. I know you will want to please her." He bowed. "I will return shortly."

Delphine waited until Ivan had closed the door before saying, "I can't meet the princess if I haven't got my clothes! I just can't."

Marianne pulled off her sealskin gloves. She stared at her hands as if they were entirely new to her, and sank down onto a bed. It creaked as the rusty metal gave under her weight.

"We'll need to help each other change," Sophie said, taking Marianne's name off her pile. "Ivan got us into these coats and he's not here to help us get out of them!"

Delphine scrunched the piece of paper with her name on it into a ball, then stroked the rich fabric thoughtfully. "These clothes are very old," she said. "I wonder who they belonged to? Do you think it was one of the Volkonsky princesses?"

What if it was the last Volkonsky princess? Sophie thought. The young woman who had left the palace with her child on the night that had shattered the history of this family?

She unfolded a heavy, wine-colored tunic, covered in embroidery, from the pile of clothes on Marianne's bed.

Delphine traced the intricate patterns with her finger. "I've never seen stitches so small," she said. "Come on, Marianne — let's see how it looks."

The two girls wrapped Marianne in the long tunic and slipped her stiff feet into pointed shoes.

"It's called a *sarafan*," Marianne said.

"Oh, save us the guidebook nonsense!" Delphine said. She took a step back and looked at Marianne critically. "If you are going to meet a princess — even a princess you've never heard of — you need to make an effort," she declared. "Will you wear some lip gloss? Just this once?"

Marianne sighed. "It won't make the slightest bit of difference, Delphine. And it just makes me feel awkward. As if someone's smeared sticky wax over my lips." She made a face and jerked her head away as Delphine, ignoring her words, put a glossy finger to her mouth. "Do you think Ivan's story about the prince is true?" she continued. "I'm not sure how he could know exactly what happened. He described it as if he was actually there."

"Perhaps someone saw it — or heard it — and wrote it down," Sophie said. She wanted to believe what Ivan had said, that Prince Vladimir died laughing. She didn't want to imagine him begging for his life.

"Well, one part of it must be true . . ." Marianne mused.

"What?" Sophie wanted to go on discussing the extraordinary Volkonskys until they had exhausted every angle of the story.

"The part about his wife and child escaping into the forest."

Delphine walked across to the mirror in the long emerald-green tunic that had been placed on her bed. With her hair hanging loose, she looked like a character out of a fairy tale. "How do you figure?" she said, looking intently at her reflection.

"Because if he hadn't managed to save them, there'd be no more Volkonskys. I suppose the soldiers must have thought they'd died in the forest so didn't bother to follow them."

Sophie got out of her *shuba*, still thinking about the princess. How sad she must have been, and yet how brave. And how had she survived in the forest this far north? The cold was, as Ivan said, as sharp as a wolf's bite. Someone must have helped her in the woods, given her food, offered her a warm hut to sleep in.

Sophie peeled off the rest of her clothes and folded them neatly, just as she would have done at school. They looked ridiculous: flimsy and cheap. For the first time, she saw them through Mr. Tweedie's eyes. No wonder he had been so insistent on her getting a new sweater. She felt ashamed suddenly: She didn't want to be the girl in the scruffy clothes anymore. She pushed them onto the floor and kicked them under the bed.

She turned her attention to the clothes that had been left for her. A long skirt, a soft undershirt, and — like the others — a long tunic, which was simpler than theirs but made of the most exquisite silver material. She pushed her feet into silver slippers (how had they known her size? she wondered), then stepped into the skirt, and drew the waist tight with the cords. Then she slid the pale shirt over her head. It smelled of lavender. And then she pulled on the silver *sarafan*.

It was cut narrow across the shoulders, with long, wide sleeves. She felt, suddenly, quite remarkable, and yet more herself than ever before. None of Sophie's clothes had ever been bought with much thought or care; Rosemary had never seen the need for anything but the basics. This tunic, however — cut with precision, sewn with knowledge of the fabric, and somehow, so strangely, of the body that would inhabit it — was unlike anything Sophie had ever worn. She looked down and watched it ripple with light.

She walked over to the mirror. Could that really be her? She looked like someone else, someone who was used to wearing delicate fabrics cut into clothes that fit perfectly. Would it be too much to hope that she might, wearing this beautiful garment, look a little like a Volkonsky? She raised her arms and the sleeves fell down like a waterfall. How hard it would be to go back to wearing a shabby school uniform after this.

"Why do you have the best one?" Delphine touched the silver cloth longingly. "Could I try it on?"

Sophie hesitated. She didn't want to let go of the *sarafan*, realizing for the first time that perhaps clothes could be magical in the way they could transform your appearance, the way you felt, and even everything around you.

"I did swap sweaters when you were in trouble with Mrs. Sharman, remember," Delphine said as she pulled off her own tunic, placing it on the bed and holding out her hands. "You could take a photo of me? For my visual diary? We'll swap straight back. Promise."

Reluctantly, Sophie took off the silver *sarafan* and handed it to Delphine, who quickly put it on and then danced away from Sophie, looking as if she had been cut from moonlight. "Do you think I look like a Russian princess in my *sarafan*?" she asked.

Sophie stood awkwardly, Delphine's emerald-green tunic over her arm.

There was a smart knock at the door. Ivan appeared. He, too, had changed and was wearing a blue tunic, the shoulders covered in large silver tassels; ropes of silver braid were swagged across his chest.

"It is time." He bowed. "The princess will greet you formally in the Winter Ballroom. Please follow me."

Delphine's eyes lit up with excitement. "I *love* princesses!" she said. "All this stuff about winter ballrooms and formal greetings! My mother is going to be so pleased when I tell her. How much better is this than tramping through Dorset?" She put her head to one side. "Only thing is, there's no time to change, Sophie. Sorry." She swished past.

"You might have known she'd do that," Marianne whispered. "What a show-off she is."

"It does look beautiful on her," Sophie admitted.

"It doesn't fit her properly," Marianne said. "On you it was perfect." She smiled reassuringly. "But you'll look lovely in the green one, too."

Sophie pulled on the tunic. It was slightly too big. She didn't feel the same in it.

Marianne linked arms. "We don't care, anyway, do we?" she said. "It's only Delphine who wants to make an impression."

Sophie nodded, but, just this once, she couldn't agree with lovely, sensible Marianne. She realized that she *did* want to make an impression on the woman who lived in this forgotten palace, who had given Ivan a new life and had vowed to restore the Volkonsky fortunes. A woman who came from a family where people were happy to die, bravely, to save a child.

They followed Ivan back down the grand staircase and then through a series of rooms that would once have been beautiful. There were carved gilt pediments at every window, painted ceilings, and ornate tiled stoves. But there was very little furniture and most of what remained was damaged. After shooting the prince, the soldiers must have run through the palace setting fire to things, smashing down doors, and looting.

But some rooms had hardly been touched, and Sophie found these the saddest of all. In one, curled and yellowed papers had fallen from a writing desk to the floor. In another were a card table still set with a decanter and glasses — the sediment of wine like dried blood — and a chess table with broken pieces. Sophie bent down, blew dust off the white queen, and set her on her square. In these rooms, it felt as if the inhabitants had only just left, as if Sophie — if only she could listen with the right sort of attention — would be able to catch their voices from the next room.

Outside, the wind sighed. Their heavy garments rustled and Ivan's boot leather creaked as they walked.

"What was that?" From somewhere quite distant — the other side of the palace? — Sophie had heard a sound. It was not the voice of a long-dead Volkonsky, even though they seemed so present. No, it was a sound she had never heard before. She strained her ears, willing the wind to die down so that she could really listen.

"I didn't hear anything." Delphine frowned and peered into the shadows behind her.

"I did." Sophie slowed down and turned her head slightly. "There it is again."

"What?"

"A moan . . . or a cry, or something." How could she describe what she had heard . . . if she had indeed heard anything? Perhaps she had just been affected by the beautiful sadness of these ravaged rooms.

"I didn't hear anything, either," Marianne said. But Sophie saw her friend shrink back into herself, as if she were frightened.

Ivan said, "I think it is the wind that you hear, little Sophie." But his eyes flicked nervously as he said it.

Sophie knew what the strange moan of the wind sounded like. And this sound was different. This made the hair on the back of her neck prickle and her heart race. It was wilder, more desperate than even the most savage storm. It was the sound of something *alive*, a desolate cry, and she felt that she had heard it somewhere before. But where?

Ivan walked quickly on, as if he wanted them to move away from the sound. "Let us not delay!" he cried, striding ahead, and the three girls ran after him.

Finally, they reached the end of a corridor. Ivan swung open the rosewood doors in front of them and light splashed out. Beyond, Sophie saw a looking-glass world made up of mirrors reflecting candlelight.

Ivan bowed deeply and announced, "Her Serene Highness, the Princess Anna Feodorovna Volkonskaya!"

CHAPTER ELEVEN

The Princess

She was wearing a pearl-gray woolen dress with silver embroidered leaves on the sleeves and a high-necked fur collar. Her hair, bright gold and pulled high off a smooth, luminous forehead, was wound in a thick coil, as heavy as a ship's rope. She wore high-heeled shoes, with long narrow toes like serpents' tongues. As she paced the scuffed parquet floor, there was a flash of bright red sole.

"I can't go in."

"Go on, Sophie, please," Marianne whispered. "I don't like it when you're scared. It makes me scared, too."

Sophie was going to explain that she wasn't scared, but overwhelmed. It was Delphine who came back from weekends away and described how she had met a *comtesse* at lunch or a cabinet minister at tea. Sophie never met anyone, let alone a princess, and she felt this lack of confidence as surely as Marianne would miss her glasses.

She felt Marianne's damp hand grab hers and yank her into the wrecked beauty of the empty ballroom.

All around them, gilt mirrors, and above them, enormous chandeliers, great ropes of crystal strung in extravagant loops, dazzled. Sophie looked up into one as they passed beneath. The way each crystal held the entire room made her feel dizzy.

She must have faltered, because Marianne's grip became tighter. Ivan led them toward the woman, who stopped pacing now and turned to face them. Her dark gray eyes settled on each of them in turn — then, without warning, the cold expression broke into a devastating smile. It was as if someone had opened the curtains too quickly on a sunny day.

"If you only knew how I've been waiting for this moment . . ." She closed her eyes. "It has been impossible for me to concentrate on anything else. My work has suffered." Eyes open, brighter now. "But that is nothing now that you are here safely, all three of you. It's almost more than I can bear."

Sophie realized she was holding her breath. There was an energy, a brilliance about the princess . . . a sense that she could explode at any moment, like a firework, in a shower of glittering sparks.

Sophie caught their reflection in the mirrors. Delphine stood very straight, shaking her hair back from her face.

She did look remarkable in the silver tunic. Marianne was flustered and ill at ease, tugging at the sleeve of her wine-colored *sarafan*. And was that really her in green, all eyebrows and mouth, her face as white as the moon? Sophie stopped looking.

The princess clasped her hands together under her beautiful cleft chin. Thin white fingers painted with mother-of-pearl polish were covered in a mass of intricately set diamond rings. A heavy scent of tuberose coiled around Sophie's face as the princess drew nearer. The perfume was intensely sweet, with a velvet denseness that made Sophie's head spin.

The princess stopped in front of Delphine. "You are so pretty! I had no idea you would be so pretty!" She put out her hand as if she would touch Delphine's face, but then checked herself and took a step back. "I like you already," she declared. "I was nervous that I wouldn't . . ." She sighed and the smile broadened. "How silly of me. I should have known."

Sophie saw Delphine smooth the beautiful silver *sarafan*. If only she hadn't let Delphine wear it! Before she knew what she was doing, she said, "You really *were* expecting us after all?"

It was a stupid thing to say, but something made her want the princess to stop staring at Delphine, to look at *her* instead.

The princess turned her gray eyes on Sophie. "Of course!" she replied.

"It's just, we thought there had been some sort of misunderstanding."

Sophie could have kicked herself. She stuck her teeth deep into her tongue. Why had she said that? She was usually good at being invisible, knowing it was better to stay quiet, not to let anyone notice her. But there was something so mesmerizing about the princess . . . she wanted to grasp the woman's full attention and have it only for herself.

"Is it my dreadful English?" The princess put her head to one side, clearly amused. Her English was perfect, with only the trace of a Russian accent.

"No. It's not about not understanding what you're saying." Why didn't she keep quiet? But it was so wonderful to have the princess take her eyes from Delphine and look at her, only at her . . . "It's just that we don't understand . . ."

The princess's eyes were on Delphine again. She looked the girl up and down, and her mouth tipped up in a lazy smile, as if she liked what she saw. Delphine blushed.

Sophie saw all this and felt suddenly shy. Should she speak again? It was clear the princess had no interest in her. But then the woman looked at Sophie once more, as if wanting to hear what she had to say.

Sophie swallowed hard, stared at her fingers, which were gripping each other for courage, and said far too quickly, "You see, we are here on a school trip. We were supposed to be staying with Dr. Starova in Stary Beloostrov . . . that's a suburb of Saint Petersburg, I think . . . but there was some sort of mix-up. And we got left on the train. We had the wrong tickets and we were made to get off . . . and our teacher, Miss Ellis . . . well, I'm not sure she knows where we are . . ."

"Or our parents," said Delphine.

The princess was nodding slowly, still smiling at Delphine.

Marianne added, "And we are meant to be at School 59 on Monday morning."

The princess raised an eyebrow, as if this was all news to her.

"It's just that no one told us about coming here," Sophie finished.

"I can see that you are a little confused," the princess said, although Sophie didn't feel confused at all. They had explained everything just how it had happened, hadn't they? The only thing she hadn't said was that she was sure that Dr. Starova was the woman who had visited her school and taken her photograph in the playground. But perhaps she was not so sure about that anymore. Marianne hadn't been convinced when she had told her.

The princess continued, "Ivan Ivanovich has explained everything to you."

Ivan nodded, but the princess had spoken as if there were no need for him to confirm anything, as if what Ivan had told them had explained their being left on the train, thrown off onto an isolated platform, and brought here to this forgotten palace.

The princess's mouth slid up playfully, a one-dimple smile. "But you can't possibly want to go back to Saint Petersburg! Boring lessons at School 59?" She shook her head as if someone had suggested she allow herself to be stung by bees. "Oh, and perhaps there are trips to museums you are longing to go on? Believe me, the Yusupov Palace is overrated, wouldn't you say, Ivan?" Ivan nodded as if such a visit would, indeed, be more of a punishment than a pleasure.

"And anyway, I have *extraordinary* things planned for you." She clenched her fists as if she couldn't contain her excitement. "Do you think anyone will take you for a midnight picnic on a frozen lake if you go back to your Miss Ellis? Or arrange for an orchestra of automata to play to you as you gamble for diamonds? Or take you for rides in a *vozok* through the Volkonsky forest? What about skating by twilight? Do you think you will get to do any of these things in boring Saint Petersburg?"

Sophie felt her pulse quicken. A midnight picnic? She

looked across at Marianne, who was fidgeting uncomfortably. Back in London, Sophie felt uneasy when her friends weren't entirely happy. But right now, it was as if she wanted to do these things with the princess more than worry about Marianne.

"Perhaps Russian grammar lessons are more to your liking?" the princess teased. "There will be plenty of those if you go back to Saint Petersburg. I warn you that the Russian language is very hard: Would you really prefer learning short-form adjectives or the perfective aspect of the verb to being wrapped in furs and bearskins and drinking cherry cordial in the snow?" She whispered, "Of course, I will send you back if you really don't want to stay . . ."

"Can we at least phone our parents?" Marianne said, not looking up. She seemed unable even to meet the woman's gaze. "I promised I would call when I arrived. My phone doesn't work."

"Nor mine," Delphine added.

"Marianne" — the princess stepped toward her — "of course you must phone your parents." Her voice was like being wrapped in velvet. Warm, reassuring, making everything right. "As soon as we can get the phone lines working . . ."

She said something in Russian to Ivan. He nodded as if he would take care of the request.

The princess shook her head. "The snow . . . and we are so remote . . ." She took Marianne's hand in both of hers. "There is no need to look so anxious!" She laughed and Sophie found herself smiling, just because it was such an appealing sound. "We are going to have the most wonderful time."

The princess spoke quietly to Ivan in Russian once more. He bowed and opened a pair of mirrored doors. The glass shivered in the panels, and their reflections shook, too. The princess let go of Marianne's hand and disappeared into the room beyond.

"What are we meant to do?" Marianne asked Delphine.

"Stay where you are," Delphine said, trying to peer into the room. "You have to wait until you are summoned."

"Why does it have to be so formal?" Marianne mumbled, pulling at her tunic. "This thing is really scratchy. Do you think I can take it off?"

Ivan coughed discreetly and indicated that the girls should follow the princess. Delphine walked forward confidently, the silver *sarafan* swishing on the floor. Sophie could see it was too long for her. She and Marianne followed her into a much smaller, darker room, almost entirely taken up by a large round table. In the center was a large candelabrum, the candles glowing, the wax dripping down the gilt branches. All over the table were piles of paper, some bundled and tied with ribbons, others in perilously high stacks. The princess was sorting through a small pile in front of her, looking slightly distracted. Ivan leaned across to push the candelabrum closer.

"Thank you, Ivan, but I don't need your help," the princess said. The sharpness of her tone seemed to wound Ivan, and he stepped back from the table into the gloom. "Just a little boring paperwork," the princess muttered to herself, still shuffling papers. "Ah yes, here we are!"

She pulled out several sheets of paper.

"Your Miss Ellis is extremely strict! Extremely thorough." She smiled as she laid a piece of paper in front of Marianne. "She would only allow me to take you skating if you signed these papers."

"Shouldn't it be our parents who sign them?" But Marianne took the pen that was offered and put her name at the bottom of the paper.

"I think your signature will do nicely."

The princess turned the paper over without bothering to read it and put it on top of a different pile. Then she smiled broadly as she beckoned Delphine forward. "It is just a formality. I am not expecting any accidents!"

Delphine took the silver pen she was offered and signed her name where the princess indicated. The princess nodded and picked up the paper. Sophie watched her

every movement, fascinated: The angle of her head, the thick rope of hair, the cut of her clothes made her look quite different from anyone Sophie had ever seen before. She was smiling as she scanned the page, but it was a quiet, private smile. Then, as she read quickly to the bottom, the princess's forehead crumpled in a frown. "But there has been some mistake . . ."

She tore her eyes away from the page and looked up at Ivan. Sophie saw anger flare in the depths of those large gray eyes.

"You are the wrong girl!" The princess spoke quickly.

Delphine took a step back. "I . . . I . . ." she stuttered.

"What are you doing here, dressed like that? That is not your *sarafan*."

The woman crunched Delphine's consent form into a ball and threw it on the floor.

Sophie panicked. She wanted to pick the paper up and return it to the princess so they could go on as before. But could it be that perhaps they weren't meant to be here after all? Perhaps it was Lydia Sedgwick who had been invited. Or Nadine? Perhaps they would be sent back to Saint Petersburg straightaway and some other girls would get the joy of skating with the princess.

"I'm not the wrong girl. I'm Delphine."

She looked at her friends as if she suddenly doubted

who she was. Sophie wanted to help her friend, but she couldn't get her tongue to work.

"I'm here with my friends," Delphine managed to say. "The school trip."

"Is this some sort of joke?" The princess's face was blank, but her lips looked thinner and her voice was sharp. "Ivan?"

Ivan looked distraught. "I followed your instructions," he started to say. "I brought them here safely . . ."

The princess was staring at each of them in turn again, as though if she looked at them hard enough she could find something she had lost. Her gaze rested on Sophie. The frown dissolved, a smile spread slowly, and Sophie again felt as if she couldn't hold the woman's gaze. It was too bright, too penetrating.

"So *you* . . ." the princess whispered, stepping toward Sophie. "*You* are Sophie Smith."

"We swapped clothes," Sophie heard herself say. "Delphine looked nicer in that *sarafan*, so we swapped."

The princess nodded slowly. "No more tricks," she said. "We won't have so much fun if you play tricks on me."

"I'm sorry," Sophie mumbled, although she didn't know what she was apologizing for. There had been no "trick."

"It's nothing!" The woman smiled at her. "I have a copy."

She turned and pulled another piece of paper out of the pile, then pushed it toward Sophie.

Sophie looked down at the paper. Everything was in Russian, fat black capital letters she didn't recognize or back-to-front letters that made no sense. The paper was thick and had a watermark in the middle. It all looked extremely official, not at all like the slips that the school usually sent out for parents and guardians to sign back in London.

"Sign the form," the princess said quietly.

Sophie hesitated, then wrote her name neatly at the bottom.

The princess snatched the paper out of Sophie's hand, folded it in half, and slipped it into a large leather wallet. Then, as if suddenly remembering the other forms, she picked them up and slipped them in with Sophie's, hurriedly smoothing the crumpled sheet Delphine had signed.

For the first time the princess laughed — a loose, rapturous, full-throated laugh. "Now the fun can begin!" she cried. "I want to find out all about you! I want to know every detail of your lives. You are my new London friends!"

She tucked the leather wallet securely under her arm.

"But now, I must leave you for a little while. I have paperwork to attend to, and it is almost the end of the day. You must eat and rest."

Sophie looked out of the small window. She saw the twilight had deepened. The stars were brighter, like pinpoints of light through a prism. Time seemed to operate differently in the Volkonsky palace. History swirled around like snowflakes; the daylight was held prisoner by the winter. Sophie sighed. It seemed so wonderfully, beautifully, romantically *different* from anything she had known. And yet, she felt, somehow not different at all.

The princess smiled at Ivan. "You will take care of my precious guests for the moment?"

"Of course, Princess."

"Think of them as lost diamonds I have found in the snow . . ." The princess raised the leather wallet to her lips and kissed it, then gazed at Sophie. "Thank you for coming," she whispered, and ran lightly to the door.

CHAPTER TWELVE

The Dinner

The White Dining Room, surely capable of seating at least a hundred diners, was almost entirely empty, apart from a table at which just three places had been set. There were shadows on the walls where paintings had once hung. At the far end of the room, snow had blown through a hole in a high, broken window and lay in a drift on the dark floorboards. Candles guttered in the candelabrum, the wax already dripping down onto the curved silver branches.

"This place is so run-down." Marianne leaned across to speak to Sophie and Delphine, dropping her voice as Ivan glanced around. "I suppose the princess has lost all her money."

Delphine shook her head. "She must have money," she said. "Did you see her dress?"

Marianne shrugged her reply.

Delphine said, "That dress was expensive. Definitely *haute couture*."

"Perhaps she's too cheap to do the place up," Marianne said as she picked up a large starched linen napkin and put it on her lap.

Sophie watched as Ivan moved silver dishes around on a large sideboard. She wondered about the other servants he had mentioned. And could a princess, could *this* princess, be cheap? She didn't want to think it of her, just as she didn't want to think of Prince Vladimir dying like a coward.

"If the palace has been empty for so long," Sophie said, "and if the princess has only just returned . . . perhaps she hasn't had time to make any repairs." She looked at the faded pattern on the walls.

"You can tell she's a princess," Delphine said, glancing across at Ivan's back. "Just by the way she looks. Did you see her rings? But I wonder why she wants to live here. She'd have much more fun in Saint Petersburg."

"Perhaps she doesn't want fun," Sophie said.

"What else could she want?" Delphine looked around, her quick gaze taking in the almost empty, no longer grand room.

"I like the way that everything was once so beautiful, but now it's so neglected and sad. It seems so much more romantic that way," Sophie said, more to herself. "And the story of the last Volkonskys. I wonder how the princess and the child survived in the forest?" She couldn't seem to stop thinking about it.

"But what's the point of being a princess," Delphine said, "unless you winter in Gstaad and spend the summer on Cap Ferrat? Who's going to see you here? There's no point."

"Not everyone is interested in 'being seen,' Delphine," Marianne said, sounding peevish.

But Sophie thought Delphine had a point. It must be a strange existence living in so isolated a place. Perhaps not if you were Marianne and interested in books. Sophie knew she would be happy here, too — there was so much to discover, so much history, and the park was beautiful. She could walk for hours in the snow. But the princess? What could have made such a woman come back to live alone in this ruined palace? She seemed so alive, so vibrant, the sort of woman who could enter a room and have everyone under her spell. Sophie could just imagine her in Saint Petersburg, at the heart of the city.

She picked up a spoon. It had the head of an animal engraved on it, not a lion or a dog . . . another wolf, perhaps. Sophie thought that it must be things like these that had drawn the princess away from life in Saint Petersburg. The knowledge that she belonged to a family who had wolves engraved on the cutlery. She didn't think she would ever feel that way about Rosemary's flat. Her guardian was suspicious of anything ornate.

"You have found the wolf!" Ivan smiled.

"Is it the family crest?" Delphine peered at her spoon. "There's a family I know in Paris who have porcupines on everything!"

"Why did they choose a wolf?" Sophie asked.

"For the Volkonskys, it is like a signature," Ivan explained. "Instead of writing their name, they use the symbol of the wolf head." He smiled at Sophie. "If you look around the palace, you will find wolves carved into the moldings, their paws cast in bronze as door handles . . . those that weren't stolen . . ."

"The nursery door," Sophie said. "I saw it! And on the train. But why a wolf?" She looked more closely at the animal. His mouth was open and his teeth were bared in a snarl. He didn't look at all friendly.

"That's what Volkonsky means!" Ivan said. He brought a large tureen and bowls to the table.

"So the Princess Volkonskaya is a wolf princess," Sophie murmured.

"There's a wolf on the china, too," said Marianne.

"The white wolves of the Volkonskys," Ivan whispered. "Guardians of the palace." Then he stopped, as if he had said too much.

"Guardians?" Sophie felt a thrilling sense of terror. For her, the word *guardian* meant Rosemary. How much more extraordinary to have a guardian who was a wolf! She traced the shape of the animal's head on her bowl with her finger.

"After the prince was shot" — Ivan looked uncomfortable — "as the soldiers set about destroying the beauty of the palace, the wolves came in and took their revenge. Not many soldiers survived that night."

Marianne shivered. "I'm not keen on wolves," she whispered.

"It all happened so long ago," Ivan reassured her, ladling ruby-colored soup into Sophie's bowl. "You have nothing to fear now."

Sophie picked up the heavy metal spoon and dipped it into the middle of the soup. She took a sip. It was warm, sweet, smoky.

"What is it?" she asked Ivan as he ladled more of the soup into Delphine's bowl and then Marianne's. "I've never had this before."

"It is *borscht*," he said. "Beet soup. The princess wants you to taste a real Russian feast!" He moved cutlery and glasses around with quiet, controlled movements. The room began to fold in around them, as if it were able to welcome them as warmly as any person. Was it the deliciousness of the soup, or the softness of the candlelight, or the heavy tiredness in her bones that made Sophie feel so comfortable?

"*Canis lupus linnaeus.*" Marianne stared straight ahead, her eyes unfocused.

"Canis whatus?" Delphine said.

"*Canis lupus linnaeus,*" Marianne repeated. "It's the Latin name for wolf. Millie Dresser did a project on wolves for Life Sciences." She shook her head. "But she's so lazy, she didn't bother to find any proper information." She put her soupspoon down in her empty bowl. "It was all just drawings." She chewed her lip, sounding mystified. "But I do remember she'd found out the Latin name and written that in mad, squirrelly writing, to cover more of the paper. And she wrote that each wolf has its own howl, like a signature, or a fingerprint." She closed one eye as she tried to remember. "Their fur is called a 'pelage.'" She opened her eye. "And they are intelligent hunters that can kill their prey with ruthless efficiency."

"Millie Dresser wrote all that?" Sophie said, surprised.

"I don't believe it," Delphine said.

They looked at each other and laughed, reminded of the hapless Millie Dresser and her attempts to fool the teachers. London felt a long way away. And less real than the place they were now. It felt good to be here, together, after their long journey, with Ivan taking such attentive care of them. Sophie felt her limbs become heavier as she allowed herself to relax in the certainty that all was as it should be.

Someone had been in their room: The furs and quilts had been turned back and nightgowns laid out.

Their luggage from the train had been put in a neat pile. Delphine started to unpack. "I don't think I brought any trousers suitable for skating," she said. "If only I'd brought those camel cords!"

Drowsy from their meal and tired after the excitement of arrival, Marianne and Sophie undressed quietly. Delphine took off the silver *sarafan* and laid it on Sophie's bed.

"Thank you," she murmured. "Although I'm not sure it made any difference." She gave Sophie an appraising look. "The princess and you . . . I can't figure it out."

Sophie climbed into her narrow bed. "I like it here," she said. The sheets had little specks of black on them, damp spots, although they were clean and well aired. "I know it's not grand anymore . . . but that makes it feel more like a home."

"I wonder how big it is," Marianne yawned. "I can't get my bearings."

On the wall next to Sophie's bed were sheaves of paper glued to the wall. They were covered in Russian handwriting and had been placed there randomly, mostly

overlapping each other. They looked as if they had been torn from a child's exercise book. Of course! Ivan had said this was the palace nursery. Perhaps this was the writing of one of the Volkonsky children.

A few of the pages around the edges were coming unstuck, and Sophie couldn't resist sticking her nail underneath the edge and trying to peel them back. She traced the letters: C, O, and then an O with a line through it, and a back-to-front N and R. СОФИЯ. What on earth did that mean?

Behind the pages were splints of pale wood and then something black: a large hole. So the pages had been stuck there for a practical purpose. A draft sighed through the gaps and rustled the corners of the pages she had pulled away. Sophie wondered where in the palace it came from. There must be so many rooms beyond this one. All of them locked. All of them forgotten.

"Do you think the princess is lonely?" Sophie asked the others. "Living here on her own like this?"

"I'm not sure about lonely," Delphine said. "But she must be bored. There's nothing to do!"

"Apart from the skating and the picnics by moonlight and the rides into the forest?" Sophie suggested.

"If you like snow," Delphine muttered. "Which you do. I miss the south of France."

"But don't you think it's interesting to be staying somewhere with such a history?" Sophie said.

Marianne frowned. "I'm not sure. Terrible things happened here, Sophie."

"But good things happened, too . . ." Sophie felt the words tumble out of her. She knew she was speaking too quickly. "The last prince saved his family!"

Modern life seemed so limited, so ordinary, so small, when compared to the lives of the last Volkonskys. Yes, it was *tragic* (how she loved that word) but surely not as tragic as living a life where nothing much happened? Just going along in the same boring way, never risking anything — would that not be more of a waste of this one marvelous life she'd been given? She didn't want to die like the prince, but she knew in that moment that she wanted a life filled with love and courage. How wonderful for the princess to be related to someone so brave and noble!

There was a knock at the door. Marianne gasped. "Who is it?"

The princess appeared in the doorway, carrying two large books. She had changed into a heavily sequined dress. As she crossed the room, moving quickly, Sophie had the impression that she was made from sequins.

"I have trouble sleeping, my little English girls, and so, at night, I walk through the palace. I have brought you some treasures." She went to Marianne's bed. "For you, a book on cosmology, written by Prince Anton Volkonsky. He built the observatory on this estate."

"You have an observatory here?" Marianne's eyes lit up. She took the large book and opened it reverently.

"Of course!" the princess answered nonchalantly. "Would you like to visit it? I sent for new telescope lenses from Saint Petersburg."

Marianne nodded eagerly, turning the first page with extreme care.

"The skies are dark and a winter long this far north," the princess said. "The Volkonsky princes always had time to examine the stars."

She turned to Delphine, who smoothed her hair. "And for you, Delphine, I have brought some early fashion plates, engravings of the dresses the Princess Maria Volkonskaya wore in the 1850s." She put the leather-bound volume on Delphine's lap. "She was just a poor peasant girl, but she danced like an angel. Prince Alexey gave up his position at court to marry her. He built the theater . . . sadly the roof was blown off, but it was noted for its painted ceiling. She danced for him every night. She was considered a flaming beauty, with a waist the prince could encircle with his hands, and she was much admired by the Tsar."

The pages crackled as Delphine turned them. She gasped as she saw four evening dresses on one page.

"Some of these dresses are probably still in the attics. They wouldn't have interested the soldiers who stole so much. We could go and look for them, if you like?"

"I'd love to," Delphine breathed, gently lifting another leaf of tissue paper guarding the illustrations.

The princess approached Sophie's bed. The voluptuous scent of tuberose made everything around her seem richer; even the water-stained wallpapers looked like moiré silk. She sat down on the edge of the bed and spoke very quietly, so the other girls could not hear. "I puzzled over what to bring you. I was not sure what you would like. I feel as if I should get to know you a little better . . ." She glanced at the other girls, who were now engrossed in their books. "Can I trust you?"

"Yes!" Sophie felt a rush of excitement. It wasn't just that she had been invited to stay with a Russian princess whose world seemed at once glamorous and mysterious. The way the princess spoke to her made her feel special. Sophie wondered if this was why her father had wanted to take her to different places — to meet people as extraordinary as the Princess Anna Feodorovna.

The princess played with the gray diamond rings on her finger, then slipped one off and slid it onto Sophie's middle finger.

"I can't!" Sophie said. "I can't possibly accept anything so valuable!" She felt panicky. What would Rosemary say? What would her friends think? They knew she had nothing of value to her name. They might think . . . oh it would be horrid . . . that she had stolen the ring! No. Better not to take such things.

"It was a gift to me. And now I am giving it to you. Is this not what friends do?" The princess's gray eyes looked cold. "You would make me feel unhappy if you don't accept it."

"But —"

"One day you will give me something in return," the princess said. She sounded very certain.

"I don't have anything to give," Sophie replied.

Delphine looked across, suddenly interested.

"It can be our secret," the princess whispered as she slipped her hand across Sophie's, hiding the ring. "And as for thinking you have nothing to give me . . . you have more than you think, Sophie." She paused, a calculating look in her eyes. "The Volkonsky diamonds are quite distinctive, don't you think?"

Sophie looked at the gray diamond on her finger. She felt quite overwhelmed to be wearing something so beautiful and precious.

"Of course," said the princess, "there are other Volkonsky diamonds. You might have seen them?"

"I've never seen any diamonds at all," Sophie said truthfully.

"Are you sure?" The princess's expression turned sour, as if Sophie had disappointed her in some way. "You shouldn't lie to me."

"I'm not lying," Sophie said.

"There are no diamonds in London?"

"Yes, of course there are, but I've never seen any," Sophie said. She had a sudden sense of shame. Perhaps the princess had picked her as a guest thinking that Sophie had the same kind of background as most of the other girls at her school. There really must have been a mistake, then.

"I think if you want to know about diamonds," Sophie muttered, "you should ask Delphine."

The princess's eyes flashed with the same sudden anger Sophie had seen in the ballroom. "I'm not interested in Delphine's diamonds," she said, then looked as if she was considering something. "Ivan told me that you had spoken to the boy."

"I'm so sorry." Sophie had known it couldn't last. She had upset the princess. "He looked so cold . . . I just thanked him . . ."

"Don't speak to him," the princess snapped. "He will tell you lies about the Volkonskys. Like all the old servants who stayed here, he's just a dirty *domovoi*." The way she said the last word was horrible. As if she had mentioned something disgusting.

"*Domovoi?*" Sophie asked.

"In Russian folklore, *domovoye* are evil spirits," the princess said. "They live in people's houses and cause trouble. They are meant to help with the chores: look after the horses, clean the stove." She leaned closer. "But they are not like us. They are not to be trusted."

"He's a spirit?" Sophie asked.

The princess laughed, but there was no warmth in it. "Oh, he's not a spirit! But he creeps around the palace just like one. You must be careful. A *domovoi* will come to your bed at night and suffocate you! You have to ask them, 'For good? For bad?' And then they are forced to tell you your future."

"But does he have anywhere to sleep?" Sophie felt upset that this boy was thought of so badly by the princess. She remembered the way he had waited for them, the frost on his shoulders, his hand on Viflyanka's bridle. He hadn't struck her as someone who would do anyone any harm. What was it he had said to her? *Voy Volkonsky?*

"Where does he sleep? Probably under a step." The princess laughed again. "Or inside the stove . . ." She looked at Sophie as if she were deciding what to say next. "I should have got rid of him when I returned to the palace," she said slowly. "But Ivan seemed fond of him."

"Why did you bring us here? Why us? Miss Ellis . . ." Sophie's words dried up. She thought she had seen the princess's expression change, just for a second.

"I thought you would like it." The princess's voice was calm. "I thought we might be . . . *friends.*" A blue vein ran down her cheek, like a thread of cotton.

"I'm so pleased you invited us," Sophie blurted, then immediately felt stupid.

"You like the Volkonsky Winter Palace?" The princess spoke very quietly.

"Yes!" The word came out on a rush of breath.

"But it is so neglected," she mused, looking up at the water stains as if she couldn't quite believe what Sophie had said. "There is nothing here that would interest you."

"But everything about the Volkonskys is interesting!"

"You'd never heard of them before you came here, had you?" the princess said slowly.

Sophie shook her head. She wanted to be able to say something fascinating, to keep the princess's attention, but couldn't think of anything.

The princess leaned across to turn off Sophie's bedside lamp, and the heavy, velvety scent wound around Sophie once more. "We shall talk more tomorrow. You will tell me everything about yourself. Every little detail, everything you can remember . . . but now, you must sleep . . ."

She stood and moved to the door. "Good night, my dear guests! Sleep well on this, your first night in the Winter Palace. Tomorrow we will picnic in the snow and skate on the frozen lake!"

"I can still smell her perfume," Delphine said, once the princess had closed the door and the sound of her footsteps had faded. She wrinkled her nose.

"She doesn't seem real." Marianne put the cosmology book down on the floor and plumped up her already plump pillow. "I don't think I've ever seen anyone who looks like her."

"But it's not just how she looks," Sophie said, sitting up and hugging her knees. "There's more to it than that . . . it's everything. This palace . . . her family . . . even the wolf cutlery! It all makes her so fascinating." She tried to forget the sudden flares of anger, the cold gray eyes that had looked so calculating.

"The princess seems very interested in you, Sophie," Delphine said.

Delphine hardly ever gave compliments. But it did mean that when she said something, it was usually true. *Was* the princess interested in her? Sophie wondered. Why would a Volkonsky princess be interested in an ordinary schoolgirl?

"You're never the center of attention," Delphine went on. "It's always me . . . and I'm not being vain when I say that, it's just a fact. Or else it's Marianne because she's so smart. But ever since you gave that tour at school, things have been changing," she said slowly, as if she were trying to figure something out. "Perhaps . . . perhaps the princess sees something in you that others don't . . ." She shook her head. "But what? What makes *you* so special?"

"I'm not special," Sophie said. "We know that!" And yet . . . since she had arrived in Russia it was as if a spark had been ignited inside her. She might not be special, but she felt more alive, as if her life now had unimagined possibilities.

Marianne took off her glasses, always a clear sign that she was tired. "Maybe it's just like that woman who visited the school and convinced Mrs. Sharman to let you come on the trip," she yawned. "The one you thought was Dr. Starova. Maybe she feels sorry for you."

Sophie nodded. That was the most obvious explanation.

"I'm glad we came," Delphine said. "Everyone will be so jealous on Monday when we go to School 59 and say we've stayed in a palace and been skating with a princess."

"They might think we've made it all up," Marianne said.

Sophie thought she might not believe it herself, once they had left this place. And would they even be back in Saint Petersburg on Monday? She tried to remember what the princess had told them when they had signed their skating permission forms, but the memory of what she'd said wasn't clear.

The gaps between the girls' sentences became longer and longer. Sophie thought about the journey that had brought them here, running the images through her mind. The dainty train carriage and the *vozok*. The wild

Viflyanka and the boy with the crescent-shaped scar. The wolf cutlery and the beautiful silver *sarafan* that seemed to have been made just for her.

She asked Marianne the time, but there was no answer.

Sophie hauled her rucksack up off the floor and got out the wooden pencil box. She took the ring off and laid it inside. It would be much safer in there. A diamond ring! She couldn't believe the princess had really given it to her. How worthless her piece of glass looked next to it. It was too big and it didn't sparkle like the princess's intricately set ring with its dusting of tiny diamonds around the large, flashing central stone. She wondered now where that piece of glass had come from, why her father had kept such a poor trinket, though thinking that seemed disloyal somehow.

She picked up the piece of glass and put it in the palm of her hand, then, on a sudden impulse, hung it around her neck, tucking it under her nightgown. It felt cool on her skin and the string tickled the back of her neck. She felt better wearing this than the ring. It felt somehow right because it made her feel close to her father. After all, it might be worthless, but he had given it with love. The princess's gift was more puzzling. As if she wanted something in return.

There was a white square of moonlight on the floor. The blizzard had blown itself out. Sophie slipped out of bed and tiptoed to the window. She saw the waiting-to-be-shot statues, dressed against the frost in their wrappings of burlap. She saw the Volkonsky forest, stretching off as far as she could see.

So that was where the last Princess Volkonskaya had fled with her child, that terrible night of her husband's death. Sophie was not sure she could have left her home like that, to face such a perilous and uncertain future. *But she did it for her child,* Sophie told herself. Both the young prince and his brave wife had sacrificed everything they had to save the life of their child.

As Sophie looked into the woods, wondering which path the princess had taken, she saw a single snow-covered statue at the edge of the tree line. How odd that it was on its own like that. She breathed on the glass and rubbed it clear of the frost flowers. What was it? A lion, crouched down on its haunches? No. Not big enough for a lion and the head was the wrong shape.

As she watched, the statue unfolded itself, stood up, and threw back its head at the moon.

A wolf!

And now she saw that it wasn't covered in snow . . . it was white. A white wolf! Just like the ones Ivan had told them about, that had once guarded the palace and avenged the murder of the prince!

The howl climbed up her spine. This, *this* was the sound she had heard as they had walked through the decrepit palace, on their way to meet the princess. Desolate and wild.

Should she be scared? Of course! The cry was even more savage than the one she had heard before. But why, then, did she feel more excited than frightened? It was as though she somehow understood, without knowing how, that this wolf was a guardian of the palace . . . that it might also have come to the palace to protect Princess Anna Feodorovna. Perhaps excitement was not such a strange emotion after all, when the imagined world of her dreams had come to life . . . when she had met a princess living alone in her deserted palace, the ghosts of her family all around her.

Sophie pressed her face to the window and closed her eyes. More than anything, she felt suddenly that she wanted to be outside, in the snow, running wild with the wolf whose cry only she seemed to hear.

But when she opened her eyes, the wolf had gone.

CHAPTER THIRTEEN

The Frozen Lake

"Geiiiiiiiii!"

Ivan had the whip. Princess Volkonskaya tore the reins from his hands, laughing, and let the horse have his head.

The furious snort of Viflyanka, the jangle of the bells, corresponded to the lurch of the *vozok* on the snow. The girls hung on to each other, their shawls tied tight around their faces. Sophie felt invigorated by the crisp, freezing air and being driven at such speed through the tremulous half-light, though she had reasoned it must be mid-morning by now. The windows of the palace slipped by, and Sophie turned her face upward to the light, snowflakes spiraling down onto her face and the bearskin that covered the girls.

They had been woken by the princess herself, already dressed in a long coat, a white mink turban on her head.

They had breakfasted on spiced apples, the princess telling them to hurry, and before they could finish, she had led them through corridors, tying lace, rather than a shawl, across her face against the cold.

As Ivan had opened the wide front door to the morning twilight, the snow sparkled and the wind sighed. Sophie had thought about the wolf she had seen the night before. Should she say something? Surely, if there was a wolf in the woods, they would need to know?

Then why *didn't* she say something? Why did she want to keep the knowledge to herself? This morning, she told herself, she couldn't be sure what she had seen. Had there really been a white wolf, or was it just her imagination? Had she been affected by the romance and savagery of the palace's history, the mesmerizing presence of Princess Anna Feodorovna? What was it about her? Sophie wondered as she watched the woman climb into the driver's seat. Why did the princess affect her in such a way? She wanted to be always in her company, felt bereft when the princess wasn't looking at her, yet almost frightened by that penetrating gray gaze.

"Stop staring," Delphine had whispered as they were called forward to climb into the back of the *vozok*. "The princess will think you're being rude."

The *vozok* lurched around the corner of the palace now, and Delphine and Marianne squealed in alarm.

Viflyanka headed for the woods, charging past the stables set behind high, ornate railings. Sophie glimpsed the dilapidated buildings where Viflyanka must sleep. She thought of the boy, Dmitri, and as if she had conjured him out of the air with her thoughts, he walked across the deep snow, an ax in one hand, a large metal bucket in the other. Yes! It was the boy! Dmitri! They raced past, and he looked up at the sound of the bells and Ivan's cries of encouragement to the fast-moving horse. His face was alight with curiosity.

Sophie wanted to wave and laugh and tell him they'd be back soon, that they were going skating with the princess, and she didn't care that she wasn't supposed to talk to him . . . But she didn't dare, even though the princess was looking straight ahead, intent on making Viflyanka charge even faster toward the forest. Sophie remembered the look on her face when she had called the boy a dirty *domovoi*.

Dmitri stood quite still, watching them. He had a kind expression, Sophie thought. Like the best sort of older brother.

"That's the boy from yesterday," she said to Marianne.

"What's he doing with an ax?" At least, that was what Sophie thought she had said. It was hard to hear above the bells and with shawls across their faces and ears.

She watched him take something out from the bucket. It was wrapped in burlap. Then he stood back, and raised the ax with a loose, practiced swing. She thought he must be chopping wood. But when he brought the ax down, she saw it was not wood at all, but the limb of a dead animal. She turned her face away, horrified, just as the *vozok* lurched to one side.

Ivan put his hand on the princess's arm as if to restrain her.

She shook it off. "Leave me alone, Ivan!" she cried. "I drive this *vozok* better than you!"

The girls looked at each other.

"How can she think that?" Marianne said in a low voice.

"It doesn't matter what she thinks," Delphine replied. "She's a princess. She can do what she likes."

"No one can do what they like *all* the time," Sophie said.

"Maybe you can if you own all this." Delphine looked at the forest looming ahead of them. She pulled down her shawl and leaned forward to speak to the princess. Her nose was already pink with cold. "How large is the estate?"

The princess, reining Viflyanka in to a brisk trot as they entered the woods, shrugged. "It goes on for many miles," she called back. "No one really knows anymore."

Sophie looked deep into the scarred trunks of the silver birches. Was this where the wolf had run to last night? Was he in there still, watching them?

"The Volkonskys came here to hunt." The princess flicked the reins. "Wolves . . . and bears . . ."

"Wolves?" Sophie said. "But Ivan said —"

"Has Ivan been telling you stories about the Volkonsky wolves?" The princess didn't sound amused.

"Princess, I —" Ivan began.

"The next story he will tell you" — she took a moment to wrestle with Viflyanka, who was sweating, waves of white foam on his neck — "is about the Volkonsky diamonds!"

"Diamonds?" Delphine looked interested. "There are diamonds?"

The princess was quiet for a moment, then said, "The Volkonskys owned a necklace of priceless diamonds — long enough to hang a man. It was given to the last princess by her adoring young husband on the occasion of their marriage."

"Will you show it to us?" Delphine asked.

"Perhaps," the princess said, looking at Sophie over her shoulder. "If I find it."

Ahead was a clearing in the woods and what looked like a small circular temple with a frozen ornamental lake in front, surrounded by birch trees. Smoke rose from the

temple's domed roof. Sophie was struck once more, not only by the extravagant architecture tossed carelessly into a Russian forest, but by the thought that some long-forgotten Volkonsky had wanted such a building as a simple skating hut. It seemed romantic rather than foolish.

Ivan turned around, his beard rimed with frost. "You see?" he said. "I have had the stove lit. We will not freeze on our skating pond!"

The princess pulled Viflyanka to a halt. "He goes well, this little horse of yours, Ivan."

"But you would do well not to let him have his head so much, Princess." Ivan collected up the reins she had thrown carelessly to one side. "He is fast . . . but he is not steady. You should be more careful."

"Careful? Did you hear that, girls?" The princess stood up. "Ivan wants me to be careful!" She jumped down into the snow, laughing, then held a hand up to Sophie. "Fetch the picnic, Ivan! We will soon be hungry."

Sophie threw back the bearskin and took the princess's hand to jump down. Ivan pulled a thick blanket over Viflyanka and unloaded wooden crates from the back of the *vozok* without saying anything.

The princess hurried the girls into the little temple. Inside, the walls had been covered in tiny diamond-shaped mirrors. A tiled stove in the corner gave off plenty of heat, and a large round table was already laid with a crisp white cloth. It was as if the room itself were waiting for its guests, pleased to be used after years of neglect.

Delphine gasped. "It's so pretty!"

"Like stepping inside a crystal," Marianne said, stamping her feet on the floor to shake the snow from her boots.

"Another example of Volkonsky madness, you mean." The princess was looking through a pile of ancient skates in a box; the blades were rusted, the leather cracked and dry. "We must find you skates!" She seemed to be speaking more quickly than yesterday, as if the ride through the woods had excited her as much as Viflyanka. Her eyes glittered like the gray diamonds on her fingers as she pulled off her sealskin gloves with her teeth.

"Here, Delphine" — she handed her a pair of skates by their tangled laces — "these should fit you." Sophie watched the princess's reflection refracted in the tiny mirrored panes as she started rummaging through the pile once more. "Marianne? I think your feet are slightly smaller than Delphine's." She picked up a battered pair of brown skating boots. "You'll need to put them on outside." The two girls tramped outside into the snow.

"As for you . . ." She looked up at Sophie's face, as if Sophie's expression might tell her the size of her feet. "I think you can take these." The skates were like little brown ankle boots with slim blades attached to the bottom. "They belonged to the last Princess Volkonskaya."

"The one who escaped? With her child?"

"Who told you that? I thought you didn't know anything about the Volkonskys." The princess looked sharply at Sophie.

Sophie hesitated. Had she said something wrong? "I don't, except what Ivan told us. How could I?"

She wondered why this should have upset the princess so much. Perhaps there were things in the Volkonsky family she didn't want Sophie to know about. Things she might be embarrassed about. But how could that be? Everything to do with the Volkonskys was so fascinating, if sad.

"He seems very keen on telling you the Volkonsky history." The woman tossed Sophie the skates. "When I think perhaps he should mind his own business! What about *your* family?"

"I don't have a family," Sophie said. "My father —"

"He died?" the princess cut in. "Do you remember anything about him?"

Sophie was taken aback. "Just strange things. Blurred pictures. Sometimes the sound of his voice." She didn't mention that she had heard it since she'd been here in Russia.

"What sort of pictures?" The princess leaned closer. But Sophie couldn't think how to describe the images of her father reading to her, or the meticulous way he peeled an apple, or the careless way he slammed a door. When she didn't say anything, the princess pressed, "What about the rest of your family? You must have other relations?"

"No."

"Surely someone?"

"Just my guardian. But she was my mother's friend."

The princess nodded slowly. "How awful to be so entirely and completely alone." But she didn't sound that sorry.

"I try not to think about it," Sophie mumbled.

They followed Marianne and Delphine outside to a large stone bench to put the skates on. Sheltered under the portico of the temple where the snow could not fall, Sophie saw that the legs of the seat on which her friends now sat ended in carved stone wolf paws.

The snow had begun to fall again. Sophie watched as Ivan carried the last of the crates into the hut.

"Unpack the picnic, Ivan!" the princess called out to him. "I need a glass of vintage *shampanskoye* from the Volkonsky cellars before I skate!"

"I think it would be better *after* your exertions on the lake, Princess," Ivan said quietly.

As he turned his back, the princess stuck her tongue

out at him. "Always trying to spoil my fun!" she said. "But what point is there in being a princess if you can't have what you want?" She leaned forward to lace up her skates. "He'll do as I ask," she said, her chin jutting out. "He'll have to!"

Sure enough, Ivan came out carrying a small horn beaker. He handed it to the princess. She looked inside, laughed, and drank the contents.

Ivan, taking the beaker out of her hand, knelt down in front of Delphine. "You must lace your skates more tightly," he said. He took off his outer gloves and retied her laces. When he had finished, Delphine stuck out her feet and flicked them from right to left. "I don't have my phone!" she said, making a mock sad face. "Now I can't film my feet!"

"Will *you* skate?" Sophie asked Ivan as he knelt in front of her to check her skates. She was going to make a fool of herself, she knew, but felt that Ivan's presence and calmness would be reassuring on the ice.

"You must not be afraid!" Ivan smiled so that his eyes crinkled at the corners. "While I am on the ice, no harm can come to you."

Sophie felt strong hands pull tightly on the laces and then mold the leather to her ankle. "They fit you perfectly," Ivan said, sounding surprised. "Your feet must be quite small and narrow."

"I had some silver slippers yesterday," Sophie said. "They fit, too." She became aware that the princess was watching them closely. She looked cross. Did she think Sophie was getting above herself? But there was no reason for her to be angry because Sophie's feet were the same size as a Volkonsky princess's, surely?

"What's taking so long?" the princess snapped, then stood up and took small neat steps down to the edge of the frozen lake. And then she launched off, with long athletic lunges, skating faster and faster. Laughing, she turned her face upward into the light flurry of snowflakes and swooped about the ice as if she were a bird that had been too long in a cage.

Sophie took a breath of the forest air. *Peppermints and diamonds,* she thought, just as she glimpsed a figure through the trees, slipping slightly as the snow gave way underfoot . . . But this was not the cloaked figure of her dreams, with snowflakes in her hair. This was Dmitri, a bag slung across his chest, two dead hares hanging from wires on his back. So he was a hunter as well as a groom.

As if he had heard her thoughts, the boy turned and looked at her. He seemed at home in the forest, almost happy. But the image of the ax swinging up and cleaving the animal limb in two made Sophie shiver and look away. When she looked up again, the boy had turned his back and started to move away.

Ivan strode onto the lake in heavy black boots, ribbed soles keeping him from slipping. He planted himself a few feet away from the edge. "Marianne!" he called, clapping his hands together in large rabbit-fur gloves.

Marianne stood, uncertain and wobbling, in the snow at the edge of the lake.

"Small steps!" Ivan called. "Like a baby! Walk toward me . . . keep looking up! Do not be scared! You will not fall!"

All the while Sophie could hear the scoring, swishing sound of the princess as she tore around the lake, now bending forward to gain speed, then standing up as she changed direction.

"She's so good," Delphine whispered to Sophie. "I can skate, but nowhere near as well as her . . ."

Marianne took tiny steps, her body hunched.

"See? I have my arms out to you!" Ivan called.

Marianne, still looking extremely cautious, took two more tiny steps.

The princess had been observing the scene and laughing. Now she began to race toward the girl. Marianne was unaware of the woman coming toward her, so intense was her concentration. Her gaze was fixed on Ivan's open, encouraging face. Just as she was about to reach out to Ivan's hands, the princess whooshed between them.

Marianne shrieked in alarm and almost fell backward, but was grabbed by Ivan, who pulled her back up.
He put his arm around Marianne. "Princess! Enough!"
he roared.

The princess laughed and turned a defiant pirouette.
"You can't stop me!" she called from the other side of the
lake. "And admit it! You don't want to!"

Delphine had now stepped onto the ice and was glid-
ing toward Ivan and Marianne.

"Excellent, Delphine," Ivan said, smiling his approval.

Sophie saw her friend look toward the princess to
make sure she had seen how easy it was for her, and was
rewarded with applause. Delphine adjusted her scarf and
skated confidently around the lake.

And now it was Sophie's turn. They were all looking
at her. Ivan, still with one arm around Marianne, held out
his other to her. Sophie knew she lacked Delphine's ability and the dogged determination of Marianne. She was
going to be the worst.

"I'll just watch," she called to Ivan.

The princess swooped across. Her skates grated on
the ice as she came to a graceful halt in front of Sophie.

"Walk toward me!" She put out both her arms.
"Don't be scared!"

Her face, with its deep gray eyes and flushed cheeks,
banished any feeling of shyness or shame. All Sophie

knew was that she couldn't skate, but that she wanted to do whatever this woman asked of her.

"Keep looking at me!" the princess said, skating closer. And then, whispering, *"Trust me."*

Sophie took another breath of the dream-laden forest air. It felt as if she had very little choice. She must either try to skate, or risk looking foolish. Last night the princess had trusted Sophie. Now she must do the same.

She stood up and felt her legs tense as she tried to balance on the narrow blades. But she could stand, just, if she took tiny steps. The trick was to keep moving, like when riding a bicycle. The princess was paying attention only to Sophie, and she sensed a furious concentration in the woman's whole body.

I'll just take two more steps, Sophie thought, *then one more . . .* She knew she must fall, surely, the next step, or the next? She had been walking across the snow, her ankles wobbling, for far too long. She seemed no closer to the princess.

Delphine and Marianne were giggling, but she daren't look at them. She had to keep her eyes fixed on the princess's face.

"Bigger steps, Sophie," urged the princess. "See? You have nearly caught me . . ."

Then, in one delicious second, Sophie understood what she was meant to do. She pushed rather harder with her right leg and transferred her weight, and felt the skate glide on the ice. Then she transferred her weight and pushed with the left. She had a sensation of feeling free and weightless, of flying and spiraling, of not knowing where she ended and the snow and the forest and the frozen lake began.

"I'm a snowflake!" she laughed, putting back her head and opening her mouth to taste the snow on her tongue.

And then she fell. Flat on her back.

But it was so funny. It was all so funny, with Ivan's face above, smiling broadly, his eyes crinkled with mirth, and the princess, her white fur turban above her arched eyebrows, laughing with genuine amusement. She saw the daytime stars above their heads, the branches of the birch trees that seemed to pin them there, and felt she could have burst with happiness.

A light mist rolled along the base of the trees. Except mist didn't move like that. Mist wasn't as dense as that. It didn't assume the shape of . . . the shape of . . .

Appalled, Sophie knew she must shout out. She was no longer in the palace, looking down from the safety of the nursery.

The white wolf crept forward, quiet as snowfall, edging closer to the princess, who continued to smile down at Sophie, oblivious to the danger behind her.

"Sophie?" The princess offered her gloved hand.

The wolf stopped, sniffed the air. His eyes looked red against the white of the snow. Sophie could see now that there were patches of pale gray on his pelage. *Oh, gray wolf* . . . But this was a real white wolf, not the old gray wolf of the fairy tale. And there was no comfort to be had from her father's voice. With a wave of panic, Sophie realized that this animal was wild and would not be hemmed in by a mere story. He was entirely his own master.

Sophie couldn't move, couldn't speak. She sensed, as keenly as an electric shock, that the wolf saw, felt, experienced the woods in a completely different way from her. He could see deep into the night. He could feel the quality of the snow with his paw, understanding how long winter would be by the depth of the ice crust. He could smell Viflyanka's sweat, hear the pulses of every one of them and know who would be the slowest runner, the weakest prey. But he didn't just take in this information; it was as if he *became* whatever was around him. He was a part of the world he inhabited. He seemed to be looking right at her. She felt drawn to him, but the fear would not leave her.

It was Viflyanka fretting and stamping that gave her a voice.

"Wolf!" she cried. "In the woods!"

Why weren't they running? Why were Ivan and the princess just staring at her like that?

The princess's face beneath her mink turban didn't show any surprise, any fear. She shook her head.

"No, Sophie."

"Yes! I saw it!" She struggled to sit up, looked again into the trees. There was nothing there.

"Inside!" roared Ivan.

"But Ivan!" The princess shook her arm from Ivan's grip. "You know there's nothing in the woods! We have them all." But when she couldn't free her arm from Ivan's hand, she said, looking uneasy, "Don't we?"

They half skated, half stumbled back to the temple, Ivan striding to the *vozok*. He pulled out a hunting rifle.

"Get inside!"

"But Viflyanka!" Sophie yelled.

The princess shoved her in the back and she fell into the temple.

Marianne and Delphine, looking shocked, clung to each other. The princess took off her skates and paced the room. Sophie jumped when two cracks from the rifle split the air.

An instant later Ivan threw open the door. His fur hat had slipped back off his forehead. His face was white. "Nothing," he said. But he was breathing heavily, and for the first time Sophie could see worry in his eyes.

The princess nodded. "I told you!" Then she pulled Sophie toward her. Her fingers dug into Sophie's arm. "Don't try that again."

"What do you mean?"

"You've frightened your friends." The princess spoke so quietly that Sophie had to strain to hear her. "There are no wolves. The wolves have been taken care of."

"But I saw —"

"You saw nothing."

They ate their picnic in silence in the temple: a loaf of fresh rye bread from a large embroidered napkin, bowls of pickles, and dishes of mushroom dumplings, which Ivan said were called *pirozhki*.

"We must go now," announced the princess the moment they had finished. "I shall drive."

The velvety denseness of the northern light had intensified in the time they had been inside. It made the silver birches stand out more clearly, and the stars appeared lower in the sky, touching the highest branches.

Ivan helped the girls into the *vozok*, then slipped the thick blanket off Viflyanka's stout body. The little black horse snorted his approval and swished his thick tail.

"Did you really see something in the woods, Sophie?" Marianne whispered. She looked around her, as if they might be surprised at any moment by a wolf leaping out from the trees. "You looked like you'd seen a ghost rather than a wolf."

Sophie saw how frightened she was. "It was nothing," she lied.

"Of course she didn't see anything," Delphine said. "She's just the girl who cried wolf. No one will believe you next time, Sophie," she laughed.

The bells jangled, the runners slid through the snow, and the princess turned the *vozok* toward the narrow path through the woods.

The moon had risen, but little could be seen of it through the black branches. Viflyanka trotted on smartly, his breathing regular. Sophie looked back at the little temple until she could no longer see it.

"We should not take this path," Ivan said. He kept his hand on the rifle. "The path around the woods is safer."

"You said there was nothing," the princess said. "Or were you lying?"

"I would never lie to you, Princess," Ivan said, but he looked uneasy.

"Remember what will happen if I can't trust you, Ivan," she hissed. Then, realizing that Sophie was watching her, the princess changed her mood instantly. "But see how well I am driving?" she teased. "Or perhaps you think I am still driving too fast?" And she pulled on the reins and slowed Viflyanka to a walk.

It was over so quickly that Sophie wasn't sure what she had just witnessed. Was the princess angry with Ivan?

He didn't seem to be untrustworthy; in fact, Sophie would have been glad to have Ivan if she had been a princess.

"I think we must keep moving in this part of the forest, Princess," Ivan warned.

Sophie could not think of the wolf now. She sensed he was no longer nearby. She felt the tears well up and blinked them back, forcing herself not to cry. She had made a fool of herself in front of the one person that mattered. She had been offered a chance of magic, beauty, friendship, and, like the idiot she was, she had ruined it. The princess didn't want to know about wolves in her forest. Of course she didn't. It was all very well having wolves on your cutlery, but that didn't mean she wanted them around the palace. They were dangerous, wild animals that would rip out her throat if given the chance.

Sophie watched the trees slip past and felt miserable. Would she ever regain the princess's good opinion?

The princess drove them to the front of the palace. Dmitri was waiting under the portico. He looked cold and wretched, not like he had in the forest; Sophie felt sorry for him. He stepped forward to take Viflyanka's bridle, without looking at anyone.

The princess, stepping down, stared at the boy. She walked around and spoke to him quietly. The girls watched as Ivan got down. The princess appeared to be explaining a problem to Ivan and the three of them spoke in short, intense sentences. The princess looked angry, although she didn't shout. The boy, who at first spoke forcefully, fell silent and sullen.

"He must have done something wrong," Marianne commented, still under the furs.

It looked that way. *But what?* thought Sophie. *What could Dmitri possibly have done?*

CHAPTER FOURTEEN

The Chandelier

Inside the palace, the princess appeared distracted, distant. She behaved as if the girls were invisible. She spoke to Ivan, in Russian, her voice conveying increasing frustration. When Ivan stammered what sounded like an excuse, she stalked off up the stairs.

Ivan looked defeated, weary. "Would you mind if I left you alone until dinner?" he said. "The princess has work to do. And I . . ." He frowned. "I, too, have urgent duties."

The girls walked up the staircase to the nursery, unwrapping scarves and undoing the belts around their *shubas.*

"What work could the princess have to do?" Delphine wondered.

"Perhaps she wants to crack on with the dusting!" Marianne said as she ran her finger along the balustrade.

"I can't figure it out," Delphine mused. "Why did the princess invite us?"

"There doesn't seem much point to us being here," Marianne agreed. "We're not going to see much of real Russian life."

Being here didn't affect the others in the way it affected her, Sophie realized. She felt already that she understood so much more about the people who had lived and died here. But how could she say this? She knew they didn't feel the same, and she felt awkward after the episode at the lake.

"Perhaps she wanted company," she said. "Friends."

"She makes a funny sort of friend," Marianne retorted.

"What do you think they were arguing about?" Delphine asked.

"*Were* they arguing?" Sophie wondered. "I thought they sounded as if they were just discussing something."

"Believe me, since my parents split up, I know when there's an argument going on," Delphine said. "Even if everything seems fine on the surface."

They were at the nursery door. Delphine pulled down on the brass paw. "Weird, this obsession with wolves," she said, then looked at Sophie. "That wasn't one of your better ideas," she said.

"What do you mean?"

"Pretending you saw a wolf, to get her attention. It was really lame."

"Delphine! That's so mean!" Marianne cried.

"I'm saying it for her own good!" Delphine walked into the room. "The princess looked really fed up with her."

"I think you should take that back," Marianne said, following her.

Sophie stood alone. She didn't know how to enter this room and take on Delphine. She knew she hadn't cried wolf. She *had* seen the creature. But the effort of trying to understand what she had seen and felt was suddenly too much. Feeling the tears and hearing a sob escape her, she ran back down the corridor. She needed to be alone for a little while before explaining herself to Delphine . . . No. She would not explain herself. Why should she?

She tried to conjure up her father's voice as she wandered through the palace, but he had become silent since that first ride in the forest. She didn't know why, but she wished he would come back.

She wasn't sure how much time passed before she realized she was lost. She had gone up another, smaller staircase, along a corridor, and found she was somewhere else entirely. But in front of her were mirrored doors that she remembered: the ballroom where they had first met the princess.

The candlelight flickered as she opened the doors, then settled to a steady glow reflected infinitely in the mirrors. She looked up and saw the largest chandelier shiver and tinkle. Light danced around the room and then, to her surprise, a rope dropped down.

"*Beestra!*" A voice! A *boy's* voice.

She ran toward the rope, looked up, and saw Dmitri staring down. She felt her cheeks flush. She felt embarrassed for him and found herself hoping that he had not seen her watch the princess talk to him after the trip to the lake. Perhaps he had done something the princess didn't like, but Sophie knew that it was wrong to speak to someone with such obvious contempt.

The chandelier drops chattered and the chandelier swung crazily from side to side as he bent down.

"What are you doing up there?" Sophie gasped.

"We talk! Woman not see us here!"

The princess had called Dmitri "dirty." No. It would not be good if Sophie was found talking to him.

"I can't come up there," she said. "I can't climb . . ."

"Put your foot in and hold rope! I will pull you up!" he called, his face earnest.

Miserable after the quarrel with Delphine, Sophie realized she wanted to talk. She grabbed the rope with both hands and slid her foot into the loop.

"Hold tight!" Dmitri called.

And she felt herself being lifted up into the air, the movements punctuated by slight breaks as Dmitri fed the rope through his hands.

I'm not sure I want to do this, she said to herself, closing her eyes. But it was too late. How far would she fall? Best not to look.

An arm pulled her up into the chandelier. "Sit on the side!" Dmitri said.

"I'm not good with heights . . ." Sophie looked straight ahead as she searched for somewhere to sit.

"Hold on!" Dmitri warned as the chandelier tilted. "Be careful!"

She lowered herself carefully onto a horizontal piece of metal.

"Lean back!" Dmitri said, showing her how he was leaning against a gilded metal bar. Then he stared at her. "You cry?"

"No!" Sophie brushed her cheeks with her hands.

The boy frowned, but said nothing more.

"I saw you," Sophie said after a few seconds' silence. "In the woods. You'd been hunting."

The boy shrugged. "Food. I can find everything I need in forest. Even in winter."

Sophie thought about asking him what he had done, why the princess had been angry with him. Then she thought it might embarrass him. And he *had* invited her up into the chandelier, trying to be friendly. She didn't want to break anything.

"I saw something else as well . . ." she said instead, then wondered if she should be saying this. Was she going to make a fool of herself again?

"What?" Dmitri was watching her closely, but his face showed no emotion.

She knew she didn't have to tell him anything. Perhaps she should stop now. But then what would she do? Go back to Delphine and Marianne? They didn't understand, and she needed to tell someone.

"I saw . . ."

"A wolf?" the boy whispered.

"Yes!" He understood. Sophie sighed with relief, and the chandelier shook, making the crystals shiver and clink together. "The princess didn't believe me," she added. "And Delphine said I was making it up to get attention."

The boy didn't say anything immediately. He flicked a crystal with his finger. "You like that woman?"

Dmitri wasn't looking at her, so it made it easier to be honest. "I think she's the most amazing person I've ever met. She's like a diamond, isn't she? She's so brilliant you can't take your eyes off her." She felt she shouldn't also say that she felt unnerved when she was around the princess, likely to blurt things out or be eager and gauche. She didn't mention how the woman had made her feel scared. Dmitri didn't need to know that. She didn't want to offend him by saying anything wrong about the princess.

Sophie moved her foot away from Dmitri's. They had to sit very close to each other and she felt awkward being unable to move any farther away.

He reached into the pocket of his worn trousers, brought out a battered cigarette, and held it out to her. "You smoke?"

"Of course not!"

He shrugged as if not smoking was equally fine. He stuck the cigarette between his lips, but didn't light it. Sophie knew it was just a prop, meant to make him look older. After a few seconds he took it out and put it behind his ear.

"Where are you from?"

"London," she said. "The place with the red buses?"

He nodded.

"At least, that's where I live now. I used to live in the countryside . . . I think . . . when my father was alive . . ." She knew she had started to rattle on about things the boy could have no interest in. But she wanted to talk to Dmitri; there was a quietness about him that made her feel she could tell him things without feeling self-conscious.

"My guardian, Rosemary, she said she'd tell me more about my parents when I'm older. She didn't approve . . ." Sophie stopped when she saw Dmitri frown.

"Approve?"

"She didn't like my father. He was a poet. No money!"

Dmitri shrugged as if this would be of little importance.

"Rosemary thought he married my mother for money . . . He must have been very poor if he did, because my mother didn't have any money, either." She sighed. "I'm frightened to ask her any more about him. Maybe it's better that I remember him as being someone who was kind and who sang to me. So much is jumbled up in my mind when I try to think of my parents. The more I try to remember things, the more tangled and mixed up they become. I can't tell anymore what is a story or a memory."

"Your father is dead . . . My father also."

"I am sorry."

"Your mother?"

"My mother, too." Sophie smiled defiantly. "I've been very careless . . . imagine losing *both* parents!"

"Many people have been lost," Dmitri whispered. The chandelier drops trembled as he shifted position slightly.

"What is the word for chandelier in Russian?" Sophie flicked one of the still trembling drops with a fingernail as he had done.

"*Lyustra.*"

"I like that word," Sophie said. "It sounds like *illustration* . . . like a picture in a storybook . . . as if you could look into the crystals and see things happening . . ." She knew from the faint frown on the boy's forehead that he didn't understand, but she felt it was important that she made *herself* understand, right now, sitting in this cloud of crystal that sprinkled light down onto the floor like a hoarfrost. She flicked another drop and it clinked deliciously, like the sound of Delphine's laugh.

"I have one a bit like this." She was going to pull the piece of glass out from under her shirt, but felt suddenly foolish. What would Dmitri think of her, wearing an old piece of glass as a necklace? Instead she said, "I love the way it sprinkles the light around."

She could see where one string of the chandelier had been replaced. The wire was thinner and the glass was dirtier, grayer than the other strings.

"Woman upstairs makes me clean. Clean chandeliers! Me! Dmitri! She said they had not been cleaned for a hundred years! She said it was good punishment."

"Punishment for what? What have you done?" Would he tell her what the argument was about?

The boy looked away. "I do most things she asks. But some things I *cannot* do."

Sophie felt it would be rude to ask him any more. Perhaps he had felt humiliated that the princess had spoken to him so harshly in front of Sophie. It was never very nice to admit you hadn't pleased someone or done what they had asked.

They sat quietly for a moment, looking through the chandelier.

"She said I must not speak to you," Dmitri muttered.

"She said the same to me!"

They looked at each other, but then looked away again.

Sophie said, "I don't know why she doesn't want us to talk." She couldn't look at his face because it was a lie: She knew why the princess didn't want her to talk to him. She had called him "dirty" and said the word in such a way that made Sophie feel awkward. Feeling braver, she looked back at him. "But we don't have to tell her, do we?" she whispered. "We could talk and not say anything? It could be a secret?"

"Many Volkonsky secrets," the boy nodded. "But she never find out."

They sat quietly for a few more seconds. Then Dmitri took a deep breath. "If I tell you something, you won't tell woman upstairs?"

Sophie nodded but felt slightly uncomfortable. The princess had said they must trust each other, it was true, but there was something in Dmitri's manner that made any agreement with the princess seem less important.

"There is Volkonsky song. I sing for you? But not for woman upstairs . . ."

The boy looked at her as if he could tell if Sophie would keep whatever secret he wanted to share. Then he spoke very slowly: *"V glubinye vecherom, Snyeg bypadaet, kak almazy. Volky poyut vlunnom svetye."*

Sophie wanted to laugh. Dmitri could tell her any number of secrets if he was going to use Russian.

"I don't understand your language," she said. "I'm sorry."

"You never heard these words?"

"They're very beautiful," Sophie murmured, unsure what the boy was talking about. "But I don't get to learn Russian at my school for another two years."

"So why are you here?"

"The princess invited us."

This answer seemed to puzzle the boy. "But why? Why three girls from England? What does she want with you?"

Sophie tried to hold the Russian words in her mind. *"Volky?* Is that something to do with wolf? Ivan told us that Volkonsky means wolf . . ."

The boy nodded, smiling for the first time. "I can tell you these words in English," he said slowly, "but I do not understand their true meaning . . ."

"Tell me anyway," Sophie said. Something in the rhythm of the language had delighted her. It seemed to capture beauty and sadness even though she had no idea what the words meant. And it was so lovely to sit here, in the candlelight, listening to Dmitri's voice speaking Russian. She realized that when people spoke English, she was never aware of their voices, only what they said. But in not understanding anything, instead she had listened intently to *how* Dmitri spoke.

"In the depths of evening," Dmitri whispered, "snow falls like diamonds. Wolves sing in the moonlight. We part."

"That's beautiful," she said. "But it's sad, too. Everything here seems to have so much sadness in it."

"Is words from poem, from old song said to calm even wolves," Dmitri said, smiling for the first time. And then, simply and beautifully, he began to sing. His voice, sweeter than Sophie could have imagined, caught on the end of the first phrase. He breathed in, pushed off again. He could have been skating over the notes.

She knew this song! Her father had sung it to her, in the dream of the forest. Hadn't he? She laid her head against the rope of crystals and looked into the petals of light on the floor as Dmitri sang, his voice weaving itself around the chandelier. She saw their faces reflected hundreds of times over. And she realized that she was fooling herself. She must be wrong. How likely was it that her father would know the same song as Dmitri? She sighed, and watched as the reflection of her face in the crystals tipped to one side. She might not know if this was her father's song or just an echo of some other melody, but what she did know was that she felt more at home in the ropes of crystals and the sad comfort of Dmitri's voice than she had felt for years.

"You are so lucky to have a place like this to hide," Sophie whispered when he had finished. "I don't think I've been in such a beautiful hiding place in my life."

"But even in *lyustra*, you can't hide from time." He picked up a dirty rag. "And I have to clean this *lyustra*."

"I was trying to find the gallery," Sophie said. "Ivan told us about Prince Vladimir. I wanted to see where . . ."

"When she arrived, the woman locked up the gallery," Dmitri said. "She found the keys to many rooms and locked them." He was silent for a moment. "But at night, I hear her. She walks through the palace. She is looking for something."

"But what?"

"Many things were lost."

"Maybe the diamonds," Sophie said. "She said there was a diamond necklace that she would show us, if she found it."

Dmitri looked at her. "She will never find the Volkonsky diamonds. They are hidden."

Then before she could ask him what he meant, he pushed the loop of rope toward her, and she put her foot through and took hold of the rope. And then she was dropping down through the crystals, through the dancing flakes of light.

Before she left the ballroom, she turned back to Dmitri, still suspended in the chandelier. He waved his cloth at her, slowly, and his graveness and the way he watched her made her want him to be her friend. She would make him her friend. She would forget what the princess had said about him.

She walked slowly along the dim corridors, navigating herself by staircases and statues. She could hear voices: Delphine's shriek of laughter, Marianne crying, "Geronimo!" What was going on? She ran toward the noise, the happy, carefree voices of her friends.

Ivan stood by a door. He looked relieved as she ran toward him. "We came to find you," he said. As she came closer, he pulled her to one side. "Please. While you are in the Winter Palace, the princess wishes you to stay with your friends."

"Come on, Sophe!" Delphine called.

Puzzled by Ivan's words, Sophie looked into a large room dominated by an enormous mahogany slide. At the top was Delphine, waving enthusiastically. "Have a go at this! It's so funny!" She lay down, facing backward, and slid, headfirst.

"It is where the Volkonsky children would take their

exercise when the storms were too wild to play in the forest." Ivan smiled as Marianne shot past.

"Together! Holding hands!" Marianne laughed, climbing up the stairs after Delphine. "Let's wait for Sophie!"

Delphine, beaming, held out her hand.

And Sophie, suddenly realizing how much she adored these two girls, ran happily to join them.

Delphine hugged her. "Friends?" she said. "Even though I was a fool? I don't know what came over me."

"Always," Sophie laughed.

Supper had already been laid out in their room. Relieved that they were now friends again, the girls took great care with each other, laughed at the slightest hint of a joke, and talked only about things that would not cause offense. Sophie hoped that the princess might visit them again.

But she did not appear, although Sophie thought she had heard footsteps outside. And just as she drifted off to sleep that night, she thought, too, that she heard the cries of many wolves, as though they were singing her to sleep.

CHAPTER FIFTEEN

The Under Palace

Something woke her.

"Hello?"

There were squares of moonlight on the floor. Someone laughed and Sophie heard muffled footsteps running, but it was all subdued, as if it were coming from another room.

"Delphine?" she called, sitting up. "Marianne?" Both girls appeared to be fast asleep. "Look, if this is some kind of joke, it's not that funny."

The palace fell silent once more. Only her breathing to be heard.

Sophie closed her eyes, but she was wide awake, every nerve tingling.

Scuffling again. Did someone cough? She thought she heard a door open, but it was not the nursery door. More footsteps, and then shallow breathing right next to her pillow.

"Got you!" she said. Her eyes snapped open as she grabbed the hand that was reaching out to her face.

A startled cry. *"Atpusti menya pajaluista!"*

It was a young girl. Sophie was so surprised she loosened her fingers, and the girl immediately twisted out of her grip and scampered behind a chair. Sophie could see her brown hair over the top. She could see a small foot, too, shod in a felt slipper, sticking out into the room.

Trying to keep her voice as calm as possible, Sophie said, "You don't have to hide. I won't hurt you."

The girl stayed where she was.

"You don't speak English?"

"Da, I speak Pangeleesky!" The voice was high, musical. "I learn with my brother from book." She pronounced the word "boooooork."

Sophie thought about turning on the light, but decided it might scare her.

"I like you," the voice said. "You pretty face."

"Thank you," Sophie answered, craning her neck to try and see the child behind the chair. The foot in the felt slipper was drawn out of sight with a giggle. "But," Sophie added, "I can't tell if *I* like *you,* because I can't see you. Why don't you come out from behind the chair?"

There was no movement, no sound.

"Are you cold?" Sophie asked. "We could share this glass of tea that someone kindly brought me while I was asleep."

"But that was me, that was me!"

The voice was accompanied by a furious clapping of hands. A thin white face with thick dark eyebrows peeped out from behind the chair. Sophie smiled and the face disappeared again.

"I bring tea . . . and jam." She talked as if she was listening to every word she was saying and was fascinated by how those words sounded. "They let me come. I promise go back straight." A sigh. "Then I see your face!"

"What about my face?" Sophie could now see a slice of embroidered purple skirt.

"I like very much!"

The girl peeped out from behind the chair. Her brown hair hung in two long, straggling braids. She unfolded herself slowly and, as if drawn by threads, walked toward the bed. She came right up to Sophie, as though she couldn't help herself, and stared hard. She had long black eyelashes and dark blue eyes.

And then the words of the princess came back to Sophie. What if this girl was . . . a spirit? What was it she was meant to say?

Sophie whispered, "For good? For bad?" really quickly under her breath.

The girl gasped. "You think I *domovoi*?" she said. She took a step back from the bed, shaking her head.

"No!" Sophie said too loudly. She dropped her voice

again, not wanting to risk waking her friends. "I'm sorry. I've never been to Russia before. I get things wrong!" She smiled in apology.

The girl nodded, as if she accepted the explanation. Sophie decided she had a kind face, curious and intelligent. Certainly not the sort of face that belonged to someone who would suffocate her.

The girl carried on staring at her. Sophie picked up the glass of tea. "Why don't you tell me your name?"

"Masha," whispered the girl. Her hand crept toward Sophie's. She was clearly struggling with the temptation of stroking Sophie's arm.

"I am real," Sophie laughed. "Look." And she pinched herself.

The girl laughed as well. And then, as if she still didn't quite believe her eyes, she put a finger out to Sophie's arm and prodded it.

"How old are you?" Sophie asked. The girl was staring at her own finger as if it might speak to her.

"Ten!"

"Are you Ivan Ivanovich's daughter?" Sophie smiled.

"I no from him!" She shook her head vigorously.

"I'm sorry," Sophie said quickly. "I didn't mean to offend you."

The girl snorted. "I serve Volkonskys!" Her eyes flashed.

"You know the boy? The boy who looks after the horse . . . the boy who met us with the *vozok* . . ."

"Dmitri!" The girl smiled with delight. "He my brother. He see you, talk to you!" She said this as if it was quite the most amazing thing that anyone could have done. "He tell us you arrive."

"And you both work for the princess?" Sophie asked.

The girl shrugged. "Princess?" She blew air through her lips. "We live too near the woods to be frightened by owls."

Sophie, to hide her confusion at the girl's words, took another sip of tea. A horrible thought. The girl might not be an evil spirit, but was she mad? How did she get into the room? Sophie glanced at her over the top of the glass. The girl was picking at the fur pelt that was Sophie's blanket.

"You tell no one you see me? I not allowed in Over Palace."

"Over Palace?"

"I live in Under Palace." Masha was backing away from the bed. "And I have many busy work to do."

"Watch out," Sophie called, as Masha was about to bump into the wall. The girl's hand reached and pressed something. A panel slid away to reveal a shadowy passage-way. A sour draft stirred from the unseen depths.

The girl hovered, then, smiling, beckoned to her. "You come?"

Sophie looked across at the sleeping forms of her friends. Marianne was curled up like a conch shell. Delphine lay on her back, her hair tumbling over her pillow. The thought of being in the room on her own with only two sleeping girls for company suddenly seemed unbearable. Sophie pushed back the heavy quilts and bearskins, swung her legs out of bed, and hopped onto the floor. The silver *sarafan* lay on the chair beside her. She threw it on, ran across the room through the squares of moonlight, and before she could think whether it was a good idea or not, Masha had grabbed her hand and pulled her through the wall.

They ran down a narrow staircase, Masha's felt-clad feet making no sound. Flickering pinpoints of light illuminated the way. But the speed of the girl! Sophie could scarcely keep up, and she had to keep her head down and her elbows in just to get through the cramped space. Her chest hurt.

"I can't bear this," Sophie gasped. "I have to go back."

"No time!" Masha yanked on Sophie's arm. She was

surprisingly strong. "If feel scared, close eyes. I can see for two!"

"But can't you slow down?" Sophie could hardly catch her breath.

"*Nyet . . . nyet!*" The words came at her out of the cramped darkness. "Never walk in the Under Palace. Always run. Faster! Faster!"

If the Volkonsky Palace had once been magnificent, gilded, and ornate, here — in the space behind the rooms and along service corridors — everything was the exact opposite. The Under Palace was modest and plain. Even at the speed at which they ran, Sophie could sense the pride taken in the dull shine of the floor and the wrought-iron brackets in which small torches flared. Not a cobweb or speck of dust to be seen.

Corridors crisscrossed each other, branching off in different directions. There were steps up and down, changing levels just when Sophie didn't anticipate them. And still Masha ran.

"Please, Masha, stop!" Sophie gasped. "I feel dizzy . . ."

Masha skidded up to a door covered in green felt. She turned around to Sophie, her face suddenly apprehensive. She reached out and pushed a strand of Sophie's hair out of her face, then spat in her hand and wiped what must have been a smear of jam from Sophie's chin. Then she nodded her approval, turned, and knocked twice on the door.

The sound was muffled by the felt, and Sophie wondered if anyone had heard. But a second later, a high, wavery voice answered. Masha opened the door slowly, talking to someone inside. A smell of smoke and vinegar made Sophie's nostrils itch.

Just as they were about to step through the doorway, Sophie having to bend her head slightly because it was so low, Masha turned and stared hard at Sophie's face. She grasped Sophie's hand tightly.

"My family waiting . . ." she whispered. "They wait to see you."

A candle burned on a small wooden table, the pale light licking at rough wooden walls. No furniture to speak of; no possessions, either. It was as if Masha's family lived in a forgotten waiting room. Sophie tried not to sneeze as the smell of vinegar, herbs, and wood smoke clutched tighter at her throat.

A middle-aged woman with bright, round eyes and high, broad cheekbones put down her sewing and looked up. She put her hand to the headscarf, which was tied tightly under her chin, as if to check that it was in place. She pushed back her stool and stood up to greet her guest.

"This my mother," Masha said.

The woman dipped her head in greeting.

"How do you do?" Sophie said.

Masha's mother picked up an embroidered hand towel. On top of the neatly folded linen was a loaf of dark bread and, balanced precariously on this, a saltcellar. She held it toward Sophie.

"I'm not very hungry," Sophie said. And then, not wanting to cause offense, she added, "Although it's very kind of you to offer."

The woman looked taken aback. She turned her face eagerly to Masha, nodding rapidly as if wanting Masha to translate Sophie's words quickly.

Masha shook her head as if she, too, was surprised. "Not food," she said to Sophie. "This bread, this salt . . . We greet with blessing."

"Oh. Sorry! It's not how we do things in London," said Sophie. She watched as the woman poured out some salt and indicated that Sophie should dip the bread into it. Sophie felt that her ignorance had disappointed them somehow, but she did her best to tear off a little piece of bread without knocking over the saltcellar, and dipped it into the mound of tiny crystals. A few of them stuck to the black bread, and when she put it in her mouth, it tasted strange, but delicious, too. "In London we just shake hands," Sophie explained. She swallowed the dark, salted morsel. "Although this seems a much nicer thing to do."

The woman came closer. Because of the way her headscarf was tied, low over her forehead, tight under her chin, her face was a perfect disc. Sophie had the unnerving impression that the woman's face was floating toward her on a column of embroidered fabric. Two hands came out of sleeves, picked up a lock of Sophie's hair, and stroked it. She showed it to Masha.

"My mother say: 'A maiden's beauty is in her hair.'"

Then the woman held up Sophie's hand and held it toward the candle.

"My mother say: 'Trust your own eyes more than others' words.'"

The woman turned Sophie's hand over and traced the lines on her palm. Her fingers were slightly rough but her touch was light. She returned Sophie's hand to her as if it were a present. Then she placed her outstretched index finger under Sophie's chin and, calling Masha to bring the candle closer, turned Sophie's face gently to the right and the left, inspecting every detail.

Masha nodded as her mother whispered to her. "It is true what my mother says," she explained gravely. "'Eyebrows may be pretty, but firewood is more useful.'"

"Your family is very friendly," Sophie gasped, trying hard not to pull her face away from the candle. "Is this how you greet all your guests in this part of Russia?"

"We have been waiting long time to greet person like you. No one ever comes to palace." She frowned. "Until woman upstairs." She smiled. "Now you come to palace. And now we so happy!"

A door on the far side of the kitchen banged open. Dmitri, holding one hand in the other, stumbled in, crying out for something in Russian. He collapsed onto a stool. Sophie gasped as she saw that his hand was bleeding.

Masha shrieked and leaped up, grabbing a piece of linen from the top of her mother's sewing pile. Her mother quickly pulled a bowl down from a shelf and poured water into it, which splashed onto the floor.

Dmitri kept saying the same word over and over again. *"Pamada! Pamada!"*

His mother, speaking calmly, set a small bowl of fat — the *pamada*? — in front of him. She washed the cut, which looked deep, as if he'd been bitten: The flaps of skin around the edge of the cut were ragged. Dmitri winced as she put her fingers into the fat and smoothed it onto the cut. She then wrapped the hand tightly in clean linen.

Dmitri, throughout this ordeal, had chewed his lip and not made a single sound. He cradled the bandaged hand in the other and, for the first time, seemed to notice his surroundings. Seeing Sophie, he started.

"You?" he said. "Here?"

He looked up at Masha, who stood next to him, her arm around him protectively. Sophie saw the little scar on his cheek jump.

"Da," she said simply.

He shook his head.

His mother came over and pulled off his sheepskin cap and kissed the top of his head. He growled and shrugged her off, but she laughed and kissed him again.

"My brother, Dmitri," Masha said. She spoke with fierce pride.

"Is he all right?" Sophie looked at the boy. His face was extremely pale.

"Dmitri brave!" Masha declared. "He no frightened anything!"

The boy made a face as if he didn't want his sister to boast. But Sophie could tell he was pleased she'd said it. His mother poured some *borscht* from a small pan into a bowl and put it on the table in front of him with a piece of bread. She broke the bread into chunks and he picked up his spoon with his good hand.

"He certainly knows some good places to hide," Sophie smiled.

The boy looked up from his soup, the spoon halfway between the bowl and his lips. He smiled back.

"Dmitri does many, many things . . ." Masha stood straight. "He very important!"

The boy shook his head and elbowed his sister. Sophie saw him blush and he glanced up at Sophie before attacking his soup once more.

"He chop wood!" Masha said. "Quick and fast! He groom Viflyanka! He feed —"

Dmitri made a sharp clicking noise at the back of his throat. Masha put her hand to her mouth and blushed.

Dmitri frowned. "She tell woman she see wolf!"

"A white wolf!" Sophie blurted out. "I shouted, but no one believed me."

Masha exchanged a look with Dmitri.

"I thought the wolf would attack Viflyanka . . ." Sophie's words were tumbling out. She stopped and took a breath and looked at the intent faces of Dmitri and Masha. It was easy to see they were brother and sister now: the shape of their chins, the flare of their nostrils, and their serious, intelligent eyes.

Dmitri nodded slowly. "She tell woman upstairs! And I am made to clean chandeliers!"

Sophie looked at her hands. "The princess said there were no wolves, that the wolves had been taken care of."

Dmitri leaned back. He put his bandaged hand up onto the table. His mother poured cherry cordial into three beakers, then sat down next to Masha and smiled at her children.

"What do you know about the wolves?" Dmitri spoke very quietly.

Sophie said, "Ivan told us they used to guard the palace. That they avenged the murder of Prince Vladimir."

Dmitri and Masha looked at each other, as if wondering whether to say anything.

"Please tell me," Sophie said. She had sensed, when they were sitting in the chandelier, that Dmitri would not — or could not? — tell her about the wolves. Had he been worried about being overheard? What was he afraid of?

Dmitri took a sip of cordial from his beaker. "The last Princess Volkonskaya brought the white wolves here. She found a wounded cub in the forest and she nursed it. For this the wolves stayed with her. They helped her to escape into the forest. They protected her as she protected them."

"Our family called her *volchiya printsessa* . . . wolf princess," Masha added. "The day she left palace was sad day for us — the Starovskys. All good fortune went with her and the child."

Sophie looked into the candle flame. As she stared into its blue center, the flame seemed to rise and float to one side.

"Terrible night," Masha whispered. "She told my great-grandmother she come back. She said she never forget Starovskys who served her!"

"The wolves fought hard," Dmitri said. "The next day, our family cleared the carcasses of horses . . . the bodies of men. They buried the prince."

"And then dark times come . . ." Masha continued. "But we never forget. We watch. We wait for Volkonskys to return."

"She promised our family!" Dmitri said vehemently. "Volkonskys keep their promises."

Sophie struggled to get the image of the dead horses out of her mind. "And now the princess has returned!" she said. "So you must be pleased?"

Masha and Dmitri looked at each other, as if unsure what to say.

"Woman upstairs," Dmitri said at last, his cheeks flushing, "she does not respect wolves. If you do not respect the wolf, you do not respect the forest, the wilderness!"

Masha put her arm around her brother and put her head on his shoulder. Sophie didn't know what to say. How terrible to have waited for so long for the princess to return, and then find she was not the woman they had wanted or expected.

Masha's mother took some logs from a pile in the corner of the room and opened a door in a large tiled cupboard. A delicious smell of warm yeast swept the room, and Sophie crinkled her nose appreciatively.

"We keep stove warm," Masha said. "It never go out."

Masha's mother smiled as she reached up to rearrange a pile of washing: flowered sheets, drying on the top of the large stove. Sophie had only ever seen drawings of these Russian stoves in the books she'd had as a child. Broad and square, with a wood fire inside, they gave off heat for hours. Sophie gasped in surprise as the sheets moved of their own accord, shook themselves, and became an old woman.

"My *babushka!*" Masha laughed. "She very, very old!"

"*Babushka?*" said Sophie, feeling her heartbeat return to normal.

"Grandmother," Masha translated.

Masha's mother spoke to the old woman, telling her something with great intensity. To Sophie's concern, the old woman started to cry. She wiped the corner of her eye with her scarf, stared at Sophie, and muttered something under her breath. Then she reached out a thin hand, like a glove of skin worn over bones, and took Sophie's hand in hers. She smiled and spoke to Masha.

Masha nodded. "My *babushka* glad you are here. She say a girl not come to palace since wolf princess come many years ago."

"The last princess came here when she was a girl?" Sophie asked.

Masha nodded. "She come when parents dead. Old Prince Volkonsky her guardian."

At these words, Sophie suddenly remembered her first night with her own guardian, Rosemary. The flat had seemed so cold and had smelled too clean. She was given a slice of toast and told to brush her teeth before bed. She knew she must "be good," for the simple reason that if Rosemary would not look after her, there was nowhere else for her to go.

"*Volchiya printsessa* loved forest. She loved to be outside. She was happy here. And when her guardian's son, young Prince Vladimir, returned from army," Masha smiled, "they married."

A bell rang above the door. Masha jumped in alarm. "You go now. We need work. Woman upstairs want coffee. We not be late." She tugged gently at Sophie's elbow. "Perhaps I wrong when I bring you . . ."

She opened the door. Sophie didn't want to leave the candlelight and Dmitri and Masha, their mother and *babushka*. They seemed so . . . *together*. A draft whipped into the little room, making the candle flame flicker.

"Will your hand be all right?" Sophie asked Dmitri.

He waved the bandaged hand and shrugged as if it were nothing. The old woman turned her back to them, settling herself back down on the stove. But as Masha's mother came to say good-bye, stroking Sophie's cheek gently with her work-worn hands, the old woman said something more. A look passed between Masha and her mother. The older woman smiled, but then checked herself and made the sign of the cross over Sophie.

Masha spoke. "My mother says she is glad you here."

Sophie muttered, "I'm going home soon . . ."

The word *home* sounded wrong even as she said it. She didn't have a home if that meant people who really cared for her in the way Dmitri and Masha and their mother and *babushka* so obviously cared for each other. And weren't you meant to feel safe at home, rather than in the way and an inconvenience? She only felt safe when she dreamed of her father and he linked his fingers through hers. And for a few precious seconds when Dmitri had sung to her in the chandelier. No. She could say she was going home, but the word was meaningless. Inexplicably, she felt tears well up. Something about this room, these people, felt so right to her. She wanted to stay.

But Masha had already started to run. "Perhaps yes, perhaps no . . ." She skidded to a halt and listened to a door opening and closing somewhere in the palace. Her eyes burned, reflecting the torchlight. "We are who we are," she said. "However the moon may shine, it's still not sunlight . . ."

The panel slid open, and Sophie saw the moonlight on the bedroom floor.

Masha squeezed her hand. "We not know why you are here, but you must be careful. Woman upstairs . . . she will ask you many things." The girl glanced over her shoulder as if she might see the princess right behind her. "You say nothing. You tell nothing. It not" — she frowned — "not *safe* for you to speak!"

Before Sophie could say anything, Masha pushed her through the opening, and the panel slid shut.

Delphine whispered something in her sleep. She turned over, and her fur fell to the floor. Sophie walked through the moonlight and picked it up, laying it gently over her friend.

She sat on the edge of her bed. The wind had dropped; the moon sat above the broken shutter. Her breath came out in a cloud. Shivering, she slipped under the heavy pelt, which crackled as it moved. Just the faint tick of Delphine's small travel alarm clock, the hands illuminating the twelve and the three.

She pulled the fur high under her chin and sat up in bed to watch the moon. Perhaps if she focused on that clear, bright light, it might help her to understand what had just happened, why she was here in a forgotten palace, lost in a vast, empty country with people who behaved so strangely. She was confused, unmoored, like a small boat bobbing out to sea with no hope of finding her way back to shore, prey to the tide, the current, and the wind.

The clock ticked on, the moon slipping behind the shutter as if no longer able to support its enormous crystalline weight.

Sophie waited. There would be, she knew with calm certainty, a single, lonely howl. She would recognize it now, the way it slid around the higher note. She put her fingers to the piece of glass around her neck. It was as warm as her skin. She knew she would not sleep until she had heard it: the heartbreaking cry of that wolf.

CHAPTER SIXTEEN

The Portrait

No one came to fetch them. No clothes had been laid out. Delphine unpacked the rest of her suitcase, placing piles of skirts and vintage silk blouses on a chair.

"I forgot my ballet flats," she said, sounding cross.

Sophie looked down at her own now rather crumpled clothes, then pulled on the Volkonsky silver *sarafan* over her jeans. Delphine smiled her approval.

"What should we do?" Marianne asked. "Should we go and find someone?"

Sophie rubbed a circle on the frosted window and looked out onto the park below. She let her eyes relax and felt the morning twilight seep into her mind. She thought about last night. Dmitri's hand . . . was he all right? And his sister, Masha. The image of them sitting next to each other, shoulders touching. And their story of the last, lost Volkonskys.

But there was something else about the way they talked whenever the princess was mentioned. Surely they should have been pleased a Volkonsky had once more returned to the palace? They didn't like the princess — that was clear. And what did they mean about respect for the wolves? She thought about how the princess had reacted at the lake when Sophie had shouted "wolf". . . *"The wolves have been taken care of . . . You saw nothing."* Why would she deny their existence?

"I'm starving," Marianne said, sighing. She looked around for the supper tray, but it had gone. "Who takes the things away?" she asked, blinking. "We never see anyone, do we?"

Sophie was about to tell them about the Under Palace, but felt, suddenly, that it would sound ridiculous. Later. She would tell them later.

"Ivan seems to do most of the stuff." Delphine shrugged, checking her reflection. She had twisted her hair into two yellow coils on either side of her head. "Oh, let's go and find someone!" she said. "We can't sit around here all day. Are you going out like that, Marianne?"

"Don't start!" Marianne snapped. Her hair was unbrushed, and she was wearing scuffed loafers. Her shirt hung out beneath her sweater. Her cheeks flushed and she glared at Delphine.

"I'm just saying . . ." Delphine looked flustered.

"I don't care what I look like!" Marianne pulled her sweater down. "Can't you get that through your head? And no one else cares, either. It's just *you* . . ."

"Marianne . . ." Sophie took her arm, gently.

Marianne sat down on her bed and took off her glasses. She rubbed her eyes. She looked as surprised by her outburst as the others. "I'm sorry," she whispered. "You look lovely, Delphine. It's just . . . I'm not interested in the same things as you."

"I know," Delphine said quietly. "I think when I'm nervous . . . I get more anxious about what I'm wearing."

"Look, I'll brush my hair," Marianne said and, picking up her brush, gave it two quick strokes. Hair floated up with static. "Thing is," she said, putting on her glasses, "whatever I do, I always look the same!"

In the corridor, everything was quiet.

"Do we even know where to go?" Marianne asked.

"They'll have left food for us in the White Dining Room." Delphine sounded confident. "Like yesterday."

The princess was seated at the far end of the table. She was dressed in an elegant blue skirt and high-necked voile blouse, an enormous fur draped over the back of her chair. She was wearing red lipstick, and her mouth looked as full as a peony. Her head rested in her hand as she stared straight ahead.

She pulled the fur stole around her shoulders as if she were cold, picked up a small cup stained with lipstick, stood up, and came toward them. Close up, she had dark circles under her eyes and Sophie could see tiny grains of powder on her nose. She had painted two thin black lines on her upper lids, the ends flicked up. But they seemed to have interrupted the fine dimensions of her face, making her look less remarkable.

The princess passed a hand across her forehead. "I couldn't sleep," she said. "So much paperwork!" She looked frail, not like the day before. "And we have a guest arriving today! A very important guest. His name is General Grekov."

"Princess!" Ivan appeared in the doorway, carrying a tray of bread rolls.

"Ivan?" Sophie saw the princess hastily try to control her expression.

He carried the tray toward the sideboard. His hair was unkempt and he had left several buttons on his jacket undone. He didn't meet the princess's gaze. Instead he busied himself arranging plates, putting glasses on the table.

The princess jumped when he dropped a handful of cutlery, and spoke to him sharply in Russian. He bent down to pick up what he had dropped, and Sophie saw that his hands were shaking.

The princess sat down. She asked for more coffee, then just stared at the walls, as if imagining paintings that no longer hung there.

The girls felt awkward. No one spoke. The princess checked her watch.

"I can't bear it," she said. "I can't sit here . . ." She smiled at the girls. "Come with me."

They followed her.

"What's going on?" Delphine kept an eye on the woman's back, her hair pinned in elaborate braids. But the princess did not reply.

Up a broad staircase, toward a pair of double doors, lyres painted on the panels, wolves with open mouths; snarling or singing, Sophie couldn't tell. They were outside the gallery! The princess reached into the pocket of her skirt and pulled out a key.

Sophie would see the place where Prince Vladimir had faced his murderers.

Before the princess unlocked the door, she turned to Sophie. "Perhaps you will see something I have missed," she said. "Come on!" She put her cold fingers on Sophie's hand. "Come and meet the family!"

The princess opened the door onto a musty-smelling void. Sophie heard the rasp of a match being lit and shaky plumes of candlelight danced on top of long candles. She gave each girl a single candle and then picked up a heavy, many-branched candelabrum and walked to the center of the enormous room. Faces loomed out of the darkness.

"The Volkonskys!" the princess announced, her white arm extended as if she were making an introduction.

There were hundreds of portraits: beautiful women with white shoulders and lapdogs; little boys with long hair and satin coats standing, like miniature adults, next to large hunting dogs or statues; men in arrogant poses, ignoring Sophie with their hooded eyes.

"Look at this!" Delphine called, and Marianne followed her toward a huge portrait of a dark-haired beauty in an extravagant ice-blue ball gown.

"There are so many of them!" Sophie turned around and around, holding her candle higher. The portraits covered every inch of the vast room.

"Correction!" The princess walked farther into the room. "*Were* so many of them." She fixed her gray eyes on Sophie. "Just think! At this moment, in all of Russia, there is only" — she counted the fingers on one hand — "yes, just the one Princess Volkonskaya."

"I'm sorry," Sophie said.

"Not as sorry as me." The princess chewed her lip and stared hard at Sophie. "Sometimes I think it would be better for everyone if there were not even one Volkonsky left. Perhaps things would be simpler . . ."

"You mustn't say that!"

"You are right." The princess inclined her head. "I must not say that. *They* might hear me." She glanced up at the massed ranks of Volkonskys. "But don't you think there comes a time when a family should just cease to be? A time when they have outlived their usefulness? Why shouldn't the Volkonskys move over and let someone else have a chance?"

As she said the words *move over,* she gave Sophie a little shove. It was so unexpected that Sophie's candle tilted and hot wax splashed onto her hand.

"But Princess!"

"Let me introduce you," she went on, ignoring Sophie's protest.

Sophie looked around at the hundreds of portraits. "You know who they all are?"

"I know they're all related to the last Volkonsky princess."

"To you," Sophie whispered.

"Is there another princess in the room?" There was a teasing note in her voice. "But tell me . . . which do you like the best?"

Sophie walked through the gallery, staring up at the portraits. She came to a stop by a picture of a young man with dark hair brushed across a high forehead, a smile playing at the corner of his mouth. He stood in a frogged military uniform, long-limbed and relaxed but with an easy confidence. A saber was looped to the side of his breeches.

Covering the portrait was a mass of bullet holes.

"Yes, Sophie," the princess breathed. "Our brave Prince Vladimir."

So this was the young, brave prince. He had the softest, kindest face, Sophie thought. No trace of hardness or ruthlessness in those eyes. The way the prince's head was tilted, as if he had just heard something interesting, reminded her of her father's photograph, the one on her windowsill at school. Sophie had the unsettling notion that perhaps this painted prince could hear anything she said.

"Do you think he was handsome?" the princess asked her.

Sophie said, "I'm not sure . . ."

"Does he remind you of anyone?"

Sophie stepped right up to the portrait. She could now distinguish the brushstrokes that made up his mustache, the dabs of pigment that flushed his cheeks. She gingerly put a finger up to the holes in the canvas. How many bullets there had been! She could have told the princess that something in his appearance reminded her of her father, but she knew that would sound ridiculous. Her father, an English poet, and a not very successful one at that, had nothing to do with this brave Russian soldier.

"He doesn't remind me of anyone," she said, shaking her head. "But then, he's not likely to. I don't know many Russian princes who were murdered in front of their own paintings."

Next to this portrait was another one, equally large, with a sheet hanging over it.

"They were painted as a pair," the princess said, and snatched at the sheet. She watched Sophie's face closely as the painting was revealed.

It was a portrait of a woman in a simple white gown — but the face had been cut out with ugly slashes. All that could be seen above the dress were tendrils of dark blonde hair and a rope of heavy gray diamonds that hung around the woman's neck all the way down to her waist. The necklace was so long it had been looped up to the side.

Marianne and Delphine had caught up with them.

"What happened to her face?" Delphine cried.

"What a horrible thing to do," Marianne said.

So this was the young woman Masha had called the wolf princess, Sophie thought. The young woman who had been brought to the palace as a young girl, nursed a wolf, and married a prince. How could anyone be so cruel? Sophie sensed a savage anger behind the slashes.

"I can understand it," the princess whispered. "The rage that someone else could be so rich. Why *wouldn't* you want to cut their face out of a painting?"

"It wouldn't get you very far," Marianne said primly.

The princess shrugged as if she thought Marianne's logic of no interest. She came closer and traced the rope of diamonds around the painted neck. "Imagine what one could do with those," she whispered. "A rope of diamonds long enough to hang a man. They would fetch a fortune." A single, sudden tear welled up in her eye and splashed onto her cheek. She put a diamond-laden finger up to the corner of her eye. "Oh, what's the use! They'll never be found."

The three girls looked at each other, horrified.

"Please don't cry, Princess," Sophie said, touching her arm.

"But the lost Volkonsky diamonds! She didn't take them with her! They're here . . . somewhere! They have to be!"

She turned to face Sophie, a stricken expression on her face. "I'm in such trouble," she whispered. "Don't you see?"

Sophie felt a chill crawl across her shoulders.

"What do you mean?" Marianne said.

"You're a princess." Delphine sounded confused. "You're a beautiful princess. How could you be in trouble?"

"I owe a lot of money," she whispered, "which now I *must* pay. I had hoped for more time . . . just a little more time. But the general will soon be here . . . He gave me a lot of money to search for the Volkonsky fortune. Oh yes. You need money to find money. I had to pay people for documents, bribe officials to ensure their loyalty. And it was all for nothing. I promised the general everything I have, everything I *don't* have . . . but it isn't enough. He is not a patient man."

Sophie saw a patch of red appear on the princess's cheek. She was appalled.

"But you can sell some paintings!" Marianne said. "People pay a lot for old paintings, don't they?"

The princess shook her head, twisting the diamond rings on her hand. "The paintings here are worthless. There is nothing else here I can sell. And I have run out of time."

"But there must be *something* you can do!" Sophie said. She looked at the two portraits, one slashed by a saber, the other ripped by bullet holes. Perhaps the Volkonskys were unlucky or cursed, she thought. You heard of families like that: whole generations lost or ruined due to one mishap, one mistake, which, even though small, was like a compass error, and just became greater with each passing generation. Was the beautiful Princess Anna Feodorovna fated never to find happiness?

The princess stepped toward the portrait and put a shaking finger up to the damaged canvas. The squares of gray oil paint had been enlivened by dots of white to replicate the diamonds' lazy sparkle.

"Where are they?" she whispered. "Princess Volkonskaya . . . please . . . tell me! *Where* are your diamonds? If you won't tell me where you hid them, I will look just like you. Not so beautiful then . . ." She turned to Sophie, anger and desperation in her eyes. "Why can't you help me?"

"Me? But what can *I* do?" Sophie said, shrinking, and watched the princess's expression turn ugly.

"You really do know nothing," she said. "You're no use to me."

"Princess!" They turned and saw Ivan in the doorway. He had smoothed his hair and his jacket was properly buttoned now.

"Is it time?"

Ivan nodded. "He is here."

The princess didn't move. It was as if she had been paralyzed. "Already?"

Ivan nodded again. He looked almost as desperate as the princess. What was it about the general's arrival,

Sophie wondered, that could have upset both of them so much?

A door slammed below.

"Anna!" A man's voice bellowed out, strong, sonorous. "Ann-aaaaaa!"

Sophie saw the princess put her hand to her chest as if to calm herself. She glanced back at the portrait of the last Princess Volkonskaya and her lost diamonds. Then, taking a deep breath, she walked unsteadily toward the door. Ivan offered her his arm, but she pushed him away and disappeared into the gloom of the palace beyond.

CHAPTER SEVENTEEN

The General

At the bottom of the broad stairs, a man in gray military uniform waited. He stood with his legs planted slightly apart, as impregnable as a gun battery. He took off his cap and gloves, put the gloves into his upturned cap, and smoothed his black hair with his hand. The light from the muslined chandelier fell onto the floor at the man's feet. He could have been standing in snow. He tapped his foot, impatient.

Sophie, Delphine, and Marianne looked over the balcony and down into the atrium.

"He's very handsome," Delphine whispered.

"They suit each other," Marianne replied.

"General!" The princess ran down the stairs to join him, her voice light and trembling. Ivan followed slowly. He looked wary of the general, Sophie thought. But protective of the princess, too: His hand kept moving toward the top of his hip in a practiced gesture, as if he might still find his soldier's pistol there.

"Anna! Anna!" the general crooned. "What have you done to me?" His voice was bright, cruel, his English faultless. He stroked the fur draped over the princess's shoulder, took her hands, and looked at the diamond rings. "Very beautiful," he smiled, but it was like a salute: something he had learned to do. "I can see that life at the Volkonsky Winter Palace suits you — and that you have been spending *my money*."

The princess snatched her hand away as if she had touched something hot. The general laughed. And then, even though he had not once glanced up and did not appear to have noticed the girls standing in the shadows on the balcony, he looked up now and stared straight at Sophie.

"Don't sulk! Don't hide! Come down!" he cried.

The girls looked at each other. They knew already he was the sort of man who gave orders and expected to see them carried out quickly. They walked down the stairs toward him.

The general put his arm around the princess. "Anna Feodorovna is the only woman in Russia who could make me travel so far!" He squeezed her shoulder and she winced. "I swear! No other woman in all of Russia can command General Grekov!"

"Grigor," the princess whispered. "Please . . . I hate it when you make fun of me."

The man ignored her; he seemed to enjoy showing off to the girls, displaying his power over the princess. "She snaps her fingers, stamps her foot. I say . . . 'Woman! I have wars to fight! Do you think I can divert my military train just to pay you a visit?'" He laughed, dropped his arm, and stepped away. "But what am I to do? When Anna Feodorovna summons me, I *must* come!"

He took a deep breath, expanded his chest, and seemed to fill more than the space surrounding him. He surveyed the atrium with a long, appraising stare and said, "So! This is the magnificent Volkonsky Winter Palace that I have been told so much about!" He sauntered over to a large gilt mirror, its glass mottled and watery. He leaned closer to his own reflection. "She promises me bears and wolves and diamonds!" He turned around. "But so far all I find are three schoolgirls!"

He strolled toward them.

"You must be our French guest," he said to Delphine. "Just as I imagined you would be . . . very stylish."

Delphine flushed. She was about to speak, but the man had already taken Marianne's hand, raising it to his lips in an old-fashioned gesture of courtesy. Marianne, flustered, grabbed it back.

"Marianne? The clever one!" He laughed. "It's the

glasses! They give you away!" Marianne blinked and moved closer to Delphine.

"So this . . ." He took a step back, as if to admire a painting. "*This* is the enigma! The famous Sophie Smith!" He reached over and pinched her cheek. Sophie flinched. On his fingers was the perfume of a heavy eau de cologne. With a shock she saw that his eyes were only pupils, with no color. "Not much to look at and all alone in the world, with no one to protect her." He brushed a speck of dust from his immaculate jacket.

Sophie felt her heart in her throat. This man was dangerous. A wolf.

He turned his head slightly toward the princess. "I hear from my associate that three girls have arrived at the Volkonsky Winter Palace as guests of the Princess Anna Feodorovna Volkonskaya." He stopped for a moment, as if he might have expected someone to speak. "I await a telephone call to invite me to the party." He stared at the princess.

"I don't have any information for you," the princess said.

"But they have been here for over twenty-four hours!"

"I haven't found —"

The man's voice cut across. "If she knows nothing" — he frowned — "why is she still your guest?"

Why was the general so interested in their arrival? Sophie thought. And who was the associate who had given him the information? She looked at her friends, but Delphine shrugged and Marianne shook her head to show that they, too, were unsure of what was happening in front of them.

Ivan stepped out of the shadows, glancing at Sophie anxiously.

"Ivan!" the general cried. "The war veteran! Our noble hero!"

"That's enough, Grigor," the princess snapped. "He has helped me."

"Don't worry, Ivan!" the general said. "I am here now! The princess will be *properly* looked after."

Ivan glared at the man. "*I* have looked after her properly — and our guests."

Sophie wanted to agree, but her voice seemed to have stuck in her throat.

"But it's just a joke." Then the general frowned. "Forgotten something, hussar?"

Ivan stood to attention and saluted. The action was swift and assured, but his eyes were dead.

The general nodded and turned to the princess. "You have it? I've come a long way, and I don't want my journey to be wasted."

"I have all the paperwork," she said. She tilted her chin up, a defiant expression on her face.

The man roared with laughter. "Anna . . . Anna . . ." he cried. "Do you think I've traveled a thousand miles for paper? No. You'd better have something more substantial to show me." He leaned toward her. "The diamonds, Anna. You promised me diamonds."

"You didn't give me enough time —"

"Ah yes! *Time!*"

Sophie edged closer to Marianne and Delphine. She wanted to tell this man to stop, but even as she formed that thought she felt powerless. She knew she wasn't brave enough to make him stop, and even if she tried, he would simply ignore her and carry on.

"You sound like a dying man on a battlefield!" The general smiled callously. "Faced with a rifle and certain death, they all cry out for more time!"

Sophie knew he was wrong. What about Prince Vladimir Volkonsky? When faced with those soldiers in the gallery, he hadn't asked for more time. He had been happy to give his life, to save his family. But against words like *family* and *love*, the general would set *power* and *money*. She knew there was no point saying anything to this man whose gaze swept now across the faces of the girls. In his cold eyes, Sophie saw the expression of some ancient, ruthless god who blighted lives for amusement. Trying to change his mind would be like trying to change the course of an avalanche with a teaspoon. She took all of this in very quickly, just as she had understood the nature of the wolf at the lake.

"I should have given the job to Galina Starova," the general hissed. "Far more reliable. Far more ruthless."

Galina Starova? What was *she* to the general? Sophie looked at Marianne, but neither she nor Delphine appeared to have heard what the general had said. Had *she* even heard it?

"Let's find a quiet corner, *Princess* . . ." General Grekov spat the title. "We can discuss business matters more easily in private."

He linked his arm through the princess's and steered her up the broad staircase toward the White Dining Room.

"Bring me food, brave hussar!" he called out. "Traveling makes me hungry!"

Ivan's eyes were fixed on the retreating form of the princess.

"I can't hear you, Ivan!" the general jeered.

"Yes. Sir!" Ivan cried out. He looked toward the girls, his kind face pained. "Why did she bring him here?"

"*Did* she bring him here, though?" Sophie whispered. "It looks more as if he just decided to arrive."

Marianne added, "He doesn't look like the type who would wait for an invitation."

The general's voice floated down the stairs. "Little English girls?" It had a sickening singsong tone to it. "No plotting! Come in here and sing for the grown-ups!"

The girls walked slowly back up the stairs, candles flickering around them.

"And anyway," said Marianne, "why should Sophie know anything about the Volkonskys?" She sounded as confused as Sophie felt.

Sophie glanced down the corridor toward the gallery. The door was still open. Where were the white wolves now? The princess needed her protectors. But somehow she knew that even that savage creature she had seen at the lake would not be enough to save the princess from this man.

The princess sat next to the general at the far end of the table. He played with a knife while he waited for his food. The princess looked sullen and moody. *Her face is no longer beautiful*, Sophie thought.

"She *is* in trouble," Marianne whispered. "She's done something wrong."

"I wouldn't want to make the general angry," Delphine added under her breath.

"Don't stand in the doorway whispering!" the general cried. "I don't like females who talk in quiet voices. It makes me feel they're plotting!" He turned to the princess. "Anna knows I believe in openness and honesty.

Anything she says or does must be seen and heard by me . . ."

The princess stared at Sophie as if she wanted her to say something to the general. But what? What could Sophie say that would make this man leave them alone?

Ivan appeared with a large silver tray.

"At last!" the general cried, even though Ivan had been gone only a matter of minutes. His expression as Ivan started to unload plates onto the table in front of him was one of contempt. Sophie wondered how Ivan could bear serving such a man. She felt she would have been tempted to let the food spill all over his perfectly pressed gray trousers.

"Bring coffee!" he snapped.

When Ivan said nothing, he cupped a hand to his ear, as if he were deaf.

"Yes, sir," Ivan said. But his voice was dull, defiant.

"Hear that, Anna?" The general looked down at the princess. "There's a *tone* in his voice. If he were one of *my* men, I'd dismiss him!"

The girls walked slowly toward the table. The princess stared at them as if she had never seen them before. Sophie could tell nothing from her blank expression.

"I need your help!" The general leaped up and pulled chairs out for each of them, flicking the seats with a napkin before they each sat down. He took his place once more, and now his mood changed. He leaned forward, his face earnest and grave. His voice became softer, and with a jolt Sophie understood that if she closed her eyes and listened only to his voice, she could make herself believe that he wasn't cold and ruthless, but that he actually cared. The voice was one that you wanted to listen to.

"Sadly, girls, my dear Anna," the general said, glancing across at the woman next to him, "this beautiful princess, dressed in furs and diamonds, has problems. Can any of you guess what they might be?"

This one simple question, said in such a straightforward manner, changed the mood in the room. It was as if he was appealing for their help. How could they refuse?

Delphine crossed her legs and looked as if she might speak. Then she stopped. The general saw it. "There's no need to be polite, Delphine." He picked up a knife, ran the edge along his finger. His fingers were thick and the nails short and clean. "It's true. The princess has no money!" He put the knife down and placed his large hand over the princess's.

His eyes focused on Marianne.

"You are *clever girls*," he said quietly. "I knew that the minute I saw you, especially you, Marianne. I would have you in my spy unit, cracking all those codes."

Marianne pushed her glasses up her nose with the same pride as when she had solved a math problem in front of the class. Something flickered in the general's eyes. He knew he'd got her.

It's like a battle campaign, Sophie thought. *He's like a sniper and he's just picking us off one by one. First Delphine, now Marianne.*

"Have you any ideas how we can help the princess in her *perilous* situation? You see, she was given a substantial sum to return here to the palace and play the princess!" He stroked her fur. "She always *was* such a princess!" He sighed. "But I am beginning to think that she is just playing a game. She has had her money and is living here with no intention of repaying her debt."

He let the silence swell in the room until it became unbearable. When no one said anything, his mood changed again.

"I have given her every opportunity to pay and, sad to say, she has treated me with contempt." He squeezed the princess's hand as if to comfort her. She winced. His voice no more than a menacing whisper, he added, "But what she does not realize is that while she plays the princess at her estate, I will not play the fool!"

"It wasn't like that, Grigor." Her voice shook. "There were no conditions attached to the loan."

"But it *was* a loan, Anna. Not a gift." He sighed. "We are faced with a very difficult situation. We have to find the money somehow. Of course, we could shoot wolves!" He laughed and sliced into a lump of meat. "In the days of the Tsars, you could get three rubles for each wolf tail! Do you know how they used to hunt wolves in the days of the Tsars, Sophie?"

He smiled at her lazily. The meat on the end of his fork was rare, a blurred circle of pink in the center. Juice dripped onto the plate.

Sophie wanted him to stop, wanted to look away. But she couldn't.

"The huntsmen would string nets around one part of the forest and set the peasants at the edge to yell and wave heavy clubs," the general went on. "Then they would enter the forest with their packs of ravenous hunting dogs driven mad by the smell of dead horseflesh . . ."

Sophie's chest felt tight. She thought of Dmitri and his kind, intelligent eyes. She thought of the wolf at the lake, outside her window. She didn't want to listen to this man; she wanted to think of how the last princess had saved a wolf, had brought that wounded, wild animal into the palace and nursed it. The wolf princess wouldn't have allowed a wolf hunt here, she just knew it. But the general's voice bore into her, taunting her, forcing her to listen.

"The huntsmen chase the wolf, crazed by the cries of the peasants, the excited, tormenting barks of the dogs. They run him at great speed toward the nets . . ."

The general stopped. He seemed to know that all of

them were listening intently. Even Ivan had become still; Sophie could see him out of the corner of her eye.

"*BAM!*" He slammed his hand down on the table.

Marianne yelped.

"The wolf, running so fast, is caught. He thrashes wildly, desperate to escape."

Sophie tried to keep in her mind the image of Dmitri in the chandelier, his song about moonlight and the white wolves, his respect for those animals. How his scar would twitch if he were in the room, sitting next to her! Surely he would stop the general from saying any more?

"The huntsmen look into the wolf's eye, the eye of a ruthless killer, but they are not afraid. As the wolf snarls and snaps, thinking he will surely be free in an instant, another net drops on him! Hah! He is caught."

Sophie felt tears stinging in her eyes as she thought of the wolf in the net. She understood how the yells of the men and the insane barking of the dogs would tear through the perceptions of the wolf and the landscape he was moving through. He would be propelled by panic and fear alone. And toward what?

The man put the lump of meat into his mouth. There was something so revolting in this one act.

Sophie said, "That's disgusting."

The general didn't appear to hear. And the fact that he ignored her so totally, as if she had been air, silenced her more completely than if he had shouted at her to shut up. Swallowing his meat, he continued, "The men string the wolf on a pole and he is taken in a wagon to the Tsar's woods. Those brave huntsmen! They break his leg so he can't run, and the Tsar himself hunts him and is given the privilege of the kill!"

"Idiots!" Sophie looked the man straight in the eyes. "They're all idiots! How can you say they're brave? They're just cowards! It's not even a fair fight!"

The general shook his head. "Why does something have to be fair if it gives you pleasure?" he mused. "Those men don't just shoot the wolf. They *enjoy* the hunt. The wolf, the men, they join in the hunt together, don't you see?"

"But what can the wolf do?" Sophie could feel her cheeks burning. He was twisting everything around. "The wolf can't fight back!"

"So you would prefer a duel?" The general picked up his knife, flicked it into the air, and caught it again with a neat action. He jumped up. "Come on then, little English wolf girl." He strode toward Sophie and put his hand on the back of her chair, tipping it so Sophie had to stand or fall forward. She stood.

"Grigor!" The princess suddenly snapped out of her reverie. "Stop!"

"She wants to defend the wolves? She needs to know how to fight!" the general laughed.

Sophie was aware of Marianne's face, her glasses lop-sided. Delphine's hair had become half tucked into the collar of her shirt. Something made her want to pull out that lock of hair, but the general had come around behind her and was moving her arms into position.

"Stand like this!" he said, his voice so confident and self-assured that she had no power to tell him to stop. "Hold the blade like this!" He put the knife into her hand. Sophie looked at the wolf head on the handle. The general walked around to face her.

"General!" Ivan's voice. He had stepped forward. It felt as if events in the room were running away and Sophie no longer had any control over them.

"Back to your place, hussar," the general snarled. "I give the orders here!"

Perhaps Ivan's training meant that he could not defy him. He retreated, but looked as if he wanted to take Sophie with him.

Sophie's heart raced.

The general, his eyes now sparkling with the certain knowledge of his own power, cried, *"En garde!"*

She heard Marianne shriek. A plate must have fallen to the floor because she heard a smash. And the word, "Grigor!"

The glitter of his eyes, the clenched jaw. And then Sophie's arm was twisted high up behind her back by the man's quick, strong grip. As the pain tore through her shoulder, she could see the knife at her temple, a hairsbreadth from her skin. She, too, was the wolf driven into a net and unable to escape. She wanted to thrash about and snarl, take revenge. This was unbearable. The second net would fall. She had been tricked just as surely as the wolves hunted for the Tsar's pleasure.

I hate this man, she thought. *I hate everything he stands for.*

Then another noise shattered everything.

It set the pulse racing but stopped the heart. It made blood sweep and crash in the ears. The sound started at the base of Sophie's spine and began to climb up and up until it hovered just above her head. It seemed to swirl around and pull everything toward it: snow, forest, wilderness, loneliness, despair, the thrill of warm blood from a fresh kill, and a fierce protectiveness toward every other member of the pack. It was a cry that made her entire being turn toward it, every cell tuned to listen to it, and yet it made her want to run and run until it stopped.

It was the same wolf. She knew it. The old white wolf from the woods. It was as if he was calling out his name.

But, Sophie realized as her pulse raced, it sounded like a warning, too. Yes, he was coming to rescue the princess. He was coming to save a Volkonsky!

"What was that?" Marianne grabbed Delphine's arm.

"Volky!" the princess whispered. "A wolf has escaped!"

"Escaped?" she heard Delphine repeat. "From where?"

Ivan ran to the door. "Dmitri!" he yelled. And then something more, in urgent, despairing Russian.

"You promised me wolves, Anna!" the general cried, taking the pistol from his hip. "By God, I'll have them!" His face was alight with the sort of joy seen on the faces of saints and martyrs. He pushed past Ivan, and they heard his footsteps running down the corridor toward the broad marble staircase.

Another howl tore through the palace as the princess ran after him.

"Princess! Wait!" Ivan called.

And then, from the general at the bottom of the stairs, the insane yell of the hunter: *"Loup! Loup!"*

CHAPTER EIGHTEEN

The Hunt

Ivan stood immobile in the doorway.

"What has she done?" he said, shaking his head. "What has she done?"

"What do you mean, Ivan?" Sophie felt the palace splinter around her.

He hesitated, as if unsure what to say, then seemed to make a decision. "When the princess returned to the palace," he said slowly, "the wolves frightened her. Dmitri said they were used to the freedom of the forest. She went crazy. Said she'd throw his family out into the snow if he didn't lock them up. There's a courtyard on the far side of the palace where they're kept and Dmitri feeds them. She wasn't brave enough to have them killed — she said the Volkonskys would haunt her if she killed a wolf."

"But you said there were no wolves. You said that was all history!" Sophie put her arm out to the door to steady herself. "I *told* the princess I'd seen a wolf at the lake! You went to look and said there was nothing!" She looked up at Ivan's troubled face.

"I saw the tracks," Ivan said. "I knew then that there was still a wolf in the forest. But I couldn't tell her. It's Dmitri's job to keep them here, in the palace. To feed them. Keep them quiet. If there was a wolf loose, the princess would have blamed him. She wanted an excuse to get rid of him. I had to protect him."

Sophie remembered how sharply the princess had spoken to Dmitri when they had returned to the palace from the lake. The three of them had stood under the portico, deep in discussion. Of course! What had Masha said Dmitri did? *"Groom Viflyanka, feed the . . ."* she had stopped before she said the word, but she knew. Everyone knew.

All these thoughts came to her in a heartbeat.

Ivan snapped out of his reverie. As if waking up from a dream, he only now seemed to be aware of the danger of their situation.

"Princess!" he cried as he ran down the stairs.

And before she could think about the danger she was about to put herself in, Sophie ran down the stairs after him.

"Sophie!" It was Delphine's voice, wound tight with panic. "What are you doing?"

"Don't leave us!" Marianne wailed.

But Sophie couldn't cower in a room. They were going to hunt the wolf! And yet the creature was here in the palace because of the princess. He knew she was in danger from the general and he had come to save her. She couldn't let the general hurt him.

"Lock the door!" she called over her shoulder. She could see the blonde head of the princess and the black head of the general as they ran down the white balustraded staircase that threaded down below her. There was no sign of Ivan or the wolf. She felt nothing other than the breath hurting her lungs as she lunged down the stairs, two at a time. Why couldn't she move more quickly?

"Please let me get there," Sophie said aloud. "Please don't let them harm him."

But the voices were becoming fainter and drifted into nothing. The palace was quiet now.

There were wolves in the palace. She had heard them. White Volkonsky wolves, just like the pack that had avenged the death of Prince Vladimir. But how could the princess be frightened of them? They were the guardians of the palace.

Sophie stopped. She had been running without thinking about where she was going: down long corridors, through dilapidated rooms, following the echoing voices. They had led her on, but now they had stopped and she was lost. She was at the head of some stairs she didn't recognize. Statues in niches guarded every few steps, but some had been smashed and had fallen forward like dead men. She looked back the way she had come. No. It was hopeless. She could run for hours through empty rooms. Without any voices to follow, how could she even know where to start?

Out of the corner of her eye, she saw a white mist at the far end of the corridor.

The creature hadn't seen her, she knew, but she saw how the sense of her presence wrapped itself around him. And then, silently, he turned.

Weaving through the blank, cold statues, his red eyes now fixed entirely on her, came the white wolf.

Sophie pressed herself against the marble balustrade, trying to make herself as insignificant as possible, but her legs were giving way. The blood swept around her head. There was a door across the corridor, but she would never make it there in time. And anyway, would it even be open? Or would it be locked? Could she jump? She peered over the balustrade and the floor leaped up toward her. She thought of herself falling, loose, easy, through the air . . . and landing like one of the broken statues.

The animal came on, his jaw hanging open. He was hungry and desperate, but Sophie sensed his strength, the muscle and bone, and the terrible, shocking length of his teeth, bared now. He could see all around him, Sophie knew, and beyond, too, as if he could enter every room in the palace at the same time. A different way of seeing.

He stopped a few feet away. How could Sophie tell him that she was no threat to the Volkonskys? That he should not harm her?

And then, behind him, appeared the princess.

Sophie, so intent on the wolf, hadn't seen her creeping silently up the corridor. She held her tiny pistol in her two hands and took aim: Sophie could see the black pout of the barrel. What was she doing?

"Don't shoot!" Sophie tried to say, but her voice was just a croak.

The wolf, still motionless, snarled.

The princess flexed her hands around the pistol, became perfectly still. She was preparing with ruthless precision to take her shot, slowing her heart, controlling her breathing so she would not miss. Except — Sophie looked at the barrel — the pistol was surely too high for the bullet to hit the wolf. It was on the same level as Sophie's eyes . . .

"Princess . . . *Nyet!*"

It was Ivan, a hunting rifle on his shoulder, his hand outstretched, pushing the princess's pistol away.

Crack!

Sophie stared at the floor. The wolf was on his side at her feet, the blood pooling on the floor. He tried to raise his head, but the effort was too much. He whimpered, and the sound was so pitiful when compared to the power of his howl that Sophie wanted to cry.

"Saboteur!" screamed the princess. "You've ruined everything!"

Ivan, chisel-jawed, his face drained of color, muttered, "I have ruined nothing. I am giving you a choice, Princess."

The princess raised her pistol as if she would smash it across his temple. Ivan stood his ground. And then, a horrible sound: The princess laughed at him. Beneath it, Sophie heard another, quieter noise. A moan or a whimper.

The wolf. He was not dead! He lumbered to his feet despite the wound, and limped down the staircase with a yelp of pain, blood pouring from his side.

"Still alive?" The general strode up the corridor. He leaned over the balustrade and aimed his pistol.

Sophie threw herself at the man. The pistol fired with a quiet, velvety pop. A statue toppled and fell. Sophie saw the startled wolf run on.

The general shook her off. "You stupid little wolf girl!" he whispered. "What do you think you're doing? A wounded wolf is more dangerous than a healthy one."

From deep inside the palace, the howling started up. The Volkonsky wolves! Terrified, but understanding their cries, Sophie listened as these creatures began their wild chorus, no longer content to be written off as characters in a fairy tale. Their cries blended, twined, and fell apart.

"They know!" Sophie cried. "They know what you've done!"

"We saved you!" The princess's eyes flashed. "Without us here, you would have been torn to pieces!"

The general shoved Sophie roughly away. "Ivan! It's time to leave these weeping women. Get that boy. He can become a man." He smiled at Sophie, a twist of his lips. "This time, without the little wolf girl, we'll shoot them all."

"Don't you dare!" Sophie screamed into the man's smiling face. "Don't you touch the wolves! Don't you harm them! They are here to protect the princess . . . from you! They are guardians of the palace! You can't shoot them!"

The general didn't seem remotely bothered by her outburst. "Princess?" he said to the woman standing next to him. "What do you think we should do with this noisy English girl? She's quite useless!"

He gave her an unfathomable look before turning to run down the stairs.

"You've got to stop him, Princess!" Sophie cried.

"But what can I do? The general likes to hunt," she said, her eyes following him.

"But *you!* How could you hurt a Volkonsky wolf?" Sophie felt the tears splash onto her face. "They live to protect you!"

"But you must understand," the princess said, "I couldn't leave that creature loose!" She laughed, but sounded nervous. "It was for your safety!"

"What do you mean?" Sophie felt the room spin. "He wasn't going to hurt anyone!"

The princess shook her head slowly. "If only that were true," she whispered. "But I have seen a wolf when he kills. He would not be kind." She leaned toward Sophie. "You think it would be quick? One bite and it's all over? Not with a wolf. A snap, a bite, and he would sit and wait, watching you bleed before he came and licked up the pool of your blood. Tell me, would you enjoy that?"

Sophie stared at the beautiful face, lips as red as wolf blood.

"If only I could find the diamonds, Sophie" — the princess put her hand to Sophie's face and moved a strand of hair out of her eyes — "I could live here happily, with no worry for the future. We could be friends!"

She glanced at the wolf's blood on the floor. "I am sorry about today. The general has made me a little crazy with his demands for money . . . What I need now is a friend."

She smiled, but it made her face look unbearably sad.

"Just one friend," she whispered. "I had hoped it would be you . . ."

"Tell him to go!" Sophie said. "Tell him to leave you alone!"

"Only if you will stay." The princess was already moving toward the stairs. "And help me?"

As the princess ran after the general, Sophie leaned against the wall. How could she help this woman?

CHAPTER NINETEEN

The Ring

The White Dining Room was empty. The remains of the general's unfinished meal were still on the table, Sophie's chair still on its side. But where were Delphine and Marianne?

Sophie ran to the nursery and pushed open the door to see her friends sitting on her bed by the window. Masha was pouring them tea from a *samovar* on the table.

"We heard shots!" Marianne ran toward her. "We were so frightened."

"Masha brought us here," Delphine said. She smiled at the girl, who blushed. "She's Dmitri's sister."

"Dmitri so brave!" Masha said as she handed Sophie a glass of tea. "General say he must shoot wolves!" Her eyes were round. "But Dmitri spit on general's boots!"

"And the other wolf?" Sophie whispered. "The wolf that escaped?"

Masha shook her head. She turned away.

"What happened?" Marianne asked. They all sat together on the bed. "Honestly, Sophie, we're worried. It's all gone weird."

Delphine stroked Sophie's arm. "I'm so glad you're here," she said. "We need to leave." As if everything had suddenly been decided in the saying of those words, she ran to the dresser and started pulling out sweaters, jeans, a pile of underwear, moving as fast as if she risked missing a train. "Let's just pack up everything. Come on, Marianne! You too, Sophie. Let's just get ready and tell her she has to send us back to Saint Petersburg!"

Marianne, looking stunned, blinked up at Delphine. "I don't want to go to Saint Petersburg," she said slowly. "I want to go back to London . . . I want to go *home!*"

Delphine refolded T-shirts. "Fine. We'll go home. Just get a move on!"

"But . . ." Sophie swung her legs down onto the floor. Was this how it was going to end? The princess wasn't the person she appeared to be, she had let them down, but she was still in terrible trouble. "She asked for help."

"But that's just it," Marianne sighed. She looked crumpled, as if someone needed to shake all the creases out of her. "We can't help her."

"But just to leave her with the general . . ."

"It's not safe for us to stay." Delphine's voice was firm.

They would be like the Volkonsky princess, then, Sophie thought . . . fleeing the palace . . .

"Delphine's right." Marianne bent down and pulled her rucksack from underneath her bed. "We need to get out of here."

It was as if none of them wanted to voice the problem in this apparently simple solution: *How?* How would they leave the palace? They packed the rest of their things silently.

Sophie, sitting on her bed, pulled the pencil box out of her rucksack. She opened it and took out the diamond ring. A gift from a Volkonsky princess. She would return it. Even if the princess did not think it so valuable, it might buy her some time with the general.

"Where did you get that?" Delphine's hand shot out, and before Sophie realized it, she had the ring on her finger. "Is it real?" she asked.

"Let me see," said Marianne.

Reluctantly, Delphine slid it off her finger and handed it to her. Marianne took it to the window and scratched it against the glass.

"What are you doing?" Sophie protested.

"Pretty it may be," Marianne said, offering it back to Sophie, "but a real diamond would have cut the glass."

Sophie put it carefully back in the pencil box. Somehow she wasn't surprised. And she didn't mind, not really.

It was just odd, she reflected, how she had brought her piece of glass here to remind her of her father, but she would be taking back another to England to remind her of Dmitri, the wolves, and the Volkonskys.

Delphine, her beautiful tweed coat over her shoulders, announced, "Let's find the princess."

From the top of the staircase they could hear the general's voice in the atrium. "Ann-aaaa!" They looked over the balustrade. He was standing as he had when he had arrived, legs planted apart. There was a pile of carpets and paintings heaped in the middle of the floor. He threw a battered silver *samovar* onto the heap.

"Don't sulk, little girls!" His voice made them jump. "Don't hide in the shadows! Show yourselves!"

"He's seen us!" Delphine gasped. "What do we do?"

"Come on!" Sophie said, forcing herself to sound determined and sure. "He's a bully. Like Natalie Bates at school. You just have to stand up to him."

Marianne pulled on her sleeve. "Are you mad? No one ever gets the better of Natalie Bates. You're better off just walking away."

But they descended the staircase slowly.

"So. A delegation! What could you possibly want, dressed in your coats, carrying your bags?"

Sophie cleared her throat.

"Not you!" the man snapped. "I'm not interested in

what you've got to say! You've had your chance . . . and you wasted it!"

Sophie was so shocked she took a step backward. Marianne was right. You never won against people like this man. They could always make you feel weak and desperate, and in that split second of feeling unsure, they'd finish you off.

"We want to leave," said Delphine, very bravely. "We were just going to tell the princess."

"We really do have to go!" Marianne blurted out. She shifted her battered rucksack a little higher on her shoulder.

The man looked at them and nodded, as if he were considering their request. Then he clapped his hands together. "Of course!" He smiled broadly and checked his watch. "You must leave! You are bored. You are wanting to return to Saint Petersburg. You must accompany me on my train!"

"We won't go with *you!*" Sophie said.

"There is no other way to leave!" the general said. "But it's up to you."

Sophie looked at her friends. They seemed desperate. It was as if she felt the palace collapsing around her. The general was right; they had no idea where they were. Their phones didn't work. They were at his mercy.

"Ivan will take us to the train in the *vozok,*" he added with a sly smile.

Sophie felt Marianne and Delphine sigh with relief. Yes, Ivan would make sure they were all right. He would get them home. The *vozok* could be outside right now! They would be bundled into it and they would be gone.

The princess appeared at the top of the stairs.

"I am leaving," the general said to her.

The princess looked distraught. She ran to him. "No, Grigor, no. I can find them. Don't leave."

"I have taken anything of any worth."

"No, Grigor," the princess whimpered. "Please. Take me with you."

"Why? You are worth *nothing*." He pushed her away. "You disappoint me, Anna. You should have taken that shot — made the kill, as I asked you to. It makes me think you are weak. Come, girls!" he cried then. "Let us get into the *vozok* — let us all go home!"

He ushered Marianne and Delphine toward the door. Sophie stayed where she was. The princess had asked for her help. She was in tears. How could Sophie leave her?

CHAPTER TWENTY

The Gift

The princess would not look at her. "Just go . . ."

"But, Princess . . ."

"It's over." She looked defeated. It was horrible, worse than when she was being cruel. Yes, Sophie had hated her for trying to kill the wolf, but she knew the princess had been trying to save her. And she felt more upset now that the princess, whom she had thought so mesmerizing, looked as feeble as a bird with a broken wing.

"It isn't over. It can't be. You're still a princess." Sophie felt tears welling. She widened her eyes to stop them from spilling onto her face. "We'll think of something to give to the general. To make him leave you alone."

"*Nyet.*" The princess crossed her arms around her body as if she were suddenly cold. "No one can help me now. You think the general is a bad man? Compared to the men he will send now, he is an angel." She was shaking.

"I could leave the palace, of course. But they will find me. Believe me, wherever I go, those men will find me." Her voice cracked. "I am undone."

Sophie knew she no longer existed to the princess; the woman was talking to herself.

"We have to think!" Sophie said. She couldn't leave her like this, not without offering some words of hope. "The princess . . . the *other* princess . . . well, she wouldn't have wanted to hide the diamonds from *you*, would she? I mean, you're a Volkonsky, too, so she must have put them somewhere that you would know about. She must have left clues!"

Anna Feodorovna raised her head. "Go on," she whispered.

"Well, is there anything you've found that might lead you to where they are? Anything you've heard? Perhaps your parents told you something when you were a child, that you didn't understand at the time?"

"They told me *nothing*." The princess's voice caught on the last word.

"Where would *I* leave diamonds if I didn't want anyone to find them? Where they would be safe?" Sophie paced up and down. "Have you asked Dmitri? Masha? They might have information."

"Have you been feeding the *domovoye* with milk and cookies?"

"No . . . I . . ."

"They're not your *friends*. And if they knew where the diamonds were hidden, they would have *stolen* them!"

"But they know so much about the palace," Sophie insisted, even though the princess looked so upset. "They told me a story about how your grandmother, the last Volkonsky princess, nursed a white wolf cub."

"I told you not to speak to the servants!" the princess cried. "They fill your head with stories, with lies!"

"But Dmitri is kind, Princess. He wouldn't steal from you. He loves his family and he's proud of working for the Volkonskys. He wants to look after the wolves . . . he even knows the words to a sort of lullaby that calms them. He told me . . . he told me the words . . ."

The image of the two of them sitting high in the chandelier, watching the light sparkle onto the floor . . .

"I don't have time for this madness!"

"About snow and wolves and tears on the ballroom floor in the moonlight," Sophie said.

"You can't help me." The princess turned away.

"My father used to sing me that same tune when I was a child . . . isn't that strange?" Sophie said. "Of course, I didn't know the words, though . . . how could I?"

"How could you . . ." The princess turned back, slowly.

"But the light on the floor is so beautiful," Sophie whispered. "It does look like tears, except . . ."

She remembered hooking her fingers through that long, gray, dull strand of crystals. Delphine standing in their room at school, her father's crystal drop held up to her ear, and now strung on Sophie's neck . . .

She looked down.

The princess's eyes glittered, then her fingers darted into the neck of Sophie's blouse and tugged hard at the string. Sophie felt a sharp burning sensation on her neck.

"It's just a piece of glass!" Sophie said. "Please don't take it. My father gave it to me . . ." She thought of how he would hold the glass up to let the light sprinkle around . . . *sprinkle around* . . . She saw the princess hold up the glass, looking closely at it, and as it began to twirl, the colors in it danced and a tiny memory fell into place.

Sophie gasped, then laughed. Had her worthless piece of glass given her the clue to finding the Volkonsky riches?

"I know!" she said. "I know where they are! Perhaps Dmitri and his family knew all along, too — except they didn't realize it!"

"You know?" The princess's voice seemed to catch again. "Are you sure? Is this some childish game?"

"This isn't a game."

The princess wrapped her fingers around the glass. "I can tell the difference between glass and diamonds," she whispered.

"This is no game, Princess," Sophie repeated. "Get Ivan. And Dmitri . . ."

The princess looked at Sophie. There was a confused look on her face, as if she didn't know what to do. But then she picked up an old-fashioned telephone and spoke tersely into it.

They ran through the shadows toward the ballroom, Sophie's heart bursting with happiness. "It's so simple," she laughed. She, Sophie Smith, would save this Volkonsky princess!

Ivan stood at the door to the ballroom. Dmitri was there, too. Sophie ran toward him, excited. But Dmitri just looked at the floor, not smiling.

The princess strode into the ballroom and stood, impatiently tapping her foot. Sophie took no notice of Dmitri's sullen face. He might be cross that the princess had set him such a demeaning task, but all would soon be explained and he and his family would be so happy . . . the history of the Volkonskys would come full circle.

"Pull down the rope!" she said. "Quickly! There's something I have to show the princess!"

The boy frowned, then walked slowly, so slowly, to the side of the room and picked up a long pole. As he hooked the end of the pole into the chandelier, the rope slipped down and danced in the air for a few seconds.

"The wolf princess was so clever . . ." Sophie said. "She cleaned the chandeliers in 1917 — on the eve of the Revolution! She wasn't mad — she was making preparations!"

"What are you doing?" the princess whispered.

"Dmitri!" Sophie shoved her foot into the loop. "You'll have to help me." The boy didn't respond. "I can't get up there on my own!" Without someone to haul up the rope, she would have to climb, sailor style. Dmitri groaned. He was being really silly, thought Sophie.

"Anna! Ann-aaaaa!" The general appeared in the doorway. "What's going on?" he snapped. "Anna? What are you all doing here? What are you whispering about?"

"Nothing!" the princess said fearfully. "We're not talking about anything!"

"Are you plotting together?" He walked toward them slowly.

Sophie took a step closer to the princess.

"I am loyal!" The princess spoke fast. "You know that! I gave you the papers the minute you arrived. Everything is yours!"

The man crossed his arms. "And tell me," he sneered, "how does an empty palace help me?"

"I need more time!" The princess ran toward him, grabbed his arms. The man stood impassive. "Please, Grigor! Everything I've done, I've done for us!"

"Us? You've done everything for us? And what is this 'everything'? You've bought yourself furs . . . set yourself up here . . ."

"Grigor!" the princess sobbed.

"And who is this 'us'?" He uncrossed his arms and roughly pushed her toward the large mirror. "Here we are!" he cried, pulling out his pistol. "The happy couple!"

A soft popping noise, like a champagne cork, and the mirror shattered in a torrent of splintering glass.

"Get me the diamonds, Anna. *Then* we'll talk about 'us.'" With a casual flick of the smoking pistol, he waved toward Ivan. "Put my things in the *vozok*."

"I won't take orders from you any longer," Ivan said quietly.

"Then you'll die where you stand." The general held up the still-smoking pistol, aiming for the middle of Ivan's chest.

Sophie's breath caught in her throat. He wouldn't . . . he couldn't . . .

"*Nyet!*" The voice came from high up, in the chandelier, which quivered above them.

Sophie looked up. Dmitri was sitting there.

Ivan said something to him in Russian.

"Get out!" snapped the princess to Ivan. "You're of no use to me now. I rescue you from the gutter and this is how you repay me?"

Ivan staggered slightly. "No use?"

The woman laughed. "Don't imagine for one second you were ever going to be anything *more!*"

Ivan shook his head, his eyes pleading, but when the princess said no more, he stumbled to the door.

"Pull me up!" Sophie cried out. "Dmitri! Do as I say!" He was taking too long.

She saw the princess look up into the chandelier, her hand to her mouth. Sophie knew the general, too, had flicked his gaze upward, but she was too excited to take anything in other than her desire to climb up into the cloud of crystal. Soon she could rescue the princess, get rid of the general. The princess would be so grateful to her, and . . . yes, they would be friends, wouldn't they? She would talk to her about the wolves, explain why they must not be locked up . . .

Dmitri pulled her up.

She scrambled up onto the metal branches. The chandelier tilted and rocked. Swaying, Sophie clutched on to the gilt bars to steady herself. Dmitri sat opposite her. He didn't look up.

"Help me!" she said. "I need to reach across . . ."

Dmitri followed her gaze to the rope of gray crystals with the rusty wire. His eyes filled with tears.

As she put her hand out, he grabbed her wrist. A tear splashed from his eye and onto his scar. "Think what you are doing!" he said.

"I know exactly what I'm doing!" she said. "Let go of my hand. You're hurting me!"

As Sophie wrenched her arm free, the chandelier shook again. The particles of light flew around them. It was all so beautifully clear to her. She unhooked the rusty wire and wrapped the rope of crystals around her wrist, her arm, her neck. Then, putting her foot in the loop, she smiled at Dmitri to let her down. His face was frozen now.

She heard the voices of the general and Anna. They were discussing something. The princess sounded anxious, as if the general might leave at any second.

"If you don't help, I'll just jump!" she cried. And she put her leg into the air. This seemed to send a charge through Dmitri's body.

"*Nyet!*" he cried. He let out the rope, feeding it through his hands, and Sophie was lowered to the ground, jumping off at the last minute.

"See?" Sophie called up to him. "They were here all along! Right where we first met. The wolf princess was so smart." She unwound the rope of stones from her arm. They were too large to be diamonds, surely? The necklace was too long. There couldn't be many stones in the world as beautiful as these.

The princess and the general were standing quite still. The princess's eyes glittered and she said one word in Russian: "*Brillianty!*" The word sparkled and threw light around the room.

In a smooth, quick gesture, she plucked the rope out of Sophie's hands.

There was the sort of silence you hear after you have dropped a beautiful antique glass. You know that something precious is about to be broken, something that, once it is smashed, can never be replaced . . . and you wonder, in that instant, if somehow, against all odds, you could catch it before it shatters.

The princess stared at Sophie, her eyes cold, almost black. The chandelier shivered and Sophie looked up at Dmitri. He had his head in his hands. The diamonds spilled over the princess's arm like a rope.

"Long enough to hang a man," she said.

And then, sweeping Sophie with an expression of icy disdain, she dropped her head back. Closing her extraordinary eyes, she laughed. Everything in the room changed.

"You are very generous. Are you sure you want me to have them?" she said teasingly.

What's she talking about? Sophie thought. *They're hers.*

The princess continued, "Are you *quite* sure?"

The general, who had been observing everything without speaking, strolled across. The princess swung the diamonds in front of his face, laughing.

He hooked them off her finger and ran them through his hands. "They're just what you said they would be!" His voice was full of wonder. He held the rope up and looked closely at each stone. "Candlelight-cut, exquisite, no flaws, each one at least fifty carats!"

"They're not for you!" Sophie screamed. "Give them back! They belong to the princess! Those are the Volkonsky diamonds!"

The man looked surprised. "Anna," he said calmly. "The little wolf girl says these diamonds belong to the Volkonsky princess!"

The woman smiled up into his eyes. "They do!" she whispered.

They looked at each other and something like a current of electricity seemed to pass between them. The princess smiled as the general reached into his breast pocket and pulled out a sheaf of papers.

"Perhaps these will be useful after all," he said. He waved them in front of Sophie's face.

She saw the watermark on the thick white paper, the heavy black Russian letters . . . and, at the bottom, looking ridiculous in her own handwriting, her name: *Sophie Smith.*

"There's no need to tease her, Grigor," the princess laughed, and took the papers from him.

The general threw the diamonds around his shoulders. They winked in the candlelight, seeming to hold the entire room in hundreds of facets. "Hurry, Anna!" he barked. "We are leaving!"

"I can come?" the princess gasped.

The man shrugged, pulling on leather gloves. He balled his fist. "Just make sure you dispose of the *evidence* first." He took a couple of steps, then turned around. "Don't make any mistakes this time, Anna," he whispered. "The only wolf you can trust is a dead wolf. That goes for wolf princesses, too."

CHAPTER TWENTY-ONE

The Wolf Princess

"I won't come with you!"

"I don't think you have a choice!"

As Sophie was pulled toward the door, the chandelier shivered. She looked up. Dmitri parted heavy ropes of crystal and stared down at her. The expression on his face made her feel ashamed. She had disappointed him. But what could she do? The diamonds were Anna Feodorovna's, and although Sophie hadn't wanted them to be given to the general, they were not Sophie's to keep. Dmitri turned his face away. Anna Feodorovna held Sophie firmly by the elbow and they walked down the corridor. In her other hand, she held the papers tightly.

"I don't understand." Sophie had a sour taste in her mouth. She swallowed.

"You are a silly, stupid little darling," the princess told her in that musical peal of bells that was her voice. "I had hoped that I would bring you here and then . . . oh, then . . . the magic would start!" She sighed.

They were moving down a narrower corridor with a much lower ceiling. It was more desolate than anywhere Sophie had seen in the palace.

"I should have got rid of you when I had the chance," the princess continued.

Why couldn't Sophie understand? The princess was speaking English. They weren't difficult words. But what did she mean by them?

"Got rid of me?" Sophie said slowly.

The princess sounded exasperated. "But Ivan interfered. I would have said it was an accident, of course, that I was aiming for the wolf and you got in the way, but I suppose there would have been too much fuss anyway. Even though we are so far away, stories get out. Your idiotic friends would have told tales. How annoying that your stupid headmistress insisted they come, too. And then who knows? Someone might have remembered something about you. They might have claimed to be related to you and the whole situation would have been unmanageable."

"Princess," Sophie whispered. "You're hurting my arm."

The woman took no notice. Her face was set straight in front of her. Sophie tripped and almost stumbled, but the woman's grip held her up. A draft soughed up the blighted corridor. Shadows flung themselves over the two figures like cloaks.

"Please let me go." Sophie thought she might cry.

Perhaps the wolves had heard them, for they sent up a lupine chorus that became louder as the princess dragged Sophie on, laughing as the wolves cried out.

"I should have had them shot when I arrived," she said. "I've had a constant headache from their stupid noise!"

There was a sour, dank smell in the corridor.

"What have I done?" Sophie felt her arm burning from the princess's tight grip. At Sophie's words, the princess looked as if she had been slapped on the cheek. She pulled Sophie closer to her and stared into her face. Sophie saw a blue vein throb in the woman's temple.

"Don't you understand?" she whispered. Sophie watched the woman's pale tongue. "All these stories about the wolf princess. *You* are the wolf princess, you little fool!"

"But . . ."

"Do you think I would give a damn about you if you weren't? Why do you think I brought you here?"

Sophie tried to twist her elbow out of the woman's grasp. But she was unable to move. Was this what Dmitri had meant when he had asked her to think what she was about to do? Had he been trying to warn her? But if he thought she was in some way related to the Volkonskys, why hadn't he said anything? Had he, too, realized only at that moment what he had done?

"How can I be . . . how can I be the wolf princess?" She didn't want to cry in front of the woman.

"The lost Volkonsky child!" Anna Feodorovna spat at her. "All the other Volkonskys dead! Killed, murdered, gone! But there was one, just one child that escaped!"

"But how can that have anything to do with me? I am English!"

She snorted. "You might be English now . . . but like so many people in your stupid, tiny, ridiculous little country, your ancestors came from somewhere else!"

"That can't be true!"

Anna Feodorovna didn't answer immediately, but looked at Sophie as though deciding what to say. She bit her lip. "That is what was so thrilling about you when you first arrived here. I thought you would know something of who you were. Would even guess why you had been brought here." She laughed. "But it was the most amazing thing! You knew nothing. *Nothing!*"

"But there isn't anything to know." Sophie wished that her throat didn't hurt so much. And that her head would stop throbbing.

"Of course not." She leaned in closer. "But haven't you ever been curious about your family? And what a family! Such a sad story, too . . ."

She frowned as if she felt genuine sorrow. "It made me so unhappy when I first found out. How Princess Sofya Kyrilich Volkonskaya, our dear, sweet wolf princess, had to leave her home in the middle of winter nearly a century ago. Such ugly, blood-soaked times, worse if you had a title or land or money . . . or a set of priceless diamonds hacked out of your own mine." She shook her head. "And that should have been the end of the Volkonskys!"

She took a step backward from Sophie, although she still held her tight. With her other hand she grasped the handle of a door. "She got nearly as far as the White Sea and then the snow claimed her. She was a fool to travel alone like that. Only a desperate woman would have considered making such a journey." She shook her head. "Perhaps if she had left the child behind, she would have escaped. But she was a devoted mother." The woman sighed. "They never found the child, you see. And that's what interested me. It would have been the first thing that a wolf or a bear would have eaten. But nothing was ever found. Not a boot or a hat or a cloth to wrap the child in. Where had he gone?"

She ground her foot into the loose stones on the floor. It made a rasping, grating sound.

"I found myself thinking . . . what if someone had found the child, in the woods, and taken it to safety? There might be some Volkonsky prince living up near the White Sea!" She raised an eyebrow. "But I couldn't find any child, and I did look . . . and so then I thought, what if someone took the child and put it on a ship . . . I didn't know where he might have gone, but I started to look around, see what I could dig up." She laughed. "And I found an old woman, very old. Living alone. She would die soon, but did she have any relatives?"

The woman looked at Sophie, her eyebrows raised. "Did you ever meet Xenia? She was still alive when you were born."

As the princess said the name *Xenia*, an image did fall, quite perfectly formed, into Sophie's mind. Stairs to a flat. Spider plants on a windowsill. A Pekingese that yapped and yapped. A woman so old that Sophie had been frightened; laughter because Sophie refused to sit on her lap. Sparkles at the old lady's throat. Diamonds? A present pressed into her hand as she left, *a piece of glass* . . .

The princess sighed. "But Xenia had never known that she had escaped from being murdered in Russia, had barely remembered being plucked from the frozen arms of her mother in a silver birch forest. How could she tell her son? Or her granddaughter? How could she tell them what she didn't know herself? But somehow, between the forgetting and the loss, there was a song and a child named Sophie. And I thought that, in time, Sophie and I might meet . . ."

"But that means" — Sophie shook her head — "that we are related. If I am a Volkonsky and you are a Volkonsky . . ."

"Who said *I* was a Volkonsky?" The woman looked at Sophie as if she had said something completely stupid.

"But that's your name," Sophie whispered.

"It's the name I *use*." Anna Feodorovna raised one eyebrow. "After all, I found the palace, I uncovered the history. I set myself the task of finding the Volkonsky diamonds . . ." She put her finger to her lips. "Oh!" She smiled. "Have I said too much?"

Her eyes glinted. She leaned forward and grabbed Sophie's hand.

"Don't shrink back into the shadows like that," she purred. "Once I brought you here, it occurred to me that you were so pretty, so amiable, that perhaps we should *become* related." She grabbed Sophie's chin and tilted her face up. "I could just get you to give everything to me!" She held up Sophie's piece of glass. "And now an extra diamond! This alone is worth a fortune."

"But that's my father's." Sophie tried again to twist away from her grasp. "It's glass."

"It's a Volkonsky diamond, you fool," she hissed. She put it around her own neck, knotting the string where it had been snapped. "And now it's *mine*. You . . . and the Volkonskys . . . really have lost everything now."

"Give it back!" Sophie tried to snatch back the glass drop that the princess shook in her face, taunting her. "My father gave me that!"

"You are so stupid!" the woman crowed, dropping the diamond into her pocket. "Everything about you is just like a Volkonsky! Of course I soon realized who you were, even though you swapped *sarafan*s with your silly friend. That's when I took the knife to that stupid, smiling portrait; I had plenty of time to look at her face. You are so like her . . ."

"*You* ruined the portrait? But why would you do that?"

"I saw the way Dmitri looked at you. I knew what they were thinking, down there, in their stinking kitchen. It wouldn't be long, despite my threats to throw them out or shoot them, before they'd realize, before they'd say something."

She turned her face and spat onto the floor. Sophie gasped.

"Don't like my rough ways?" she laughed. "Well, that suits me. Because *I* don't much like *you*!"

She reached into her pocket and got out a key. The wolves kept up their chorus, louder now, as she unlocked the door.

Sophie took a step back, but Anna Feodorovna, without turning around, reached out and grabbed a handful of Sophie's hair.

"Not so fast," she muttered. Snowflakes hurled themselves over the two of them as she opened the door an inch. "If only you had done as I asked, and not spoken to Dmitri," she whispered into Sophie's ear, "I might have kept you here for a couple of years. I might have let you play princess for a while before I got bored of you . . . and did . . . *THIS!*"

She pushed Sophie through the door and out into the snow.

CHAPTER TWENTY-TWO

The Wolf Garden

Sophie hammered on the closed door as the snowflakes whisked crazily around her. "Princess!" she cried. "Please. Don't leave me!" She rattled the large iron door handle, but heard bolts being thrown and realized it was hopeless.

She turned. She was standing at the top of steps in an enclosed courtyard in what seemed like an even older and more neglected part of the palace, filled with enormous stone animals. She looked up at the high walls. Every window was shuttered. Even if anyone was looking, no one could see her.

For a moment it was silent. The howling she had heard in the corridor had stopped.

And then she heard the sound of crying. Behind a rusting metal grille that looked like a claw gripping the courtyard wall, Marianne and Delphine crouched, wrapped in furs . . .

She tried to call out their names, but all that came out was a broken croak.

"Sophie!" Marianne clung to the metal bars.

Sophie put her foot down on the next step and sent a mini avalanche of snow to the bottom.

"Watch out!" Delphine screamed. "Sophie! The wolves!"

It was as if they were speaking to her through a dream. She understood the words, but not what they meant. She saw Marianne bury her head in Delphine's shoulder and she knew this meant something bad.

"Princess!" Sophie scrabbled back up the step and hammered again at the door. "Please . . . let me in! I'll do whatever you want . . . I promise . . . the wolves . . ." She was crying. "The wolves . . ."

It was quiet. She had closed her eyes, tried to squeeze as flat as she could to the flaking paint of the enormous door, but she knew it was no good. They were coming toward her.

She half turned, and the white shapes moving through the cemetery of stone animals stopped, as if they were playing statues. And even though they were still some distance away, she saw things she didn't want to see. Eyes that glinted red in the pale rose pink of their eyelids. Lips pulled back from teeth that looked too long. Blood on white fur, as if there had been a recent kill. She took a breath and thought, *How many more breaths will the wolves allow me to take?*

There was a peculiar noise. She could hear it above Marianne's panicked sobs. There was the sound of her own breathing, of course, and the pounding of her heart, but also a thin, inconsequential humming. Her humming. She wanted to laugh. Who would hum as wolves crept closer? Because they *were* creeping closer now, in their loose-shouldered way. She crouched down and made herself very small, putting her head in her hands.

I am a girl in a wolf garden, Sophie thought. *I am about to be torn to pieces. Those teeth will sink into my flesh any moment now! Why am I singing?*

She wanted it to be soon. She wanted it to be over. She knew without looking that they were all gathered at the foot of the steps, and this waiting was unbearable. If she had been on a roof, she would have jumped. If she were on a sinking ship, she would have hurled herself into the sea . . . anything to end this dreadful wait.

She sang louder. Her father's song. Or was it Dmitri's song? She heard his voice in the chandelier mixing with her father's half-remembered lullaby. She heard the wolves' rasping breath. Did she dare to open one eye?

At the front of the pack was their leader: larger, heavier-boned. The rest stood around him at the bottom of the steps, just as she had imagined, immobile as the statues. She noticed the way the snow clung to their pelts. One — a younger one, surely — had his tongue lolling out. Even in that blink of a moment, she understood clearly the structure of the pack, how the younger wolves waited for the old wolf to move.

She started to cry when she thought what was to come, and the song came out weirdly, the rhythm syncopated by sobs. She sniffed and tried to sing harder. It would make the last few minutes easier, surely?

Sophie closed her eyes again and sang even louder.

She could hear the wolves inch toward her up the steps, but when she opened her eyes once more, they were crouching on their haunches.

Sophie stopped singing.

Then the wolves put their heads back and, as one animal, the pack howled, the sound running up Sophie's spine. Silence. She watched them, horrified but fascinated at the same time. She heard Marianne cry to Delphine, "I can't bear to look."

Sophie put her head back and sang. The old wolf at the front nodded his head and licked his lips. He loped up the steps, regarding her with his red, flashing eyes, and stopped just below her.

Sophie tried to draw her feet even closer under her. The wolf sniffed the air above where her feet had been. Again, she tried to tuck them underneath her, wrapping her arms around herself. But perhaps it would be better to just put out her leg and let him bite it . . . would it be quicker that way? She wanted it to be quick. She pushed her foot toward the edge of the step through the snow, and cried out as the wolf stretched forward his powerful neck and brought his mouth right up to her shoe.

Then she saw the rosette of dried blood on the wolf's side where the bullet had grazed him.

"It's you!" she gasped. "You're alive!"

And as if he had understood, the wolf whimpered. He nudged Sophie's foot with his nose and then, in a languorous motion, he pressed his head into her thigh, closing his eyes. A sigh shuddered through his body.

The rest of the pack now trotted toward her, arranging themselves around her in the snow. She gasped as one leaped up and knocked her against the door in his enthusiasm. A wolf cub climbed onto her lap and licked her face. He was warm, even though the pads of his feet were covered in ice. She buried her hands in his fur.

The sound of metal grating against metal. The key in a lock. Bolts being dragged back. The old wolf put his head up and snarled. Sophie felt a rush of gratitude toward the creature; he would protect her, she realized, or die in the attempt.

"Sophie?"

"Dmitri!"

"Stand still. Don't show fear. You know they will not hurt you. I have meat to feed them so they will not hurt me, either." She heard him kick the door in frustration, then he burst through. The bucket in his hand slopped blood and entrails onto the snow. He dropped it and the wolves ran to it, yelping in delight.

He threw his arms around her. "I wanted you to be Volkonsky!" he cried. "I knew it the moment I saw you. But I could not let myself believe it!"

"That's what you said to me! *Voy Volkonsky!* When I first arrived. If only I'd understood. Except it would have seemed incredible. Impossible." She was laughing, but crying, too.

They stepped back from each other, suddenly embarrassed. Some of the wolves came back to her, leaning into her and unbalancing her. It was like wearing a long, full skirt made out of a tangle of white fur.

Dmitri steadied her. "The wolves knew. They always knew," he said, laughing.

"Dmitri . . . we must get Delphine and Marianne! They've been locked up!"

He nodded, but pulled her through the door. "But they safe behind bars! And Masha coming! She help them!" He held her arm tightly. "That woman leaving! We must hurry! We must rescue Volkonsky diamonds!"

CHAPTER TWENTY-THREE

The Ice Road

Sophie, Dmitri, and the wolves ran through the blighted, candlelit corridors of the Winter Palace. Sophie could hear the rhythmic panting of the animals, the way their claws scratched on the floor. It made her heart beat faster. It felt as if they were running with this pack, had become wolves themselves. Dmitri held her hand to run up stairs or across echoing rooms, through parts of the palace she had never seen, and as the wolves seethed around them, she felt a wave of gratitude toward this boy.

At the front door, the wolves clustered around Sophie and Dmitri, eager to be outside after months of captivity in the courtyard. It was as if the emptiness of the forest had filled their bodies and made them crazed to be free.

Sophie turned the enormous handle and pulled the door open to let in a sliver of twilight. The wolves howled excitedly.

"Careful!" Dmitri cried. "They will scare Viflyanka!"

She could see the princess and the general already in the *vozok*, which was laden with paintings, rugs, and silver. They were surely about to leave any second. Ivan ran toward them from the stable yard, yelling furiously. He pulled the silver *samovar* off the heap of stolen treasures and hurled it into the snow. The general reached for his pistol as Ivan tugged at the handle of a suitcase. It sprang open and clocks, plates, cutlery spewed out onto the snow. Anna Feodorovna, furious, stood in the *vozok* and screamed abuse.

But she stopped as she saw Sophie in the doorway. She looked shocked, then frightened, as she shook the general's arm and pointed.

"Go!" roared the general. "We have the diamonds!"

Dmitri ran to calm Viflyanka, who, terrified of the wolves in the doorway, tried to rear up. The weight of the *vozok* would not allow it. Sophie could see the animal would break his back if he wasn't freed. But the wolves did not immediately leap out into the snow. They seemed to be waiting for a signal from her.

"Poshawwwl!" Anna Feodorovna screamed as she grabbed the reins and the whip. *Crack!* The whip snapped across Viflyanka's sweating neck, catching Dmitri's face. The boy staggered back, clutching his cheek, and in that instant, Viflyanka leaped forward. The general took aim and fired at the doorway, but the erratic lurch of the *vozok*

meant that his aim was off. Sophie heard the bullet whiz close to her head.

"Don't you dare!" Ivan yelled as he leaped up at the man. He tried to swipe the pistol from the general's hand and they struggled awkwardly as the *vozok* moved forward. The general roared again. The pistol flew over Ivan's head into the snow, and Ivan was kicked and shoved until he fell back off the *vozok*.

"She will kill herself," he cried as he lay in the snow behind the now fast-moving sleigh. "There is too much in the *vozok* — it is too heavy for the ice road."

Sophie had been holding on to the thick fur of the old wolf in the doorway, so the pack had stayed with her. But as she ran forward to help Ivan, the wolves took this as their cue and they ran forward, too. It was as if they wanted the general and the princess gone once and for all as they gave chase to the *vozok*, harassing Viflyanka, snapping at his heels. The bells on his harness jangled insanely, and the *vozok* swung erratically behind the terrified horse. They saw Anna Feodorovna — no longer the princess, Sophie thought — standing up now, yanking ineffectively on the too-long reins, cracking her whip at the wolves.

"We have to stop her!" Sophie looked at Ivan. He was motionless, watching the *vozok* as it lurched toward the sunken ice road. "Ivan! How do we stop her?"

Dmitri was already running after them, calling the name of his horse in despair. Sophie could hear the tears that rent his voice: The animal was spooked now, and would gallop until he dropped dead or was shot.

But Anna Feodorovna didn't seem to think the furious pace was fast enough, and cracked the whip once more, the sound like a rifle shot. The wolves veered away from the *vozok*. Sophie heard her laugh.

Viflyanka strained for even more speed and flew down the bank. Just before the *vozok* disappeared, it careered and tipped to one side.

There was a huge crash. Silver cutlery flew up into the twilight in an arc; a small urn bounced across the ice, chased by a silver tray.

Ivan started to run. Sophie ran, too, though she soon fell behind and her chest burned as the ice-cold air went into her lungs.

They reached the bank of the ice road just behind Dmitri. The *vozok* lay on its side, Viflyanka struggling in the harness. The princess had fallen from her seat and onto the ice. She looked dazed, a cut on the side of her head already oozing blood. The general was clambering over the side of the *vozok*, the diamonds looped around his neck. The wolves were on the bank, pacing and snarling, but staying away from the ice.

Ivan stared in horror at the frozen road. "It's cracking! The wolves won't go on the ice — they know."

Dmitri, sliding down the bank to reach the horse, tried to slow himself by digging his heels into the snow.

"Get off!" Ivan yelled at him as large black lines appeared on the ice with frightening speed.

Dmitri threw himself back and lay full-length in the snow. "Viflyankà!" he wailed, and beat the snow with his fist. Everything was happening so fast.

Then a huge *boom* that sounded like a cannon cut through the sky, violent as the breaks cleaving through the ice.

The general ran swiftly across the ice away from the wolves, causing more black lines to appear. He disappeared into the trees, not once looking back.

Over the creaking noise of the moving ice, they heard Anna Feodorovna call feebly, "Grigor . . ." She managed to stand up and staggered a step or two, but slipped. She saw the wolves, howling and snarling on the bank, and cried out in terror. She slid away from them, toward the center of the ice.

Dmitri now slipped down onto the ice road. It was no longer solid.

Boom!

"Dmitri!" Ivan looked stricken, torn between trying to help the boy and the woman. "Come back! Your weight will make it worse."

But Dmitri was sliding toward the thrashing horse now, still trapped by the *vozok* on the fast-cracking ice.

"Sophie!" Dmitri shouted. "Help me!"

Sophie was too quick for Ivan, although she felt his arm brush her shoulder as he lunged to pull her back. She skittered down onto the ice and, trying hard to keep her balance, trod gingerly toward the horse, her arms in front of her. She could feel the water tilting the ice, and that dreadful grinding noise filled her head.

"Hold Viflyanka's head!" Dmitri shouted. "We must get him out of harness."

The way the ice would suddenly shift was like sitting on a train when it jolts abruptly to a halt. Sophie could see they had so little time. The black water licked at the white ice, sucking the *vozok* down. Viflyanka, snorting, eyes white, foaming with sweat, tried to pull himself forward.

"He will drown . . ." Dmitri worked with furious concentration at the leather buckles.

Sophie tried to catch the horse's bridle, but he swung his head around and tried to bite her.

"Dmitri . . . I can't get his head . . ." she called desperately.

Dmitri said nothing; he was still working on the buckles and straps. With one last gesture, he freed the props, the *vozok* sliding back into the black water with a sickening gurgle. Viflyanka, snorting and with a terrified whinny, pulled himself free. Sophie had to put her hand up to catch the panicked horse's bridle; if he stepped back he, too, would be in the water and their attempt to save him would be in vain.

She swiped at the reins and then, somehow, caught the bridle. She saw Dmitri, on the other side now, holding the horse's head as well. He was stroking him and talking to him and gently getting the animal to walk toward the bank and away from the black hole in the ice.

"Go slowly . . ." Dmitri could have been talking to Viflyanka or to her. They half slid, half skated back to the bank.

"Where's Ivan?"

Sophie looked around her for the first time since racing after the *vozok*. Through Viflyanka's hot steaming breath, she saw something she wished she hadn't.

Ivan had stepped onto the ice and, fixing his gaze on Anna Feodorovna, was walking calmly and slowly toward her, talking to her in Russian. It sounded as if he were telling her a story, and she did seem to be listening, even though her head was half turned away, to the path through the woods where the general had gone.

"Can he save her?" Sophie asked Dmitri.

Ivan reached out his hand, using the same calming movements Sophie had noticed Dmitri using with Viflyanka. She was saved! Sophie held her breath as Ivan's fingers wrapped themselves around the woman's white hands.

"He's got her, Dmitri!" she gasped.

But then two things happened. Just as Ivan was pulling Anna Feodorovna toward him, there was the shrill whistle of a train and the *shussssh* of brakes. The second thing to happen was that Anna Feodorovna·cried out, "Grigor!" and leaped backward as if Ivan's hand had burned her, toward the bank. But she hadn't leaped far enough. Sophie heard the dull sound of her breath thudding out of her chest as she fell heavily on the ice.

And then, suddenly, there was only Ivan. Anna Feodorovna, who had been lying on the ice, just right *there*, was there no longer.

"Where? Where is she?" Sophie knew the answer, but she wanted Dmitri to tell her it wasn't how it seemed.

And then she saw a white shadow slip fast along under the ice, sucked by some deep, dark, cold current. Sophie saw the woman's face. It looked surprised, and her fingers scratched desperately at the frozen water above her. There were black weeds all around her.

"We have to get her out!" Sophie yelled again. She felt two arms whip around her, holding her tight.

"Ice not safe," Dmitri said. And she knew he would not let her go.

She could only watch as Ivan threw himself onto the ice where the princess's surprised face had last been seen. He hammered at it with his fists until they bled. He shouted her name. Black and red water splashed up into the air when the ice broke.

He plunged his arm up to his shoulder into the freezing water.

But it was too late. The princess was gone.

CHAPTER TWENTY-FOUR

The Return

"Is that it?" Sophie whispered. "Is it really over? Just like that, in a second?"

She tried to break free from Dmitri's arms. "There must be something we can do . . . We have to get Anna Feodorovna out. If we don't get to her . . . Why isn't Ivan doing anything? Why is he just lying there?"

She twisted out of Dmitri's grip and slid down the bank.

"Get back!" Ivan roared, his face wet with tears. "You stay off the ice!"

"But we have to help her . . ." Sophie knew it was too late, but she felt that if she kept talking, it might not be true. "We can't just leave her to drown . . . under the ice . . . Ivan . . ."

She sat down in the snow and put her head on her knees. She heard the ice creak. A hand hooked itself under her arm and lifted her up.

"I told her it was all over." Ivan put his hand under her chin and lifted her face so that she had to look at him. "She was not a princess," he said. "*You* are the princess."

"But I *can't* be a Volkonsky . . ."

It was so painful, this dislocation of her world. Her throat ached. It was as if she were being told that she was a boy, or that her parents hadn't really died but had just been playing an elaborate game of hide-and-seek on her for all these years. It was as if she, herself, had fallen through the ice. But no, she mustn't think like that. She must find something solid to stand on.

"I am being foolish!" Ivan helped her up, put his arm around her, and started to walk her back toward the palace. "I need to get you inside. And quickly."

Sophie's legs were unbearably stiff and she leaned into Ivan's reassuring solidness as they skirted the banks of the ice road. She glanced behind her toward the forest. The wolves stood at the tree line for a moment — and then, with a yelp of joy, they streamed off into the forest.

Dmitri led Viflyanka slowly behind them. At the portico, he asked Ivan something in Russian. Ivan nodded, then leaned down and said, "Dmitri will take Viflyanka to the palace stables. The horse needs attention."

"Of course," Sophie whispered. "Will Viflyanka be all right, Dmitri?"

"Yes." Dmitri nodded. "Thank you. Without your

help, he would be like . . ." He must have seen the pain on Sophie's face, because he stopped.

Masha, waiting on the steps, ran toward them. Her eyes were wide. "I hear ice road crack. Like cannon! But you safe!"

"Oh, Masha . . ." Sophie bit her lip. "Something awful has happened. The princess . . ."

"Not princess," Masha whispered.

Ivan squeezed her shoulder. "Masha, I should have listened to you. I should have understood what you were saying to me."

Masha shrugged.

"Will you forgive me?" Ivan said.

Masha curtseyed. "I will forgive . . . and help you, too." She added, "Now we both serve Volkonskys!" She looked up at him and smiled, a little shy.

"Where are the others?" Ivan asked.

"I take them to warm room," Masha said. "I give them tea?"

Ivan smiled too, although he still looked sad. "They are in need of warmth and friendship . . . You will give them that, I know."

Masha smiled proudly. "And the princess?" she said shyly. "I will make tea for princess?"

"You will make tea for the princess," Ivan said. "But not just yet." He turned to Sophie. "There is something I must show you."

"Where are we going, Ivan?"

Ivan shrugged off his *shuba* and hung it on a passing statue. "I believed her when she told me who she was. I never questioned it." He hit the side of his head with his fist. "I was such a fool!"

"Why wouldn't you believe her?" Sophie burst out. "She was *like* a princess! She saved you, brought you here."

"I didn't understand what she wanted," Ivan continued. "I believed her when she said she wanted some young friends in the palace." He laughed, a sound more like a bark. "She said she had plans for you. But all she wanted was information to help her find the diamonds."

They had been walking up the stairs of a remote tower. Sophie had never been in this part of the palace. Ivan threw open a door to reveal a surprisingly warm and cozy room. A gilt clock ticked on a marble mantelpiece; fur rugs were draped over gilt furniture.

"When we came to the palace, she asked me to bring the least damaged furniture here." Ivan sighed. "There was something secretive in her manner I didn't understand. I kept a key to the room and, although I'm sorry to admit I did that, I see now it was better that I did."

He put his hand on Sophie's back and gently guided her inside. "When she told me to get out of the ballroom, I came here. Then I truly understood what she wanted," he said slowly. "That was why I tried to stop her from leaving."

He pulled a key from behind a gilt clock and unlocked a large marquetry cabinet. Papers slid out all over the floor: photographs of faces, which were followed by more images, charts, maps.

He was quiet for a second. "I never believed that she would harm you. But the wolf hunt . . . I knew then. She was a perfect shot — and I saw in that moment she was not aiming for the wolf. She was aiming for you."

"So you saved my life?"

"She thought you knew nothing. The general had ordered it . . ."

"She really wanted me dead?"

"In that moment," Ivan spoke quietly, "yes."

Sophie's mouth was dry. She bent down and picked up a photograph. A girl in a school uniform standing in a playground. "But . . . this is me!" She held the photograph out toward Ivan. "At my school in London."

"Anna Feodorovna did her research." Ivan took the blurred picture of Sophie and looked at it. "The general sent his secretary to be sure. He needed to know that there would be no more Volkonskys alive to dispute her claim on the diamonds. No one to come forward and call themselves a prince or a princess when she had taken that title for herself. When she found you, it must have made her desperate," he whispered. "She had thought she could have all of this without anyone knowing she had stolen it. But in the course of finding out the forgotten story of the

Volkonskys, she found a forgotten child. A schoolgirl with a lost family history."

"But I knew nothing of this." Sophie blinked back the tears. "No one had told me anything." She folded her photographed face in four and absentmindedly pushed the photograph into her pocket.

"But she didn't know that," Ivan sighed. "And if she had found you, if she had made the link, perhaps someone else could, too. She had to be sure that she wouldn't be discovered."

"So, is it really true?" Sophie said. "Am I really a Volkonsky?"

Ivan found another photograph, very old and grainy. It showed a girl, not much older than Sophie. "This is your great-grandmother Sofya." Ivan smiled sadly. "You look very like her."

Sophie looked into the grains of the photograph of the wolf princess. There was something of her own face, she could see that now. The straight eyebrows. The pale skin. But the expression! How many more years would that open, bright, curious face have before she perished in the woods?

"Her child was safe," Sophie whispered. And then she thought about Xenia. An old lady. The daughter of a forgotten Russian princess who had been brought to England. And for what? She died alone. It was so sad. Would her father, Prince Vladimir, have been happy for her to end her days like that? Would her own father be happy for Sophie to live so alone?

"Xenia was rescued, perhaps by a peasant. Probably sold for bread." Ivan found more papers. "Sofya was traveling to Arkhangelsk. There had been reports of the British navy waiting there to help the Tsar escape from the Revolution." He smiled sadly. "But the Tsar never came. Instead, the boat took other travelers . . . and Xenia Volkonsky must have been one of them."

Sophie sighed. "I'm sure my parents had no idea about this," she said. "My guardian would have told me if they'd known anything."

"Anna Feodorovna was meticulous," Ivan said, shaking his head. "She would not have embarked on such a course of action if she had not been sure. Your guardian will have papers somewhere that relate to your family."

Sophie thought of the box of files in her bedroom in Rosemary's flat. She had once looked inside, hoping to find photographs of her parents, or perhaps letters, but Rosemary had found her and become angry. There had been a particularly vicious argument and, soon after, the files disappeared. Did Rosemary still have them? Would they hold any answers?

She sank into a chair. "There's so much to take in," she said. "It feels so strange. When you think you're one person . . . and then . . . suddenly, you're another!"

"You are still the same person," Ivan said. "It's just that now you know a little more about where you came from." He put his arm around Sophie. "But this is how life surprises us," he said. "I thought I knew one person very well indeed . . . and I was wrong."

"I'm sorry," Sophie murmured.

"She was so clever!" Ivan said, struggling to keep his voice calm. "She could have made any life she wanted for herself. She didn't need to rob someone else of theirs." He turned away. Sophie glimpsed tears in his eyes.

After a second, he straightened his shoulders and said, "Let us go and find the others. There are things we must discuss. Plans we must make. We must get you back to Saint Petersburg and Miss Ellis. I think you have lessons at a real Russian school tomorrow!"

Sophie nodded, but knew that the only lessons she needed to learn would not happen in a Saint Petersburg school. Or any school.

She swallowed. "Do I have to go back?"

Ivan looked surprised.

She said again, more forcefully, "I wish I didn't have to go back so soon, Ivan. There's so much I want to find out about, so much I need to learn."

Ivan considered this. "We would have to speak to your guardian," he said gravely. "She is the only person who can decide at this time."

"She doesn't even know I'm here!"

Ivan frowned, not comprehending.

Sophie explained, "I really wanted to come to Russia. Isn't that odd? I always dreamed of snow and a forest . . . I didn't know I was dreaming my own history . . . if such a thing is even possible. But I knew my guardian wouldn't let me come . . . I'm afraid you wouldn't be pleased if I told you what Delphine and I did . . ."

"You did what you had to do . . . But" — Ivan's mouth crinkled up at one side — "it would be hard to imagine that your guardian would be happy to let you stay here once she has been told. You have no money, the palace is sinking into the snow . . ." He shook his head. "It would be hard to convince anyone that this was a suitable home for a young girl."

Sophie supposed he was right.

"What will *you* do, Ivan?" she asked. "I mean, now that the princess, I mean, Anna Feodorovna . . ."

"I will settle everything here — for you — if you would allow me to."

"But I can't pay you." Sophie felt embarrassed. "Like you said, I've no money . . . unless you want to take some paintings!"

"It would be an honor to serve you." He bowed his head. "I have no need of paintings."

"But what then?"

Ivan frowned again. "I will return to my home in Nizhny Novgorod," he said. "My mother is old. When I was a little boy, she gave everything to me, the meat from her bowl, the vegetables from her garden. She asked for nothing in return. She deserves to be cared for by someone she loves . . ."

"I wish you could stay," Sophie whispered. "Is there any way you can stay? You could bring your mother here and look after her in the palace!"

He shook his head sadly. "It is true that I have been happier in the few months I have been at the palace than at any other time, in any other place in my life. I even allowed myself to imagine that I could call it my home one day, if home is that place that you never want to leave . . . and if you leave it, you look for all your life." He sighed.

Sophie put her hand on Ivan's arm.

"I am not a prince, Sophie. I was stupid to think that this magical world, forgotten and broken as it is, would make any space for me."

"I think you should stay," Sophie whispered. "I'd like you to stay. It would make it easier for me to go back to London if I knew you were here."

He smiled at her, but his eyes were sad. "This is not a fairy tale, Sophie. How would I live? How would anyone live here without millions of rubles? The princess . . ." He shook his head. "I will always think of her that way, I think . . . Anna Feodorovna took money from the general on the understanding that she would find the diamonds . . . Without the diamonds, the palace cannot survive."

Sophie felt faint. "I had them," she whispered. "I found them. I gave them to her. For the general. He was threatening her. They were in the chandelier."

For the first time, Ivan looked angry. He controlled his face, but Sophie could see his jaw clench. His words, when they came, were calm, but Sophie could hear that at any second his emotion could break through. "He won't be able to do anything with them." He was speaking to himself. "I will make sure that the world knows that she got the diamonds by lying and that he is a common bully and a thief." He said something else in Russian that Sophie didn't understand.

"But it won't help, will it, Ivan?" she said sadly. "I mean, it won't make it possible for us to stay."

"*Nyet.*" He spoke sternly. "You will have to grow up to become even more beautiful and marry an oligarch!"

Sophie grinned. "Volkonskys marry for love, though, Ivan. Not for money!"

His smile broadened. "It's true," he said. "*Voy Volkonsky.*"

Marianne and Delphine were waiting in the White Dining Room. Masha had given them glasses of tea, and sat staring at Delphine with something like awe. They jumped up when Sophie walked into the room.

Delphine seemed to be in shock. "I think you're the first princess I've ever met," she said.

"Masha has told us!" Marianne laughed. "Do we have to curtsey or something?"

"All day!" Sophie said. "Morning, noon, and night."

"Do you think Miss Ellis has even noticed that we're missing?" Delphine said. "She'll get into terrible trouble once we tell our parents."

"I'll call mine from Saint Petersburg," Marianne said. "Ivan says we can leave as soon as we are ready. And I know they will want me back in London."

"My mother will cancel everything, and come and get me," Delphine said. She looked at Sophie. "You know you can come and stay with us in Paris for the holiday."

"Or with my family," Marianne added. "My parents are always happy to have you. We'd better go," she said, standing up.

"Will you let me say my good-byes first?" Sophie looked at her friends.

"Of course," Marianne said. "It's horrible leaving people behind without saying good-bye."

Sophie slipped toward the door. "Masha," she said, more enthusiastically than she felt, "before I say good-bye to your mother and your *babushka*, will you ask Dmitri to help me with something?"

CHAPTER TWENTY-FIVE

The Letter

She stood in front of the damaged portraits, one torn with bullet holes, the other a woman without a face. She reached out and touched the slashed canvas near the young woman's neck. This was the first wolf princess. Sofya Volkonskaya. She had lived *here*. Sophie had held those very diamonds, now just brushstrokes, in her hand. She wondered if the Customs Office would let her bring these destroyed portraits back to London. If Rosemary made a fuss, she could always put them under her bed.

She sighed as she thought about that chandelier drop, now at the bottom of the ice road . . . Could it really have been from the palace? If so, Rosemary might not be quite so keen as usual on decluttering when Sophie brought the paintings back to London.

Dmitri stood next to her. "We have found you . . ." he whispered. "We watched and waited and then you came."

Sophie stared straight ahead; she wouldn't risk looking at him because she would see the disappointment on his face, but she could see his scar twitching out of the corner of her eye.

"Why are you leaving?"

"I will come back," Sophie said. She touched the frame of the painting and added, "I promise you I will come back as soon as I am able." This promise was to the wolf princess as well as to Dmitri. She groaned. "Why do I have to be so young? Why does everyone have to treat me like a child?"

She slipped her hand into her pocket and found the photograph of herself at school in London. She pushed it behind the cobwebbed frame, but it stuck. There was something in the way. She felt around with her finger and pulled out a folded piece of paper. She opened it, but the words were just marks on old notepaper. She couldn't read any of them.

"Dmitri" — she held the letter out — "do you know what this says?"

Dmitri took the paper and frowned as he murmured through the Russian words. "It's a letter . . ." He turned it over. "But I don't know who for . . ."

"There's no name?"

"No . . . It just says . . . 'To . . . my own'?"

"What else . . . what else does it say?"

Dmitri scanned the letter. "She doesn't want to leave . . ." he said haltingly. "She is very sad . . . she sends words a very long way . . . across the sea . . . across the years . . . across . . . tears?"

"It's from Sofya."

Dmitri nodded.

Sophie gently took the letter from his hand. "This is hopeless." Dmitri's eyes clouded and he looked puzzled. "Don't you see, Dmitri? This is the only letter I have, the only words I have from anyone in my family that are addressed . . . well, not to me, but to the me they hoped would happen!"

Dmitri nodded slowly. Sophie went on. "But the saddest thing is . . . I can't understand any of it! Do you see? My father sang me the song, before he died. Perhaps he did sing the words to me and I forgot them. He didn't live long enough to teach me Russian. My guardian despised him. She never told me anything . . . if she even knew herself."

"The Volkonsky song. A lullaby. It was how the wolf princess hid her diamonds . . ." Dmitri whispered.

"Perhaps that's why it was important for my father to be a poet," Sophie said. "Although he may not have known why."

She stared at the letter again, traced her finger over the strange letters. At the bottom, though, the letters of the Russian version of her own name. СОФИЯ, *Sofya*, Sophie.

"I need someone to help me learn Russian," Sophie said. She looked at Dmitri's kind, earnest face. "Will you help me?"

His face was open and relaxed. He nodded. But then almost immediately he turned away. "How can I? You are leaving us!"

Sophie held the letter in her hand.

What should she do? What should she do?

Masha had tied a bright scarf around her head in honor of Sophie's leaving. She, her mother, and her grandmother had come up from the Under Palace to say good-bye. Sophie kissed Masha's mother. The *babushka* stroked Sophie's cheek.

"I feel I need to ask forgiveness from your *babushka* . . . and from you . . . I did a dreadful thing when I gave Anna Feodorovna the diamonds."

Masha shook her head. "The diamonds brought her no happiness," she whispered. "We knew that they would not help her."

"I'm not sure she understood happiness, really," Sophie said quietly. "She thought if she was rich, she would be happy."

Masha shook her head again. "You have to have diamonds in your soul to be happy."

"The general has them now," Sophie said. "Perhaps they'll bring him better luck."

"Volkonsky diamonds not like that." She was quiet for a moment.

"What do you mean?"

"They have to be given with love. They cannot be bought or sold." She squeezed Sophie's hand in hers. "This the way of the Volkonskys."

"But they're his now." Sophie felt exasperated with herself. "I had them . . . and I lost them."

"Better lost," Masha whispered, "if having them hardens the heart."

"What are *you* going to do, Masha?" Sophie said sadly. "You and Dmitri and your mother and *babushka*?"

Masha looked up, trying to smile, but her eyes were wet. She sniffed and wiped her nose on her sleeve.

"We'll watch," she said. "We'll wait. For our wolf princess."

Sophie ran down the steps to join the others, who were already tucked under their bearskin rug on a new *vozok*, this one smaller than the sleigh swallowed by the ice, and painted a cheerful, defiant red. Dmitri didn't look at her. She knew he was upset about her leaving. She mustn't cry; she didn't want to embarrass him or herself.

The bells of the *vozok* rang out as Viflyanka snorted through the snow. They wound around the birch forest, Sophie unable to stare at the trees without feeling a pull of deep sadness. How long would it be before she could return? Her whole life she had dreamed of having a home, and now, having found that place, she had to leave it. She wished she could have said good-bye to the wolves, but was grateful that they were out in the forest, hunting, as they should after their months of confinement. No wolf garden would ever be large enough for them, nor any meat — however expertly chopped by Dmitri — be as enticing as their own kill.

Dmitri stared straight ahead. She sensed his disappointment in her, as if she were betraying him for a second time: the first time by giving the diamonds to Anna Feodorovna, and now by leaving him and his family behind.

Marianne and Delphine must have realized how difficult it was for Sophie. They sat under the bearskin, not speaking.

The white train was waiting, steam pouring from the funnel. Ivan helped the girls down and opened the carriage door, checking his watch. Then he turned to Sophie and offered his hand to help her into the train. "Princess," he murmured.

"Give me a moment," she whispered. She traced the

lines of the wolf's head painted on the carriage door.
The open jaw, the sharp teeth no longer looked frightening to her; instead they gave her a feeling of reassurance.
It told her something about herself, the girl who had never
known anything about who she was or where she came
from: If you were a Volkonsky, you fought like a wolf to
protect what was dear to you.

She stood on the tiny platform. The snow was falling
lightly. She looked into the woods, those trees she had
dreamed about so often. And through them, now, she
could see the wolf pack. They loped toward her, each one
in its favored position. They seemed so much a part of the
forest and the snow that they could not exist in any other
place, she thought. Viflyanka whinnied, but Dmitri
calmed him. The wolves hung back.

Vladimir and Sofya, she realized in that clear moment,
had done so much — given up their lives — to ensure
there would one day be a Volkonsky on this estate. And
now she felt as if she were letting them down. They had
died to save their child, but she, their great-granddaughter,
was going back to London. Why? Perhaps she didn't
deserve to be a Volkonsky after all. Perhaps she was a
coward.

The forest and the snow and the wolves seemed to
spin around her. It was just a moment, a single moment in
her life, and yet it was like looking at everything through

the drops of the chandelier. Everything was contained in it. She wanted to be brave. She wanted to trust in what she was feeling.

Could she perhaps have another, different sort of life?

She blinked back tears and turned to her friends. This was going to be hard. But not as hard as doing the wrong thing. She realized, as she stood on the edge of the woods of the Volkonsky estate, that she was more than one person. She was Sophie, yes, but she was her father, too. She was Xenia, Sofya, Vladimir, a collection of all these people. As she looked at her hands in their sealskin gloves, moved her feet in her *valenki*, and breathed a cloud of misty breath into the clear, northern air, she was any number of lost Volkonskys, their portraits all waiting to be discovered in the gallery.

Sophie took a breath of the cold forest air that had enchanted her in her dreams. She looked at the puzzled faces of Marianne and Delphine. She smiled. Yes. Now she felt properly happy in a way she had never felt before. Because she understood something about herself. And she knew, with a certainty that knocked in her chest, what she would do.

"You were right, Marianne," she said, her voice light. "You and your theories . . ."

"What do you mean?" Marianne's glasses had fogged up, which gave her a bemused look.

"That theory you told us about. The day we found out we were coming to Russia. About everything in the universe leading to one place, and that we can only be in that one place because it's the right place for us."

"I don't think that Dicke put it quite like that." Marianne frowned. "He was talking about weak nuclear forces . . ."

Delphine nudged Marianne. "Let's talk about it on the train, shall we?" she said. "For once, I'd be happy to discuss nuclear forces with you . . . once we're safely on our journey!"

Sophie didn't move. Marianne took her glasses off to clean them on her *shuba*, and Sophie felt her stomach turn with affection for her friend.

She smiled as confidently as she could. "Well," she said. "I am here. And everything has been leading to this moment. And, when you think about it, Marianne, if I go back to London with you . . . I'll be breaking some scientific law, because this is where I am supposed to be."

Marianne's eyes were round as she pushed her glasses back on. She gave a low whistle. "That," she said, "is quite masterful! I mean, I see how you did that . . . it's good." She hugged her friend. "I don't know how we're going to explain this to Rosemary, though, Sophie. And I don't know how we will manage at school without you. But perhaps you *should* stay here . . . for a while."

"You've changed, Sophie." Delphine looked serious. "Dmitri and his family need you." She leaned closer. "We'll miss you."

Sophie's throat was so tight she didn't dare risk swallowing.

"Ivan, would you mind?" She looked up at the man, who had become very still as he watched her. "I won't get in the way . . ."

He nodded. "We will speak to your guardian," he said. "Perhaps she will allow you to stay for a while if we promise to look after you . . ."

Marianne and Delphine both hugged her at once, then scrambled up onto the train. Ivan shut the carriage door, and climbed into the driver's cabin.

"We will see each other soon," Sophie called up, but the *shush* of steam blew her words away. The wheels screeched as they started to move on the icy tracks. Suddenly, Sophie wanted to be with them, in the carriage. She ran along the short platform, but the train picked up speed and the trees swallowed it up until the only thing she could hear was the rhythm of the engine as it pulled the carriage away.

She walked slowly back to the *vozok*.

Dmitri leaped down. His face was shining with happiness. "You are sure?" he said.

"Yes!" she laughed.

"Wooooooooo!" he cried as he took off his hat and threw it up in the air. He ran to pick it up, laughing, then held out his arm to help her. She climbed up and sat beside him in the *vozok*.

"I am *so* sure," Sophie said again. "I know I can't leave the palace right now, even if I can't stay here forever."

She wouldn't cry. She would be happy. If she wasn't going to be allowed to stay here for the rest of her life — if, in fact, she might only have a few more days before she was yanked back to her life in London — she wouldn't waste it being sad. She would devote herself to study . . . to finding out as much as she could about this family she was part of. She would set herself the task of uncovering the Volkonskys.

The wolves were in the woods, yelping to each other. The afternoon starlight fell down on her. Out of a clearing, the pack came, tongues lolling, running with their loose-shouldered lope. They trotted alongside Viflyanka, who took no notice of them, sensing that the well-fed wolves had no interest in him.

"They've been hunting!" Sophie called to Dmitri. She looked for the old, wounded wolf. Where was he?

Dmitri kept Viflyanka trotting smartly on toward the portico. Only days before, Ivan had brought them here, innocent of Anna Feodorovna's plans. And now Sophie was defying sense, defying everyone, to stay in a place she hardly knew. But Ivan had said that home was the place that was hard to leave. And the place that, having left, you searched for throughout your life. She had never known a home in that way. And she wanted to.

At the door, Dmitri jumped down and walked around to help Sophie out of the *vozok*. The door shuddered and opened.

Masha stepped out and gave a cry of surprise. She clutched at her chest as if she couldn't speak, but then, her face lit with a broad smile, she held out her arms. Sophie jumped down. They stared at each other for a while before Sophie hugged her.

And as they entered, Masha's mother stepped forward with candles and laughter and bread and salt. "Come, children," she whispered. "We bless . . . we bless our princess . . ."

"You knew!" Sophie was laughing and crying at the same time. "You knew I couldn't leave you!" She took a piece of bread and dipped it in the pyramid of salt. "I bless you." She bowed her head.

And then, seeing Masha's concerned gaze, she turned to see the old wolf padding toward her. He had something in his mouth that hung down and trailed along behind him. Sophie was apprehensive; she didn't think she would care for the sort of present a white wolf might bring her from the woods.

But Masha was laughing.

The wolf came right up to Sophie; she wasn't sure what was hanging from his mouth, didn't want to believe what he had found. He opened his mouth and she heard a soft *chink* at her feet. The wolf made a satisfied yelp at the back of his throat and licked her hand as if he expected her approval. She looked down at the wolf's gift.

A rope of fat, gray, candlelight-cut diamonds, long enough to hang a man, winked lazily in the shadows of the Volkonsky Winter Palace.

The End

GLOSSARY OF RUSSIAN WORDS
AND EXPRESSIONS

babushka	бабушка	*grandmother*
beelyet	билет	*ticket(s)*
Beestra!	Быстра!	*Quick!*
borscht	борщ	*beet soup*
brillianty	бриллианты	*diamonds*
da	да	*yes*
dacha	да´ча	*weekend country house*
domovoi	домово́й	*house spirit (in Russian folklore)*
koffye	кофе	*coffee*
lyustra	люстра	*chandelier*
nyet	нет	*no*
požhalusta	пожалуйста	*please*
pamada	помада	*ointment*

pirozhki	пирожки	*dumplings*
samovar	самовар	*urn-type container for boiling water*
sarafan	сарафан	*long dress worn as traditional Russian folk costume*
shampanskoye	шампанское	*champagne*
shuba	шуба	*fur coat*
Snegurochka	Снегу́рочка	*The Snow Maiden — Russian fairy-tale character*
spasiba	спасибо	*thank you*
toska	тоска	*sadness, "a melancholy that afflicts the Russian soul"*
uchitel	учитель	*teacher*
valenki	валенки	*heavy felt boots*
volk/volky	волк/волки	*wolf/wolves*
vozok	возок	*sleigh*
Von!	Вон!	*Out!*
zdravstvuitye	здравствуйте	*hello*

ACKNOWLEDGMENTS

I am extremely grateful to my agent, Hilary Delamere, who embraced *The Wolf Princess* wholeheartedly, and understood completely the nature of the book I wanted to write. Her wise yet spirited counsel has made launching this book a joy. Also, thanks are due to Jane Fior, a wise woman and Russian soul, who understands the deep work of dreaming. Being lost in a forest is not a bad place to be with such a wonderful companion. I had a generous reader in the writer Susan Irvine, who commented with such perception on so many, many drafts. I am also grateful to the writers Sarah Jeans, Fatima Martin, Rosie Parker, and Angela Young for their continued encouragement. Snejana Tempest, my wonderful (and extremely patient) Russian teacher, might still be struggling with my inability to fully grasp the subtleties of the genitive case, but I thank her for her comments on the text. Thanks also to the artist Carolyn Quartermaine, who happily discussed the brilliance of *The Singing Ringing Tree*!

I feel very fortunate to have Barry Cunningham as my publisher. His deep understanding and passion for children's literature makes writing for the Chicken House a pleasure, a thrill, and a privilege. And his jokes are *really* funny. His team is remarkable, and I thank Rachel Leyshon, my editor, for her patience and humor and refusal to be spooked editorially when I skated off onto particularly thin narrative ice. Thanks, too, to Rachel Hickman for her calmness and ability to make the world "out there" appear manageable and, on occasion, a place of wonder and surprise; she has been a wonderful champion of the book. Elinor Bagenal did an outstanding job of introducing *The Wolf Princess* into the wider world, and I am really grateful for her enthusiasm. As for Tina Waller . . . "We salute you!" Of course, the Chicken House is a team, and there will be people I haven't mentioned by name, but every one of these lovely people has made the writing of *The Wolf Princess* an exciting, challenging, and utterly delicious process.

And of course, thanks also to my family. I grew up in a house furnished with books, and I am so grateful to have been given space and time to read by my parents. Thanks to Rhiannon, my sister, for her encouraging texts and e-mails along the way. Your jokes are also *really* funny!

I must also thank Charles, who has been so supportive, in his own entirely unique but wonderful way! And of course, Milo, Rufus, and Syrie, who have been incredibly patient whilst I stared out of the window. I love how sweet and funny and fierce and kind you are. This is a book about home . . . and you have made me understand how beautiful, and precious, that is.